PENGUIN CLASSICS

KING ARTHUR'S DEATH

BRIAN STONE wrote his first book, *Prisoner from Alamein* which had a foreword by Desmond MacCarthy, in 1944. After the war, during which he was decorated, he entered the teaching profession and taught English in boys' schools for eleven years. He then trained teachers for ten years at Loughborough and Brighton. He has recently retired from the Open University, where, as a founder member in 1969, he was Reader in Literature. He has four other translations to his credit in the Penguin Classics: modern English renderings of *Sir Gawain and the Green Knight*; *The Owl and the Nightingale*, *Cleanness* and *St Erkenwald*; Chaucer's *Love Visions* and *Medieval English Poems*. He has also published a critical study of Chaucer in the Penguin Critical Studies series.

KING ARTHUR'S DEATH

Alliterative *Morte Arthure* and
Stanzaic *Le Morte Arthur*

Translated and with Introductions by
BRIAN STONE

PENGUIN BOOKS

PENGUIN BOOKS

Published by the Penguin Group
Penguin Books Ltd, 27 Wrights Lane, London W8 5TZ, England
Penguin Books USA Inc., 375 Hudson Street, New York, New York 10014, USA
Penguin Books Australia Ltd, Ringwood, Victoria, Australia
Penguin Books Canada Ltd, 10 Alcorn Avenue, Toronto, Ontario, Canada M4V 3B2
Penguin Books (NZ) Ltd, 182–190 Wairau Road, Auckland 10, New Zealand

Penguin Books Ltd, Registered Offices: Harmondsworth, Middlesex, England

Published in Penguin Classics 1988
3 5 7 9 10 8 6 4

Copyright © Brian Stone, 1988
All rights reserved

Printed in England by Clays Ltd, St Ives plc
Photoset in Linotron (202) Bembo

CONTENTS

INTRODUCTION

The two long Arthurian poems, the alliterative *Morte Arthure* (*c.* 1400) and the stanzaic *Le Morte Arthur* (*c.* 1350), are here presented to English readers for the first time, together and in modern verse translation. The main material of both poems is familiar to readers of Malory, who presented it in shortened and significantly different forms in the unified prose work he made from collecting together many Arthurian romances, *Le Morte Darthur* (*c.* 1470, printed in modified form by Caxton in 1485). The climax of both poems, which gave them their titles, is common: the death of England's first national hero-king after the treachery of Mordred in usurping the kingdom during Arthur's absence campaigning abroad. In the alliterative poem, which presents Arthur as a heroic warrior-king in a mainly realistic political and military action, his death follows his victorious wars against the Roman emperor; Fortune deserts him at the zenith of his triumphs. In the stanzaic poem, the destruction of the Round Table and the death of its leader are the tragic and moral consequences of Queen Guinevere's adultery with Lancelot, who is the hero of the poem. Both conclusions, in my view, are superior to that of Malory, who uses both poems.

Malory's compilation offers the last important medieval treatment of a corpus of stories which had belonged to Western Europe for several centuries before he modified and re-wrote them. In origin they had not been English, but first Celtic and then French. Arthurian romance was categorized by Jean Bodel, a French poet of the late twelfth century, as the Matter of Britain, one of the three main divisions of romance subject. The other two were the Matter of France, which contained legends and history concerned with Charlemagne, including the *Song of Roland*, and the Matter of Rome, which treated classical subjects, including

7

especially those related to the fall of Troy and the life of Alexander the Great. From the eleventh century onwards, all these were elements in the stock of literary and popular culture over the whole of Western Europe, not excluding lands as far from the Celtic northwest as Sicily and Scandinavia.

The Matter of Britain seems to have begun with a hero who was probably a real person, a sixth-century 'dux bellorum' (war-leader) and possibly high king of the post-Roman period in Britain. The name 'Arthur' is derived from the Latin 'Artorius'; for some time after the Romans left Britain in 410, it had remained fashionable for noble British children to be given Roman names. As accounts of Arthur's successful wars against northern neighbours and sea-borne Saxon invaders proliferated, legends gathered round his name. A ninth-century Welsh monk from Bangor, Nennius, in his *Historia Brittonum* has a chapter on Arthur, who is credited with twelve victories over the Saxons, and with killing 960 of them himself in the Battle of Mount Badon. There are scattered references to an Arthurian figure in several other early medieval Welsh works, most of which assume popular knowledge of the Celtic hero and his exploits.

The earliest English reference is in William of Malmesbury's *Gesta Regum Anglorum* (1125), a history of England from 449 to 1120. He notes that fables have collected round the name of Arthur, and insists that he deserves to be commemorated rather in authentic history.

The key work in the development of medieval Arthurian literature is Geoffrey of Monmouth's *Historia Regum Britanniae* (History of the Kings of Britain), c. 1136. It is the most important of the many medieval works of Welsh origin in which Arthur figures, though it is of course written in Latin. In Part Seven, Geoffrey presents an amalgam of history and marvel in the glorification of an English monarch legendary for his achievement and tragic in his betrayal by Mordred and subsequent death; and it is Geoffrey's version of the life and death of Arthur which is clearly recognizable in the *Morte Arthure*. His account was translated and adapted into French by the Jersey poet Wace, whose enormously expanded *Roman de Brut* (1155) ran to 16,000 octosyllabic lines and was dedicated to Henry II's queen, Eleanor of Aquitaine. Wace's poem is the first major work to treat Celtic Arthurian matters in French. It is also the first we possess to mention the Round Table, and it stresses the hope that King Arthur will return from the Isle of Avalon. Yet we know that even that idea had long been current: in 1113 the servants of some monks from Laon expressed doubts about Arthur's return during a visit of their masters to Bodmin in Cornwall, and a riot resulted.

Wace significantly influenced Chrétien de Troyes, the most original and copiously productive of Arthurian romancers. Only the German, Gottfried von Strasbourg (early thirteenth century) wrote a greater single poem in the genre, his profound and elaborate *Tristan*. Chrétien's five long Arthurian romances, *Erec et Enide*, *Cligès*, *Lancelot*, *Yvain* and the *Conte du Graal* (Story of the Grail), were all written within about a dozen years, the last, which is a composite of two poems, a *Perceval* and a *Gauvain* (Gawain), being left unfinished in about 1182. In his elaborations of Arthurian legends, which he claimed to have derived from named sources, though none of these has been traced, Chrétien established the mode of Romance which was to remain dominant. The ruling discipline of all his heroes and heroines is the chivalric code, irradiated in its higher aspects by Christian piety and its associated virtues. The old feudal and national concerns are accordingly less emphasized, but the fury and the mystery of Celtic enchantment remains, fully harmonized in the genre. The most powerful driving force in the poems is love, and in view of the Christian moral framework, which is often presented in an allegorical way, it is intriguing that two of the hero-lovers, Cligès and Lancelot, are adulterous, as of course Tristan is. 'Courtly love' – a modern term used to translate what the French progenitors called 'fine amour' – has arrived on the European literary scene with its full apparatus. In Chrétien's romances, Arthur is not the central figure although, as head of the chivalric community, he holds the ring for the action and is interested in the outcome.

Following Chrétien in France came a group of Arthurian romances written in prose during the period 1215–30, which is known as the Vulgate Cycle (because written in the vulgar, i.e.

common, tongue, French) and includes three romances which are largely dominated by Lancelot: *Lancelot*, *Queste del Saint Graal* and *La Mort le Roi Artu*. The latter is particularly important, because the English *Le Morte Arthur* is based on it.

In the period immediately after Chrétien and just before the composition of the Vulgate Cycle, the first major work in English featuring Arthur was written. The author was a Worcestershire priest called Layamon, whose *Brut*, a versified history of Britain, was based on Wace. His transmutations of, and additions to, his source material in Englishing it are instructive because he seems to hark back to an earlier age in Britain, and to eschew to a large extent French poetic forms, words and chivalric ideas. The work is predominantly in alliterative verse, though occasional rhyme and assonance occur; it features many words with an Anglo-Saxon flavour which were already archaic; its code of conduct relates to an earlier heroic age which is ignorant of the strict courtly code; and many of its events are embellished with scenes of exaggerated prowess, detailed brutality, dreams and Celtic magic. For all its extraordinary length – just over 16,000 long lines – it most often proceeds by the concrete and the graphic; its dialogue is particularly dramatic. It seems to have been written for an English audience at a time when Norman French was the language of the ruling class; an audience which felt some nostalgia for pre-Conquest days. In its focus on a patriotic age with larger-than-life heroes like Arthur – and Lear and Cymbeline, who also figure in it – it is an early poetic marker for such a work as the *Morte Arthure*.

Robert Mannyng of Brunne (Bourne in Lincolnshire), a Gilbertine monk who adapted Wace into English verse, is the last author of concern here, as the many tales from the Matters of Britain, France and Rome which came to be told in poetry during the fourteenth century will be referred to, if at all, in the separate introductions to the two poems. In his *Chronicle of England* (1338) Mannyng sets out to repair the deficiency of the English language in works about Arthur, whom he regards as the greatest of Christian kings.

The two poems translated in this volume are products of a

longstanding tradition which has been lightly indicated above, and each is a peculiarly English example of the genre of romance. The *Morte Arthure*, in its glorification of Arthur's English rule and the prowess of his Round Table, harks back to a heroic age in our history and literature, and *Le Morte Arthur*, with its swiftly moving narrative and realistic clash of character, profitably avoids the more meditative chivalric finesse and magic of its source, the French prose *Mort Artu*. Neither poem may easily be categorized as a romance: the first is akin to an epic which ends in tragedy, and the second, with its shunning of so many standard elements of romance, and its relentless forward drive, is like an extended tragic ballad.

Each poem is accordingly a masterpiece of a special kind. My motive for performing what turned out to be a long and exacting task of translation was to enrich the stock of readily available poetic fiction in English on two Arthurian stories of prime importance in our culture. The excitement of doing the work increased as each poem moved toward final focus in the form that I found achievable in modern English. As I make clear in the separate introductions to the two poems, each presents a problem to the translator from medieval into modern English verse. In the case of *Le Morte Arthur*, for the first time in translating a long work, I preferred a slightly different stanza form from that of the original poet. In apologizing here for that, I refer to my explanation of my procedure in the introduction to the poem (pp. 170–71).

Though essential background and critical introductions are offered as normal apparatus of such a book as this, my hope is that the verse translations, which provide the *raison d'être* for the existence of the volume, will be taken, understood and enjoyed as poetry with a place in the English literary tradition.

Acknowledgements

I am particularly indebted to Valerie Krishna, for her edition and her translation of the Alliterative *Morte Arthure*, and to Larry D.

Benson, for his edition of that poem and of the Stanzaic *Le Morte Arthur*, in that I worked my first draft from their editions. My further indebtedness is indicated in the short bibliography, which lists only works that I have consulted in preparing this book. Students who work on the poems will need a fuller bibliography of the kind provided by W. R. J. Barron (see bibliography).

MORTE ARTHURE

The Manuscript and the Translator's Sources

The poem exists on a single manuscript, Lincoln Cathedral MS 91, which was written by a Yorkshire gentleman called Robert Thornton, whose seat was at East Newton, a village about twenty miles northeast of York. It is securely dated in the fourth decade of the fifteenth century, and its linguistic features suggest that though the scribe was a Yorkshireman, the copy he worked from was two removes from the original, which was in the language of the North or Northeast Midlands. *The Thornton Manuscript*, with its beautiful illuminated capitals and clear handwriting, exists in a facsimile edition (see bibliography).

The editions I have used in translating and introducing the poem are those of Brock (1871) and Benson (1974), and the two full modern critical editions, Krishna (1976) and Hamel (1984) (see bibliography). Hamel appeared when this translation already existed in first draft, and therefore influenced the revision of the poetic text, the notes and this introduction. It is the fullest edition, and usefully provides students of Malory with the relevant parallel text of Book V of *Le Morte Darthur*, which is based on the first three-quarters of the poem.

The Poet's Sources

The main story of Arthur's foreign conquests, his return to England to combat the treachery of Mordred, and his death, is taken from Geoffrey of Monmouth, but there are many other sources. It has been shown by the technique of line-by-line collation that this learned poet composed with Geoffrey, Wace,

Layamon and Mannyng (see pp. 8–10) all open in front of him. In addition to the Latin, French and English of those authors, he had read the Italian of Dante. Two works on which he drew for particular episodes are *Sir Ferumbras* (or its French predecessor) for the meeting of Gawain and Priamus (ll. 2513 ff.), and *Li Fuerres de Gadres* for the whole structure of the Siege of Metz episode (ll. 2416–3077) with its 'siege, foraging expedition, the encounter of an enemy leading a large host, the overcoming of superior forces, return to the siege and reduction of the city' (Krishna, p. 19).

The poet drew on a wide range of French works, including the *Mort Artu* for the last part of the poem, though his ending is markedly different from that of the poet of *Le Morte Arthur*, who based his whole work on the *Mort Artu*. He appears to have consulted the *Life of the Black Prince*, Mandeville's *Travels* and at least three works of classical inspiration, including two Alexander romances, besides Boethius, whose *The Consolations of Philosophy* (*c.* sixth century) influenced him, as it did many medieval authors.

This literary learning provides general and episodical narrative structures and some ideas, but besides knowing the literatures of several languages, the poet demonstrates detailed and practical knowledge of English political and military matters of the four-teenth century. 'This is primarily a poem of battles' (Benson, p. xv) – a statement which indicates how much of it deals with actual fighting. The poet accurately records contemporary tactics in massed and individual combat, armour, clothing and heraldry, and writes vividly about conduct in battle and council debate. It is not surprising that he is conjectured to have been in or close to the entourage of Edward III, and to have been personally engaged in his political and military affairs.

The poet may have been prolific in his use and transmutation of the material of his reading and experience, but consideration of his sources leads, as it usually does with major medieval poets, to pleasure and astonishment that the finished work is so original and so remote from a mere compilation. The structural placing and imaginative elaboration of Arthur's two dreams, the pervasive violence and the extended tragic conclusion, which contribute so much to the poem, are the poet's own.

The Language and the Metre

The poem is unusual in its vocabulary. It contains a high proportion of words of French origin, and in this may be compared with the finest work of medieval alliterative poetry, *Sir Gawain and the Green Knight*. Both are products of Northern England, and show in their different ways intimations of a world alien to French romance – in *Sir Gawain*, the harsh physical nature of the north, and in *Morte Arthure*, something of the tragic feudal world of Anglo-Saxon epic. This linguistic phenomenon should not greatly surprise a reader who knows that Durham cathedral was built soon after the Norman Conquest of 1066, and that Edward II and Edward III both used York as their seat of government for a time in the fourteenth century.

The language of *Morte Arthure* is rich in nonce-words and technical terms, especially those concerned with military and naval matters – weaponry, armour, heraldry, navigation, rigging; and the procedures of battle tactics, siege warfare and fortification on land and sea. It has been hard to translate terms for which modern equivalents may not exist, and harder still to give passages in which they are used clear meaning, without including annotation, some of it speculative, within the translation.

These problems are compounded by Thornton's habit of only sometimes altering words or inflexions to conform to his own Yorkshire, and his inconsistent spelling. Two further aspects of language affect the task of literal translation no less than that of verse translation. The manuscript has no punctuation marks other than those indicating the mid-line caesura and the occasional beginning of a paragraph – and the principle of paragraphing is not clear. Besides this, the structure of verse sentence is often rhetorical rather than syntactical; the force of writing goes into significant juxtaposition of phrases, not causal linking by use of connectives. So a reader or translator sometimes has to judge whether a phrase should be the last in one sentence or the first in the next, and the question of whether a sentence is simple, complex or periodic has then to be faced and solved. It is a problem dealt with by the editors cited, who do not always agree with each other in their readings.

The poem is composed in alliterative metre, the standard form of Anglo-Saxon poetry which, with some modifications resulting from language changes in the interim, reappeared in the fourteenth century as a major English form in which several masterpieces were composed. The medieval line contained four stresses, with a caesura after the first two, and the basic alliterative pattern was aa/ax. The number of stresses could be increased to five by adding to the first part of the line, and in *Morte Arthure* it is this first part of the line, however many stresses it contains, which usually carries the main meaning. The second part, which typically carries only one alliterating sound matching the first part, tends to consist of a phrase which, by apposition or qualification or addition of a component, extends the first part. Alliteration is of consonants, or occasionally of paired consonants, or of vowels, the rule in the latter case being that all vowels may alliterate with each other or with initial 'h'. Lines 2286–9 demonstrate these two regular patterns:

> They *d*rewe owt of *d*romondaries *d*yuerse lordes,
> *M*oylles *m*ylke whitte and *m*eruayllous bestez,
> *O*lfendes and *a*rrabys and *o*lyfauntez noble,
> Ther *a*re of the Oryent, with *h*onourable kynges.

> (They led away large numbers of lords' dromedaries,
> Milk-white mules and marvellous creatures,
> Noble elephants, Arab horses and camels
> Of oriental habitat, owned by high monarchs.)

The poet is a conscious artist who does not monotonously reproduce the regular pattern. He freely uses the old Anglo-Saxon patterns of ax/ax, xa/xa and aa/ax, which enhances the Old English, as opposed to the typical medieval, effect of the prosody. Often he combines different patterns in a succession of lines, thus for example: aa/ax – xx/ab – bb/bx. But his favourite resort is to write whole sequences of lines using the same alliterating sound throughout. Usually it is only two to four lines, but in one instance, in lines 2483–92, the same consonant sound, 'f' is retained for ten lines. In the translation, I have used such variations without following the poet precisely in each case, and in the interest of keeping natural word order, I have also felt free to use the irregular form aa/xa.

One further general characteristic of this alliterative verse must be mentioned. In Anglo-Saxon, the number of unstressed syllables between stresses tended to be one or two, which was possible because Anglo-Saxon was an inflected language in which auxiliary words such as prepositions were sparse, and word order was to some extent flexible. But by the end of the fourteenth century, when this poem was composed, many inflexions had disappeared or weakened, so that more prepositions and connectives were required, and accordingly it was generally necessary for a poet to include more unstressed syllables – up to three or even four – between stressed syllables. Since 1400, the process described has continued, so that a modern poet or translator using alliterative metre usually requires even more unstressed syllables than a medieval poet. Nevertheless, poets such as T. S. Eliot and W. H. Auden have profitably used the metre, which accords better with the way the stressed English language works than any metre based on Romance prescriptions of syllable-counting and strict poetic feet. The pervasive rhythm of alliterative verse in all the three periods mentioned is dactylic.

In *Morte Arthure*, stock groups of alliterating words are repeated, often with little variation, and their collective meaning helps to give frame to the poem, because each becomes formulaic: I have not counted the number of occasions on which *ch*evaliers on *ch*alk-white *ch*argers either *ch*op their enemies or are *ch*opped themselves. When Sir Kay receives his death-wound, each of the first three lines of his speech informing King Arthur ends with a formulaic phrase of the kind which typically completes the alliterative line, and it is a moment of high pathos:

I am wathely woundide – waresche mon I neuer,
Wirke nowe thi wirchipe, as the world askes,
And brynge me to beryell – byd I no more.
(ll. 2186–8)

(I have been dealt my death-blow and will never recover.
Accomplish your courtesy as required by the world
And bring me to burial; no better thing I ask.)

Frequent verbal repetition, occasional word-play and the odd heavy joke, usually ironic, are also found in the poem. The problem of translating the poem throughout has been to accommodate in modern English the barbaric fury and emotional exaltation of the original, often using words of weaker force than those of the poet.

The Story

Lines 1–1221. Resting after conquest, King Arthur keeps Christmas in Carlisle with full court panoply. As the feast is about to start on New Year's Day, an embassy from Lucius Iberius, Emperor of Rome, arrives to demand that Arthur pay tribute. Arthur continues the feast, including the ambassadors as guests, before holding a council to determine his reply to Lucius. Arthur's royal allies and chief knights counsel war against Rome and promise support, and the ambassadors return to Rome. Lucius masses support and marches into Germany. Arthur appoints Mordred as his viceroy, makes his farewells to Guinevere and embarks his army for France. While sleeping on board ship, he dreams about a fight in the sky between a dragon and a bear, and when he wakes, his sages interpret it as meaning that he will succeed in the imminent campaign. When he lands in France, a Templar secretly informs Arthur that a cannibal giant whose lair is on Mont Saint Michel is terrorizing his subjects in Brittany. Arthur climbs the rock alone and after a prolonged struggle stabs the giant to death. Then he has the giant's treasure distributed to his grateful subjects.

Lines 1222–2385. The Marshal of France informs Arthur by messenger that Lucius is ravaging the country. Arthur sends a small force which includes Gawain to order Lucius to withdraw, and when Lucius defiantly refuses, Gawain slashes off the head of the Emperor's uncle before leading a rapid retreat. The Romans' first pursuit is repulsed, but they beat Arthur's men in a further attack, capturing Sir Boyce. In the renewed fighting, Sir Boyce is rescued and Senator Peter, leader of the pursuing Roman forces, is captured, together with many Romans and much booty. The prisoners are sent to Paris to be incarcerated, and Lucius sends a force to ambush the escort before it reaches the city. In the ensuing battle, Arthur's knights suffer casualties, but eventually the Romans are beaten and the prisoners are safely delivered into the care of the Provost of Paris. Arthur weeps when he hears of the casualties, and Lucius plans to intercept Arthur's army at Val-Suzon. But Arthur reaches the town first and sets up his defence. The Romans attack, and as the battle tilts the British way, the specific vows of support for Arthur made in Carlisle on New Year's Day are fulfilled. Sir Kay is killed, and Arthur avenges him in a burst of slaughter. Arthur kills Lucius, the Roman forces disintegrate and the British kill every Roman they can catch. After the looting of the Roman baggage train, Arthur has the enemy dead honourably coffined and sent to Rome, styling them as the only tribute Rome will receive from him. Arthur then arranges for his own dead to be buried.

Lines 2386–3218. The Romans being vanquished, Arthur invades Lorraine and lays siege to Metz. He sends Gawain on a foraging expedition, and Gawain meets Sir Priamus, a knight fighting for Lorraine, by whose magical sword he is wounded. When the wounds of both are healed and battle resumes, Sir Priamus and his men change sides and fight for Gawain. Gawain kills the Marquis of Metz, but one of King Arthur's favourite squires is killed. Gawain's force gains the victory and rejoins Arthur, who is besieging Metz. The city falls to a savage assault and Arthur spares the women, priests and children, but sends the Duke to prison in England. Arthur leads his men through the Alps to

Como, which he takes. The Sire of Milan sends him tribute and promises homage, and Arthur moves down to Tuscany, where he lays waste the countryside. A cardinal comes to Arthur and pleads for the Pope, who promises to crown Arthur emperor in Rome and confirms his offer by leaving 160 noble children in Arthur's care as hostages.

Lines 3219–4348. With his aim of ultimate power and glory in his grasp, Arthur goes to bed and has a long and ominous dream. In it he travels through a wood where beasts of prey menace his knights, but emerges in a beautiful meadow into which the goddess Fortune descends from the clouds, whirling her wheel. Arthur sees six of the Nine Worthies cast down from the wheel, and two more trying to climb up it. Fortune invites him to all the pleasures of the place, but suddenly changes her mood and whirls him downwards on her wheel so that his spine is smashed. Arthur wakes, and his sage interprets the dream as meaning that his achievements are finished, and that now he must repent his conquests and shedding of blood, and prepare his soul for death. Arthur leaves his tent in anger, and on the road meets a pilgrim who turns out to be his knight Craddock, who tells him that Mordred has usurped the throne of England and taken Guinevere as wife. Arthur hurries back to England, and wins a sea battle against Mordred's heathen navy off Southampton. Gawain with a small force lands to attack Mordred's army, but they are slaughtered to a man, and he himself is killed by Mordred, who then regrets what he has done. Mordred retreats westwards. Arthur lands, laments the death of Gawain and swears revenge. Though he has only 1,800 men to Mordred's 60,000, he marches to the river Tamar and engages the enemy at once. Mordred himself fights under a false banner. Arthur notes with sorrow that Mordred is using his own ceremonial sword, of which Guinevere had charge. Mordred and Arthur meet, and Arthur receives his death-wound, after which he slashes off Mordred's sword arm. All Mordred's men are killed, and Arthur is left with 140 knights of the Round Table. The dying Arthur orders that he be taken to Glastonbury for burial; he bequeaths his throne to Constantine, orders that Mordred's children be killed, forgives all who have done him wrong, and commends his soul to Christ. The court mourns his death.

The Poem

Although there are four distinct narrative parts of the poem, which the poet or his scribe might have marked for our convenience, the theme and bearing of the whole are crystallized in Arthur's two prophetic dreams. These are placed respectively before the ending of the first part and at the start of the last. The first dream is of unalloyed good fortune, which is to come to him through remorseless battle such as that engaged in by the dragon and the bear of the dream. The second dream, in which Fortune figures, reviews Arthur's happy past in the allegory of the beautiful garden, before promising his downfall and destruction in the process of the whirling of Fortune's wheel. Fortune herself, here presented as a duchess rather than a goddess, provides an alluring and amoral focus for the concept of noble destiny to which Arthur, as a king and the representative of all nobly inclined men, aspires. After warning him by showing him the fate of the Six Worthies who preceded him, Fortune mounts Arthur richly on a throne, gives him her own never-failing sword, and seals with wine her recognition that he owns Rome. This is at once followed by his loss of her favour, which she introduces not as moral retributive consequence, but simply as an effect of time:

> 'King, you can claim nothing, by Christ who made me!
> For you shall lose this pleasure, and your life later:
> You have delighted long enough in lands and lordliness!'
>
> (ll. 3385–7)

The medieval idea of Fortune in the Christian hierarchy finds expression conventionally in that 'by Christ who made me,' but

21

the actions of Fortune and Arthur's deeds are put into a moral frame only by the sage who interprets the dream.

In approaching such a poem, it is important to confront its essence, and not to indulge expectations which might be fulfilled if it were another sort of poem. *Morte Arthure* is about warfare, the qualities in the class of men that make for efficiency in warfare, the acquisitions of loot and territory that come to its successful practitioners and the idea of the nation and its leadership which apotheosize the values of accomplished warfare. It is also about the practices in warfare embraced by those – and especially by one, Mordred – who want with such passion to win the spoils that in pursuit of their objective they break the 'gentlemanly' rules of the game. And game it is, on account of its conventions, which prescribe and so limit the ways in which the objective, the destruction of the enemy, may be pursued.

This is not a poem in which interest in love between men and women figures, or in which conflict between different psychological types of men is the centre of interest in the main subject of patriotic warfare. The love under frequent scrutiny is honoured love between male kin and kin, between knight and brotherly knight, and between feudal royal master and his liegers. This love among men spreads as far up and as far down as the medieval hierarchy can reach among those who are capable of fighting and qualified to fight; a king is at the top and an adolescent squire at the bottom. All women are on the periphery of this arena, and figure as passive sufferers who are forced into the appalling conflict, whether it is a Duchess of Brittany who is raped by the Giant of Mont Saint Michel, or Arthur's queen, Guinevere, who is appropriated and made pregnant by the usurper Mordred. Arthur is not made jealous by Guinevere's infidelity, but is affronted by her treason and the danger to the succession, which makes him decree in his dying moments that her children by Mordred must be 'secretly slain and slung into the sea'. The role of Lancelot, the greatest lover of women in the whole of Romance, is here only that of a warrior.

The forces which activate the vision in the poem are seen to breed, through time, their own destruction simply by the mode and the value system by which they operate. It may be this that has persuaded some modern critics, whose sensibilities are perhaps exaggeratedly attuned to our own dangerous times, to label the poem an anti-war work. But that is to ignore the primitive ecstasy with which battle prowess and national triumph are repeatedly celebrated. The same ecstasy goes into celebrations of the death in battle of the King's chief henchman, Gawain, who dies in an excess of rash chivalry fighting against absurd odds, and of Arthur's final disposition of his heritage as he commits his spirit to Christ.

Besides the conventional Christian framework of expression, and the two regulating dreams, the only supernatural or magical elements the poem contains are in the fights between Arthur and the Giant, and between Gawain and Sir Priamus. In this respect the poem is unusual in Arthurian literature, and is more easily defined as a realistic epic than a romance.

A single narrative formula, which is capable of much elaboration, governs the episodes in the poem, whether the term 'episode' is applied to whole campaigns like the war against Lucius and the siege of Metz, or to single confrontations like that between Gawain and Priamus and the many individual duels fought in battle. The formula produces a narrative sequence something like this: circumstance, challenge and reply, action, resolution, consequence – the final stage of consequence often being no more than the freeing of the agent, who is mostly Arthur himself, for the next episode. Every stage but the action, which has its own rhetoric, includes speech-making.

Arthur's grim encounter with the Giant of Mont Saint Michel (ll. 840–1221) follows the formula. The Templar's narration of the circumstance, which is the existence and tyranny of the giant, is horrifying in its description but concludes by pointing out to Arthur his kingly duty of revenge. As preparation for the next two stages, the dressing of the hero for combat is described in full, as elsewhere in the poem. Then the circumstance is further elaborated in the speeches of the ancient foster-mother who accompanies the Duchess of Brittany to the scene of her rape and death:

23

He forced her, defiled her, and fatal was her end,
Slain most savagely and slit to the navel!
I oiled her body here and afterwards buried her;
In anguish at her helplessness I shall be unhappy for ever.

(ll. 978–81)

This build-up of the circumstance is the most elaborate in the poem, and is buttressed by an ironic joke which runs from start to finish of the episode, in which Arthur insists on the idea that his exploit is

to seek out a saint
On the Mount of Saint Michael, where miracles are performed.

(ll. 898–9)

The description of the enemy, which is usually made at the stage of challenge and reply, is also the most elaborate of all, and fills the space of pure astonishment that the giant experiences at being challenged at all. His reply to Arthur is wordless, being represented only by his monstrous self as he prepares to club the King to death:

His body bulged, as big as a porpoise's,
And the flesh of his foul lips fiercely quivered,
Each collop curling like a cruel wolf's head.

(ll. 1091–3)

The fight, which rages barbarically for fifty lines, is memorably concluded when the pair, locked in their death struggle, roll together down the whole height of the Mount to the beach, where Arthur's attendants are waiting:

They toppled down from the top in tumult together,
With Arthur over him and under by turns,
From the height of the hill to the hard rock below,
Not ceasing though they struggled at the sea's edge.
Then Arthur stabbed him savagely with a dagger,
Repeatedly hitting into the hulk to the very hilt.

(ll. 1144–9)

24

The resolution is the giant's death and beheading, and the consequence is that Arthur's subjects are free of the menace and able to enjoy his treasure, while Arthur is free to resume his main project of repelling Lucius's invasion of France.

A mysterious and constant feature of the combat scenes is the formal poetic tribute to the beauty of the natural background of battle – flowering trees, singing birds, sweetly flowing waters and so forth. Arthur's approach to the giant's lair is through a particularly lovely landscape (ll. 920–32). Such descriptions may be placed immediately before or after a battle, often both, and may occupy only a line or two. Thus, Cador leads a charge against the Romans:

> Shattering was the shock; they shunned nothing
> Where the shrubs brightly shone under the shimmering trees.
>
> (ll. 1759–60)

More deliberate is the idyll during a lull in the fighting outside Metz, when Gawain and Priamus, both badly wounded, make for

> . . . the mountain where our men were encamped,
> Grazing their grey steeds in the goodly meadowland.
> There lords were leaning low on their gleaming shields,
> And lifting light laughter for love of the birds,
> The larks and linnets with their lovely song;
> And some slipped into sleep ensorcelled by them
> As they sang at that season in the sparkling shrubland,
> Lurking low with their lulling tunes in the glades.
>
> (ll. 2671–8)

There is a multiple effect: the beauty of ideal knighthood receives the sanction of Nature in a harmonious setting; the brutality of the knightly trade is offset by the contrasting softness of the environment; and Nature, 'dear goddess' as Lear was soon to call her, is somehow always there, expressively heaving and sounding under and around the life of the poem. Formal medieval rhetoric about nature is geared to an unusually grisly purpose.

The speeches made in the shadow or heat of battle are compounded of barbaric elements: vows of slaughter and revenge, insults and invocations of noble names and blood. Gawain's encouragement to his men outside Metz is typical:

> Fear not, my fine fellows, the flashing of shields
> As those rotten men revel on their great rearing horses!
> Bannerets of Britain, brace your spirits!
> Be not abashed by those brightly clad knaves!
> We shall abate their boasting for all their bold vaunts,
> Till they're as obedient as bedded bride is to lord.
>
> (ll. 2853–8)

The rhetoric of grief is more congenial, and reminds the reader of such tragic epic writing as that in the Anglo-Saxon Chronicle, which records the defeat of the English by the Vikings in the Battle of Maldon four centuries earlier. As Arthur cradles the dead Gawain, he speaks the very height of chivalric love:

> Dear cousin and kinsman, in care I am left,
> For now my glory is gone, and my great wars finished.
> I hold here my hope of joy and armed success;
> Wholly on him depended my heart and strength!
> O my counsellor, my comfort, keeper of my heart,
> Renowned king of all knights ever known under Christ!
> Worthy to be king, though I wore the crown!
> Throughout the wide world my wealth and my glory
> Were won by Gawain, through his wisdom alone.
>
> (ll. 3956–64)

The Gawain mourned by Arthur is the one man besides the King and his ultimate antagonist, Mordred, who is defined as a character in anything more than a vivid vignette. His loyalty, prowess and spirit of aggression are marked whenever he appears, but the special thing about the Gawain of this poem is his rashness. Unlike Arthur, who in battle sometimes shows tactical restraint, Gawain seems impelled always to overbid the hand that Fortune has dealt him, with the aim of improving his already immaculate chivalric reputation. The three particular occasions on which he does this are: on his first embassy to Lucius (ll. 1346–55), when in the middle of a parley he suddenly beheads one of the enemy; on the foraging expedition outside Metz, when with five hundred men he attacks and defeats a huge army; and lastly, when he gets killed in his foolhardy sally up the beach against the entire army of Mordred.

The latter, who is usually execrated, emerges from this poem as an interesting figure who gains some sympathy. Initially (ll. 639–92) he resists the King's command to remain in England as viceroy, and modestly makes it plain that he proposes to accompany the Round Table on its campaign against the Emperor. However, he yields to Arthur's appeals to his loyalty in kinship, and to his threats. In this poem Mordred is Arthur's nephew, not his incestuous son as in *Le Morte Arthur*.

In Craddock's report of his usurpation of the kingdom, Mordred appears about as vile as an usurper could be: he uses heathen allies to hold down and despoil the country, and he treats Guinevere as his wife. In the last battle he outrages the spirit of chivalry in two respects: he holds back his own force until he judges Arthur's men to be so tired that he can defeat them, and when he does advance to join battle, he bears false arms on his banner in order to avoid identification. Set against all that is the strange episode of the death of Gawain, which Mordred brings about first by clever army tactics, and then by valour in single combat. It is a long episode (ll. 3724–898), and besides containing the clearest account of an actual battle in the whole poem – relative skirmish though it is – it contains Mordred's heartfelt grief for having killed his distinguished kinsman. The poet does not make Mordred and Gawain brothers, as they are in Geoffrey of Monmouth.

To turn from Gawain and Mordred to Arthur is to confront the heart of the poem, with what W. R. J. Barron (*English Medieval Romance*, p. 229) calls 'its thematic emphasis on the fate of a society as conditioned by the character and personal conduct of the hero-king' and 'the structural pattern of detached, highly dramatized scenes organized in sections'. Arthur is the hero of all the main scenes, and seems to have four important characteristics. He is above all a ruler and a forceful maker of political and military decisions; he is a brilliant though often brutal warrior and general; he is a faithful and passionate lover of all who acknowledge his rule and leadership, who has a special feeling for his knights and

27

their prowess; and lastly, his knowledge of himself in these particulars makes him aspire to a chivalric and national ideal against which he measures himself all the time, and most significantly in the hour of his death.

Arthur's magnificence (a word which in the next century, the fifteenth, came to be used to define the essential quality of a powerful king) shows right at the start of the poem, in his treatment of the Roman ambassadors who, though terrified by his lion-like aspect, receive such hospitality from him that they report him to the Emperor in these words:

> 'Speak of him as a spender who despises silver,
> Gives gold no more regard than great boulders,
> Rates wine as water that wells from the ground,
> And worships no wealth in this world but glory.'
>
> (ll. 538–41)

The military application of this magnificence shows in instinctive fearlessness and savage humour, as in the battle against the Emperor, when Arthur

> Got close to Golopas, who had done greatest harm,
> And cut him in two clean through the knees.
> 'Come down!' said the King, 'And account for it to your fellows!
> You are too high by half, I have to tell you.
> You'll be even handsomer soon, with Our Lord's help!'
> And with his steely sword he struck off his head.
>
> (ll. 2124–9)

Arthur freely exposes himself to enemy missiles while reconnoitring the walls of Metz to find the best spots to place his siege engines, and more than once goads moderate performers in battle into greater bravery by mocking them. He increases loyalty and valour among his men not only by rewarding them with the spoils of war, but by making new knights, often before battle or during a lull in the fighting. Dubbing contained a religious element; a newly dubbed knight vowed not only to defend his feudal master, but also to fight for the Christian faith, a theme implicit in the poem. The poet always emphasizes the reliance of Arthur's main enemies, first the Emperor Lucius and then

Mordred, on the military support of heathens and devils' off-spring. The quintessence of this idea that Arthur is a defender of the faith against the powers of darkness is expressed in his destruction of the Giant of Mont Saint Michel, who stands for everything un-Christian and subhuman – monstrosity, murder, rape, cannibalism, disorder. And that makes the central joke of the episode – that the giant is a saint – more splendidly apposite and barbaric.

Arthur's coronation, which gave him Christian obligations as well as temporal power, must have included standard fourteenth-century rites such as the blessing of the ceremonial sword of kingship. In the final battle, Arthur laments Mordred's theft and misuse of that symbolic weapon whose secret whereabouts in the royal armoury only Guinevere knew:

> I kept Clarent as my clean darling, accounted it precious,
> And kept it for crowning consecrated kings . . .
> Now I see Clarent unscabbarded, crown of all swords.
>
> (ll. 4196–7, 4202)

The central sanctity of the poem attaches to the idea of kingship, which is based on the tenets of chivalry, kinship and patriotism. These are pursued with a fierce male love which is social as well as personal. I earlier defined the spirit of the poem as ecstatic in its celebration of battle prowess and national triumph, and confirm that epithet as applying to the hero of the poem when he knows and accepts his own doom and loss, and the doom and loss of his kingdom, without blaming Fortune or expressing the kind of penitence enjoined by the sage-interpreter of his second dream:

> I advise you to confess your flagrant misdeeds,
> Or most promptly you will repent your pitiless acts.
> Amend your mood, man, before misfortune strikes,
> And meekly beg mercy for the merit of your soul.
>
> (ll. 3452–5)

There is no response to that commonplace medieval advice about holy dying from the Arthur of this poem, who thanks God for his final victory over Mordred in his last moments, and passionately laments his own and his people's loss, together with the irony that their fate has been brought about by treachery:

> All my lordship is laid low to the ground.
> Those who gave me gifts through the grace of God,
> Maintained my majesty by their might in battle
> And set me up in honour as Earth's master,
> In a terrible time this trouble has come to them,
> That through a traitor all my true lords are taken in death.
>
> (ll. 4276–81)

The barbaric ecstasy to which I have referred lies equally in the poem's acceptance of reasonless vicissitude as a consequence of the code embraced by its protagonist, and in the form and fact of its poetry, which have no precise equivalent in prose.

Fourteenth-Century Battle Techniques

These selective notes will help readers to follow what happens in the accounts of fighting in *Morte Arthure*, and are also relevant to parts of *Le Morte Arthur*. As I have indicated above, some medieval terms defining armour and weapons have no modern equivalents, and the practice of armoury experts today is to use the medieval words. I have avoided doing so myself in order to make the passages comprehensible without driving the reader constantly to footnotes or glossary. From time to time there may be a loss of precision as a result, which it is my aim to repair by describing the chief practices of fighting here.

In tournament, deadly duel and battle, the standard form of combat is the charge of horsed knights. A mounted chevalier holds his shield and the controlling reins in his left hand and his spear in his right, and thus charges his enemy left against left, shield to shield. His spear is aimed over his horse's left ear, and is intended to strike the enemy knight obliquely as both knights gallop past each other. To take the impact, the knight strains forward in his saddle and pushes with his feet back against the stirrups. Nevertheless, that impact often unhorses one or both of the knights. In the charge, the problem with the spear is to have it aimed during the charge, and precisely levelled at the moment of impact; to facilitate this, there was a spear rest on the knight's saddle to steady it during the charge, and a further elaboration appeared towards the end of the fourteenth century in the *fewter*, which was a spear-rest attached to the breast-plate. Thus, there is no mention of the fewter in *Le Morte Arthur*, but it is often referred to in *Morte Arthure*, which was written about half a century later.

There is frequent reference, in the battle scenes in *Morte Arthure*, to knights slashing each other as they pass. Since a knight cannot hold both a spear and a sword in one hand, this means that in the first charge or at some other time in the conflict, the knight's spear has been shattered – a circumstance often recounted – and he has resorted to his sword. Gawain and Priamus so slash each other (ll. 2558–73) on the famous occasion when Gawain deals such a blow that Priamus's liver can then be seen by the light of the sun. Arthur deals such a blow to dispose finally of Mordred:

> Yet still with his sword Excalibur he struck nobly,
> Guarding himself guilefully with his glittering shield,
> And slashed off Mordred's sword hand as he surged past.
>
> (ll. 4243–5)

Of course, mounted knights may fight with swords with their horses stationary, when the spear-charge is finished or spears have been broken.

If one knight is unhorsed in the charge, he may invite the other to dismount in sheer fair play, so that the next stage of combat may be between dismounted swordsmen. This kind of sword-fight is more deadly and continuous than mounted combat, because there is little room for manoeuvre or flight, since both men are wearing heavy armour. It may end with them so interlocked that their long swords are useless, and their last resort then becomes the *anlas* or *anlace*, a short two-edged dagger carried at the girdle especially for this ultimate stage of combat. It was narrow at the point and broad at the hilt, and if driven in made a big wound. It is with an anlace while wrestling on the ground that

Arthur kills the giant, and Mordred kills Gawain. It was the practice, even during massed battles, for two knights to be left fighting their duel, which it was dishonourable to interrupt.

Readers may be amazed at the apparent unreality of speeches being suddenly made in the midst of a general melée, but that appears to have been possible in real medieval warfare. It is a historical fact that Edward III, while besieging Calais, was challenged by King Philip of France to make a decision by single chivalric combat.

There are several references to the efficacy of British longbowmen, and to the damage done by hostile crossbowmen. These, and the details concerning siege warfare at Metz, accurately reflect late-fourteenth-century practice, and can comfortably be followed by the reader.

The last important point concerns battle signals. If banners are spread, that means that fight is intended, but it seems that there were different ground rules for the use of ambush, which was generally dreaded because of the element of surprise. But in all battle circumstances, the banner of the king or leader is the ultimate rallying point, and its retention or loss is cardinal in determining the outcome of the combat. Hence Arthur's admonition before the last battle:

> Neither attend nor protect me, nor take account of me,
> But be busy about my banners with your bright weapons,
> Ensuring that strong knights sternly defend them
> And hold them nobly high for our army to see.

(ll. 4094–7)

ALLITERATIVE
MORTE ARTHURE

Here begins the Death of Arthur. In the
Name of the Father and the Son and the
Holy Ghost. Amen for Charity's Sake.
Amen.

Now may glorious God, great in His grace,
And the precious prayers of His pure Mother
Shield us from shameful deeds and shifts of sin,
And giving us grace, guide and govern us here
In this woeful world, that through worthy living
We may come to His court, the Kingdom of Heaven,
When our souls are severed and sundered from body,
Ever to abide in bliss and be with God!
May He sway me to weave some words at this time
Not empty or idle, but honouring Him,   10
With pleasure and profit to the people who hear them!
   You who love to listen and long to hear
Of our ancestors of old and their awesome deeds,
How they were loyal to their religion and loved God
     Almighty,
Hear me with good humour! Yes, hold still,
And I'll tell you a tale that's true and lofty
Of the regal and highly-ranked of the Round Table,
The champions of chivalry and chieftains of title,
Prudent in practice, powerful in arms
And doughty in deed, ever dreading disgrace.   20
Courteous and kind they were, accomplished in court
     manners,
And won in their wars a wealth of honours,
Slaying wicked Lucius, the Lord of Rome,

And conquering that kingdom by skill in arms.
Turn hither your ears and hear this history!
  After King Arthur had overcome in war
Castles and kingdoms and countries in plenty,
And regained rule over all the fine realms
That Uther[1] had owned on earth in his time –
Argyll and Orkney and all the outer isles,   30
The whole of Ireland, which the ocean surrounds,
And spiteful Scotland, which he skilfully ruled –
He won Wales by war at his will,
And Flanders and France fell freely to him;
Holland and Hainault he held wholly,
Burgundy, Brabant and Britain the Less,[2]
Guienne and Gotland and Grasse most splendid.
Bayonne and Bordeaux he brought under rule,
And Touraine and Toulouse with their tall towers.
He was appointed Prince of Poitiers and Provence,   40
Of Valence and Vienne, both of value immense,
And of Auvergne and Anjou, earldoms most wealthy.
After conquest most cruel they called him lord
Of Navarre and Norway, and Normandy too,
Of Austria and Germany, and a host of other lands.
He subdued all Denmark through dread of his power
From Sluys up to Sweden, with his sharp sword.
  Those deeds being done, he dubbed new knights,
Made dukedoms in different lands and dealt them out,
And raised his relatives to royalty anointed   50
In countries whose crowns they were keen to wear.
After riding those realms as ruler of their peoples
That royal one rested, at the Round Table presiding,
Sojourning a season to solace himself

1. 29 Uther Pendragon: Arthur's father.

2. 36 Britain the Less: Brittany.

Within the bounds of Britain the Greater[1] as best he liked,
Then went into Wales with his warrior force,
Swung to the south with his swift hounds
To hunt the hart in the high country
Of Glamorgan merrily, their mood ever joyful.
There he set up a city with consent of his lords   60
Called Caerleon, with well-crafted walls,
Beside the splendid river[2] that sweeps by;
There for battles abroad he could embark at will.

   He kept his Christmas feast at Carlisle after that,
This far-famed conqueror, re-affirming his lordship
Over dukes and dignitaries of different realms,
Earls and archbishops and others in plenty,
Bishops and bannerets and bachelor knights,
Who served under his standard, set it up where he would.
But on Christmas Day, all being assembled,   70
That mighty commander made it mandatory
On all men to remain and not make their farewells
Until the time when the tenth day ended.
Thus in royal array he ruled his Round Table
In splendour and sweet joy, with exotic feasting.
Never in mortal knowledge was such a noble triumph
As was made that midwinter in the Western Marches!
   Now just at noon on New Year's Day,
As bread was being brought to the bold men at table,[3]
There strode in suddenly a senator from Rome,   80
Escorted by sixteen knights stepping behind him.
He hailed the High King, and then the whole hall,

1. 55 Britain the Greater: England.

2. 62 The 'splendid river' is the Usk.

3. 79 Traditionally in Romance, the start of a feast is the time a visitor
arrives to initiate an adventure or other event.

To king after king in courtesy bowing;
He greeted Guinevere as her great rank required,
Then broached his business with a bow to Arthur:
'Sir Lucius Iberius, Emperor of Rome,
Salutes you as subject by his seal of royalty –
Credentials, Sir King, of cruel import!
Take it as no trifle, his true seal proves it.
Now this New Year's Day, by notaries' warrant,   90
I call on you in your court to sue for your kingdom:
On Lammas Day[1] allow no let or hindrance
To your being ready in Rome with all your Round Table!
Appear in his presence with your princely knights
At dawn of the day, on pain of death,
In the famous Capitol before the King himself
When he and his senators are in session enthroned,
To answer on your own why you occupy the lands
Which owe homage of old to him and his ancestors,
And why you have raided, robbed and held people for
    ransom,   100
And killed his kinsmen, kings anointed.
You must render a reckoning there for your Round Table,
Why you are rebel to Rome and withhold its revenues.
If you resist this summons, he sends you these words:
He will seek you over the sea with sixteen kings,
Burn Britain the Greater and butcher your knights
And bind you, as obedient as any beast that breathes,
Robbed of all revel and rest under the radiant sky,
Even though you find yourself a foxhole in fear of Rome!
For flee into France, or Friesland indeed,   110
You'll be fetched back by force and felled for ever!
Your father paid fealty, we find in our records
In the registry of Rome, as rightly seen.
No trifling! We are determined to take the tribute

1. 92 Lammas Day: 1 August, when first fruits and rents fall due.

Julius Caesar won in war with warriors of mettle!'
  The King studied the senator with his splendid eyes,
Which flamed like coals fiercely, so furious was he.
His cheeks' colour changed, charged with fierce rage,
And he looked like a lion, on his lips biting.
The Romans in rank terror cringed on the ground   120
Through fear of his face as if fated to die;
Cowering like curs before the King's majesty,
They seemed stunned by his stern expression.
To his knees rose a knight then, and cried with loud
    clamour,
'King crowned by Nature, courteous and strong!
Harm none of us envoys for your honour's sake,
Since we are in your hands here and ask your mercy.
We belong to Sir Lucius, the Lord of Rome,
The most marvellous man of might on earth:
We do our lawful duty when we do his pleasure   130
And we come at his command. Excuse us therefore!'
  The Conqueror came out with these crisp words:
'I call you a coward, a craven knight!
If some man in this mansion were mightily upset,
You'd not dare for all Lombardy to look him in the face!'
'Sire,' said the senator, 'so save me Christ,
The power of your expression pierced us with pain;
In my life I never looked on a lordlier man.
No lie, but you glare like a lion, it seems.'
'You have summoned me,' said the King, 'and spoken
    accordingly.   140
For your sovereign's sake I still suffer you.
Since I was crowned with due right and with chrism
    anointed,
No thane ever threw such big threats at me.
But come! Let crowned kings counsel me,
Doctors of divinity, dukes and earls,
Peers of the parliament, prelates and others,

And all the highest orders of the Round Table.
Thus shall I be advised the views of valiant men
And do as deem my most deep-minded nobles.
To waste wild words would win me no honour,   150
Nor would wreaking my revenge in rage wilfully.
So you must stay here in sojourn with these lords,
In solace for a seven-night, stabling your horses,
And see what life we lead in these lowly parts
Beside the royalty of Rome, the greatest ever.'

   Then he commanded Sir Kay, 'Take care of these lords!
Look after these high-hearted men as their honour requires,
Lodging them without delay in lofty chambers,
And see that they are then served suitably in hall,
And that they find no fault with the fodder of their mounts,   160
Nor with the wine or wax candles or other worthy offering.
Spare not the spices! Spend what you please!
Let largesse be plentiful, with no lack at all.
If you guard my good faith, man, by my given pledge,
High reward shall you have, to handsel you for ever!'

   Then they were given grand lodgings and regarded as
     guests,
Served quickly by courteous men within the castle walls.
In chimneyed chambers they changed their attire,
Then in chivalrous charge of the chamberlain they
    descended,
And the senator was seated in seemly style   170
At the King's own table, where two trusty knights
Served only him, as Arthur was served,
On the right of the royal seat of the Round Table,
So great was regard for the grandeur of Rome
And its royal blood, the richest ever to rule on earth.

   There came in as first course before the King himself
Bristling boars' heads brightened with silver
Taken in by trained townsmen, attired in splendour,
Of lofty lineage, a line of sixty nobles.

Flesh fattened in close season with fine frumenty was there   180
With a wealth of wild beasts and wonderful birds,
Peacocks and plovers on platters of gold,
Porcupine piglets[1] unpastured by man,
Then herons handsomely hidden in their plumage,
Fat swans swiftly served on silver chargers,
Tarts from Turkey of attractive taste,
Beef pies in plenty pleasing to the palate,
Wild boar shoulders, with the best brawn sliced,
Barnacle geese and bitterns on embossed dishes,
Young hawks *en croute* too, hard to better,   190
And brisket of pork brightly gleaming.
Then several sorts of stew were there to please;
Bluish with bright sauce they burned flickering.
On each slice the flame was leaping high,
Delighting the lords who were looking on.
There were cranes and curlews cunningly roasted,
Rabbits in rare sauce richly hued,
Pheasants flourished with flaming silver,
And pies glazed with glair, and good things in plenty.
Then claret and Cretan wines were cunningly piped   200
Through conduits cleverly made of clear silver,
Osay and Algarve wines and others besides,
Rhenish and Rochelle as rich as could be,
And splendidly strong and sweet Venetian wine
From faucets of fine gold, for any to fancy.
The King's cup cabinet was covered with silver
And great gilded goblets gloriously hued.
There was a chief chamberlain, a chivalrous butler,
Sir Kay the courteous, who was court cup-bearer;

1. 183 According to Hamel (p. 260) this is a riddle. 'The popular dish
"urchins", pigs' maws with spiced pork stuffing, studded with silver
almonds to look like hedgehogs.' Much of the ensuing menu is still a
mystery, without mention in medieval cookery books.

A set of sixty goblets served the King,   210
So cleverly and craftily made, carved with skill,
Each part being picked out with precious stones,
That should poison be privily put in them
The bright gold would break to bits in the vapour,
Or else void the venom by virtue of the gems.
And the Conqueror himself, exquisitely arrayed,
Was clad in colours of clearest gold among his knights
And, adorned with his diadem, on his dais was exalted,
For he was held the highest-mettled of all earth-dwellers.
   Then the King spoke courteously to the company of
     lords,   220
Addressing the Romans with royal words of cheer:
'Sirs, look lordly and lighten your expressions!
In this land we have learnt little of lavish cooking;
We have but this bread, in these barren lands,
So fall to without feigning, enforce yourselves the more,
And feed on such poor fare as you find before you.'
'Sire,' said the senator, 'So save me Christ,
Such royalty never reigned within Rome's walls!
No prelate or Pope or prince of this world
But would be pleased to partake of this priceless feast!'   230
   The worthy meal over, they washed and went to the
     hall,
This conqueror acclaimed and his company of knights,
Sir Gawain the Good with Guinevere on his arm,
And Sir Uhtred[1] on the other side, high lord of Turin.
Then spices were served unsparingly to all,
And malmsey and muscatel, those marvellous wines,
Went round rapidly in ruddy brown cups,[2]

---

1. 234 Uhtred: either a Roman, or one of the Yorkshire Ughtreds, in which case 'Turin' represents a scribal error (see Hamel, p. 263).

2. 237 Carved wooden cups, sophisticated table equipment.

To each titled one in turn, Romans and others,
And presently the Prince, to please himself,
Assigned to the senator steadfast lords   240
Who would show him to his chamber, should he ask,
With melody and merriment, minstrelsy noble.
  Then the Conqueror came to council afterwards
With lords whose allegiance lay with him;
To the Giant's Tower he joyfully took
His justices and judges and gentle knights.
To the King Sir Cador[1] of Cornwall spoke,
Lovingly laughing with a likable expression:
'I thank God that threat throws such trouble at us;
Either do a better deed or be dragged in chains, I say.   250
The letters of Sir Lucius lighten my heart.
We have lived like layabouts many a long day,
Making merry in our many domains here,
And forfeited the fame we formerly sought.
By God, I was embarrassed on behalf of our best men,
Who were doleful at our disuse of deeds of glory.
Now war is awake, worthy honour to Christ!
With courage we shall conquer, and reclaim our honour!'
  'Fine counsel, Sir Cador!' the King replied,
'You marvellous man with your merry words!   260
You don't assess circumstance or consider deeply,
But hurl out of your head what your heart thinks.
We must treat for a truce touching this matter,
And ponder the present news that perplexes my heart.
You understand that the Emperor is angered somewhat;
It seems from his spokesman that he is seriously aggrieved.
His senator has summoned me and said his say
Outrageously in my hall with hateful words,
Spoken to me scornfully and spared me but little.
I could not answer for anger, my heart so trembled!   270

1. 247 Cador speaks first, as heir to the throne. His son Constantine succeeds Arthur: see l. 4316.

Tyrannically he told me to pay the tribute to Rome
Sadly owing of old from our ancestors' time,
When aliens, in the absence of armed defenders,
Claimed it from the Commons, as the chronicle tells.
But title I have to take tribute from Rome:
My ancestors were emperors who owned Rome themselves,
Belinus and Brennius and Baldwin the Third;
They occupied the Empire for eight score winters,
Each heir in turn, so the old men say.
They captured the Capitol and cast down its walls,   280
And hanged their head men a hundred at a time.
Then Constantine our kinsman conquered it after that;
He was heir to England's throne and Emperor of Rome,
And captured the Cross by conquest of arms
On which Christ was crucified, King of Heaven.
So we ask the Emperor with equal justice:
"What right thus to rule in Rome does he claim?"'
    Then King Aungers[1] answered Arthur the Conqueror:
'You ought to be overlord to all other kings
For your wisdom, your worth, your wielding of power   290
And your kingly counsel, which no crown could better.
I dare say for the Scots, we suffered from them;
When the Romans ruled here they asked ransom for our
        leaders,
Rampaged round the land and raped our wives,
And without right or reason robbed us of our possessions.
So I shall swear a sacred oath to Christ
And to the divinely virtuous Veronica[2] so noble,   ⟍

1. 288 Aungers (Angus), King of Scotland and brother of King Lot of
the Orkneys.

2. 297 Veronica, so named from the 'true likeness' (vera-icon) of
Christ's face printed on a handkerchief at the Crucifixion. She is the
symbol of pilgrimage to Rome, which gives an ironic significance to
the Round Tablers' vows to support their king's plans (Hamel, p. 266).

Vowing to avenge the vile villainy
Of those wicked men with my worthy warriors.
I shall furnish you with a force well provided for defence,   300
Twenty thousand men within two months,
Paid by me to campaign wherever you purpose,
Fighting your foes who unfairly treat us.'
    Then the royal ruler[1] of Britain the Little
Held counsel with Arthur and earnestly asked him
To answer the aliens with austere enmity,
To provoke the Emperor to advance over the Alps.
He said, 'I swear a sacred vow to Christ
And to holy Veronica, I shall not retreat
In rank fear for any Roman who reigns on earth,   310
But shall always have my war-host armed and ready,
No more fearing the force of their fell weapons
Than the dew that comes down damply falling;
No more flinch from the flash of their fierce blades
Than from the fairest flower that flourishes on earth!
I shall bring to your battle my best-armoured knights,
Thirty thousand in number, thoroughly equipped.
Pick the place you propose for them,
And they shall be there within thirty days.'
    'Ah!' cried the Welsh king, 'May Christ be praised!   320
Now shall we fully avenge what vexed our ancestors.
In the west of Wales such wonders of evil they did
That all woefully weep at the thought of that war.
I shall have the vanguard[2] utterly to myself
Until I have vanquished the Viscount of Rome,
Who did me a villainy at Viterbo once
As I passed on pilgrimage by Pontremoli.
In Tuscany at that time he took some of our knights,

1. 304 King Howell of Brittany.

2. 324 A vow fulfilled: see l. 1986

43

Wrongly arrested them and held them to ransom.
No prospect of peace do I promise him   330
Till we have sternly set to by ourselves alone,
And dealt out death-blows with our deadly weapons!
For that campaign I promise to pay the best knights
Of Wight and Wales and the Western Marches,
Two thousand in total, all truly horsed,
The hardiest armed men in all the West!'

    Sir Ewain FitzUrien then eagerly spoke up,
Cousin to the Conqueror, for courage renowned:
'If we are aware of your will, Sire, we shall work to it,
Whether this campaign take place or be postponed,   340
To ride against the Romans and ravage their lands.
But give the word, we shall go fully geared and take ship.'

    'Cousin,' said the Conqueror, 'most kindly you ask
If my counsel concurs in the conquest of those lands.
By the kalends[1] of June we shall encounter finally
Those cruellest of knights, so Christ help me!
To that end I offer my holy oath to Christ,
And my vow to Veronica full of virtue and power.
At Lammas I shall leave, and linger freely
In Lorraine or Lombardy as my liking determines,   350
Then march to Milan and mine down the walls
Of Pietrasanta, Pisa and Pontremoli.
In the vale of Viterbo I shall victual my knights,
Staying there six weeks to solace myself,
Then send couriers to the city and set up my siege –
Unless they proffer me peace in process of time.'

    'Let it be so,' said Sir Ewain, 'and I swear
If I ever set eyes on the man
Who occupies your heritage, the Empire of Rome,
I shall truly attempt to take that eagle[2]   360

---

1. 345 Kalends: first day of the month.

2. 360 A vow fulfilled: see l. 2070.

Borne on his banner of bright precious gold,
Snatch it from his soldiers and slash it to bits,
Unless it is rapidly rescued by resolute knights.
I shall reinforce you in the field with fresh warriors,
Fifty thousand fighters on fine horses,
To take arms against your enemies wherever you think fit,
In France or Friesland, fight when you like!'
    'By Our Lord,' said Sir Lancelot, 'Now lightens my heart!
I praise God for the gifts these great lords have promised!
Now lesser men have leave their loyalty to vow   370
As allowed by law; so listen to my words:
I shall be at the battle with my brave knights
On my straining steed, splendidly equipped,
Before the main fight, facing Sir Lucius,
To joust with him among his giants, Genoese and others,
And strike him sternly off his steed with the strength of my arm
Despite the strong soldiers supporting him.[1]
My retinue being arrayed, I reckon it not hard
To irrupt into Rome with a ravaging force.
With six score helmets, within seven days   380
I shall be seen at sea, sail when you like.'
    Then laughed Sir Lot, loudly speaking out:
'I like it that Sir Lucius longs for misery;
Now that he wants war, his woes shall begin.
It is our fate to avenge what vexed our ancestors.
I give my word to God and to gracious Veronica
That if I see the Romans, styled so renowned,
Arrayed in rich pomp on a broad battlefield,
I shall ride for reverence of the Round Table
Right through their ranks, rearguard and all,   390
Preparing a path for my men pressing after,
My horse running in red blood as it rushes on.[2]

1. 377 A vow fulfilled: see ll. 2074-9.

2. 392 A vow fulfilled: see ll. 2088-94.

The first to follow my furious charge
Shall find behind my feet many fatally dispatched!'
The Conqueror kindly encouraged these knights,
Much praising their princely protestations:
'May all-ruling high God honour you all!
Let me never lack you while lordship is mine!
You maintain my might and my manhood's honour
Throughout the whole earth, and in other kings' lands.   400
You won me my wealth, my worldly renown
And my crown's possessions by courage in conquest.
He need fear no foe who has followers like you,
But can fight ever fresh on the field at will.
No king in Christendom need I take account of
While I see you stand strong; I set store by nothing else.'
   This trusty council concluded, amid cracking of
     trumpets
They came down in due procession, dukes and earls,
Then swiftly assembled and supped in hall,
This comely company, in courteous style.   410
Then the great governor regaled the assembly
With rich honour and revel for all the Round Table
While seven days slipped by. Then the senator asked
In harsh tones what answer the Emperor might have.
Epiphany being past, and opinions taken
From peers in Parliament, prelates and others,
The King in his council, courteous and noble,
Brought forth the foreigners and fairly told them himself:
'Greet Lucius your lord, and let him hear straight:
If you are loyal liegemen, let him know at once   420
That at Lammas I shall leave and then lodge freely
In delight in his lands with lords in plenty,
Rule there as a royal king, resting when I please,
And by the river Rhone establish my Round Table,
Truly taking tribute in that fair territory
Despite the menace of his might and his malice whatever!

Then march over the mountains to his main lands,
To Milan the marvellous, and mine down its walls.
In neither Lorraine nor Lombardy shall I leave a single man
Alive who lives by his laws in those places.   430
I shall turn into Tuscany at the time of my choice
And ride over those rolling lands with my raiding force.
Bid him be bold to get back his honour
And make good his manhood by meeting me there!
On the first of February I shall be found in France;
Let him meet me in those marches, and make his mind up
    when!
Before I am taken by force or forfeit my territories,
The flower of his followers shall be fatally felled.
I swear to him under my great seal that I certainly shall
Besiege the city of Rome within seven winters,   440
So securely encompass it, covering all sides,
That many a senator shall sigh for my sake alone.
My word is warranted and you are well equipped
With safe conduct and credentials – leave when you like.
I shall set your stages, say myself where you rest
Between this place and the port from which you pass over.
I assign seven days for your journey to Sandwich;
It seems a small stage, sixty miles a day.
You must spur most swiftly, not sparing your horse.
Make your way by Watling Street, no other.   450
Wherever you unhorse at night's onset, stop;
Be it forest or field, go no farther.
Halter your horse by the bridle to a bush
And lodge under a lime tree as you best like.
An alien ought not to be on the move at night,
Roaming with such a ribald rout as yours.
Like it or loathe it, whatever you think,
Your licence is limited, as these lords witness,
And your life and limb's safety lies upon it
Though Sir Lucius should lay the lordship of Rome on it.   460

But if you are found one foot from the fringe of the ocean
After the eighth day early in the morning,
Your heads will be off and horses will tear you apart;
You'll be hanged on high and hounds will gnaw at you.
No rent or red gold that Rome may possess
Shall readily rate, knight, as ransom for you!'
   'Sire,' said the senator, 'so save me Christ,
If with honour I could leave now,
For no emperor on earth would I again
Ever go to Arthur on an embassy like this. 470
But here I am alone with only sixteen knights:
I beseech you, sire, grant us safe passage.
If any should hinder us unlawfully on our way,
And your licence allow it, lord, you would lose honour.'
   'Have courage!' said the King. 'Your safe–conduct is
     known
From Carlisle to the coast where your craft is anchored.
Though you carried full coffers crammed with silver,
My seal would see you safe sixty miles farther.'
   They bowed to the King and begged leave to depart,
Swung up on their horses and hurried from Carlisle; 480
Sir Cador the courteous made clear their route,
Conducted them to Catterick and commended them to
    Christ.
They spurred at such speed they exhausted their horses,
And hurriedly hired old hacks as a result.
They rode in rank fear, never resting at all,
But for lodging under lime-trees when the light failed.
The senator ever sought the straightest way,
And at sunset on the seventh day they reached the city.
Of all glee under God their gladness was greatest
At the sound of the sea and Sandwich's bells. 490
Swiftly they settled their steeds on board,
Wearily to the wan sea making their way.
They helped men haul the anchors over the gunwale

And fled at first high tide; to Flanders they rode,
Then crossed that country, coming as seemed best
To Aachen in Germany, still in Arthur's domain.
W⟨h⟩en they had gone by Mount St Gothard, a gruelling
    way,
They at length came to Lombardy's lovely region,
And turned into lofty-towered Tuscany,
And in Pisa put on precious apparel quickly.   500
In Sutri on the sabbath they stabled their horses,
And by consent of all sought out the saints of Rome.
Then they spurred to the palace with its splendid portals,
Where Sir Lucius was lodged with lords in plenty,
Lovingly bowed low and delivered to him
The sealed dispatches with their solemn wording.

   The Emperor eagerly and ardently inquired of them,
Asking what answer Arthur had sent,
How he ruled his realm and reigned over the people,
And if he were rebel to Rome, what right he claimed.   510
'You should have seized his sceptre and sat above him
In reverence for the royalty of Rome the magnificent.
Seeing you were a senator sent from Rome by me,
He should have served you himself with solemn grace.'

   'That will he never for any soul in the world
But a warrior who can win a war against him.
First, many fallen on the field shall be left dead
Before he appears in this place, propose what you will.
Arthur is your enemy for ever, Sire, I tell you,
And aims to be overlord of the empire of Rome,   520
Which all his ancestors owned but Uther alone.
This New Year I made known your announcement myself
To that acclaimed conqueror in nine kings' presence.
Right by the most royal Round Table
I summoned him solemnly in sight of his nobles.
Such fear, in faith, I never felt in my life
On entering the hall of any other earthly prince.

I would lose all my loyal men and my lordship in Rome
Rather than go again to that great king on such embassy.
He might be picked as the paragon of princes,   530
Both as champion in war's chances and chevalier of
    distinction,
Most splendid, sagacious and strong of arm.
Of all men I ever met on this middle-earth so fine,
He is counted the most courteous creature in Christendom,
Fiercest of feature and fullest of fiery courage,
The noblest in knighthood ever known under Christ!
Speak of him as a spender who despises silver,
Gives gold no more regard than great boulders,
Rates wine as water that wells from the ground,
And worships no wealth in this world but glory.   540
Such decorum was never kept in a country of worth
As that conqueror keeps in his kingly court.
This Christmas I counted the kings anointed
At his table at one time – ten with himself!
War he will surely wage; beware if you will.
Recruit men of courage and keep watch on your borders;
Have them armed and on guard as early as possible,
For if he reaches Rome, he'll have it ransomed for ever.
I pray you, prepare yourself. Put it off no longer!
Make sure of your mercenaries; to the mountains send them.   550
If Arthur's health hold, early this year
He'll sternly set out, soon and in haste.'
    'By Easter,' said the Emperor, 'I aim myself
To head a host of armed knights in Germany,
Then foray boldly into France, that flower of realms,
To fetch forth that fellow and make forfeit his lands.
I shall place patrols, powerful and cunning,
Many Genoese giants, jousters of quality,
To meet him in the mountains and massacre his knights,
Strike them down in steep gorges and destroy them for ever.   560
On St Gothard we shall garrison a great watch-tower,

Furnish it fully with a fine force of men,
With a beacon above to burn when they wish,
So that no enemy army may enter the mountains.
On St Bernard shall be built another barbican,
Manned by battle-hardened bannerets[1] and bachelor knights.
No prince shall pass in at the portals of Pavia
Through places made perilous by my splendid knights.'
    Then Sir Lucius in lordly style sent letters
Off to the Orient in the hands of stern knights,   570
To Albania, Arcady and Alexandria,
To India and Armenia where the Euphrates runs,
To Asia and Africa and the whole of Europe,
To Hyrcania, Elam and all those outer isles,
And Araby and Egypt; to earls and others
Who occupied any lands in those eastern marches
Of Damascus and Damietta – all dukes and earls.
They, fearing his frown, fast complied.
From Crete and Cappadocia kings of repute
Came at once without waiting when he commanded.   580
When Tartary and Turkey were told of his summons,
Mighty monarchs quickly marched to Thebes,
As did the flower of fair folk in Amazon lands:
All who failed to take the field were forfeit for ever.
From Babylon and Baghdad bold knights came,
And barons with their battle groups held back no longer.
In Persia and Pamphilia and Prester John's lands
Each prince with his power prepared actively.
The Sultan of Syria assembled his army
From the Nile to Nazareth in enormous numbers.   590
In Gadara and Galilee they gathered together,
Those sultans who served Rome as staunch mercenaries,

---

1. 566 Banneret: 'a knight entitled to bring a company of vassals into
the field under his own banner, and who ranked next to a baron and
above other knights' (OED p. 165).

Then gathered by the Greek Sea with their grim weapons
In their great galleys, with their glittering shields.
The King of Cyprus stayed at sea for the Sultan,
The royalty of Rhodes ranged about him;
At speed the Saracens, seizing opportunity,
Sailed the salty coast in a strong wind.

    The kings came in good order to Corneto port   600
Sixty miles or so from the city of Rome.
A great number of Greeks had got ready by then,
The mightiest in Macedonia, with the men of those marches,
And Apulians and Prussians pressing on with others,
Liegemen of Lithuania with legions in plenty
Massing in their formations, myriads of men.
Thus sultans and Saracens from various states,
With the Sultan of Syria and sixteen kings,
Assembled at speed in the city of Rome.

    Then out came the Emperor in full armed order,   610
Ranged with his Romans on royal steeds;
In front were sixty giants, fathered by fiends,
With witches and warlocks to watch his tents
Wherever he went, in winter or any season.
No battle-horse could bear them, those barbarous creatures,
Only camels with mail-clad castles for saddles.
He forged forward with his foreigners, a force immense,
Hard into Germany, which Arthur had conquered,
Rode in by the river revelling in carnage,
Then harassed the high lands in huge delight;   620
He won all Westphalia by war as he wished,
Drew down to the Danube and dubbed new knights.
Castles in the country near Cologne he besieged,
And sojourned that season with Saracens galore.

    On the eighth day of Hilary[1] Sir Arthur himself

---

1. 625 Hilary: St Hilary's Day is 13 January, so the Council is held on
the 20th.

In high council thus ordered all his lords:
'Go swiftly to your seignories, assemble your knights
And rendezvous ready for war at Cotentin with me!
Wait for me on the sweet waters of Barfleur
Boldly on board with the best of your warriors: 630
I shall greet you in good faith in those gracious borders.'
He speedily sent out sergeants-at-arms
To all master mariners to muster ships for him.
His splendid fleet was assembled within sixteen days
On the sea at Sandwich, to sail when he ordered.
He proclaimed a parliament in the palace at York
For all the lords of the land, lay and clerical,
And at the sermon's end to all the nobles
The King in council clearly spoke thus:
'On a perilous path I propose to march,   640
Campaigning with my keen men to conquer yonder lands.
If opportunity offers, I shall overcome the enemy
Who occupies my heritage, the Empire of Rome.
I set before you a sovereign, assent if you will!
My own sister's son, Sir Mordred by name,
Shall be viceroy, I vow, invested with power
Over the loyal liegemen who live on my land.'
    To his cousin he declared in council then:
'I make you the master of many kingdoms,[1]
A warden worthy to wield rule in my lands   650
Which I have won by war the wide world over.
Let Guinevere my wife be given grace and honour,
And let her lack nothing she likes to possess.
Take care of my castles and keep them equipped
For her to solace herself in splendid company.
Fence in my forests or forfeit my favour for ever,
Granting rights to hunt game to Guinevere alone,

---

1. 649 Arthur's strict injunctions on Mordred, and his threats at ll. 656
and 692, give ironic point to the end of the poem.

And then solely in the season when prey is sleek and fat,
So that she has sport at those special times.
Change chancellor and chamberlains as you wish,   660
Ordain your auditors and officers yourself,
Your juries and judges, your justices of land,
And deal their due deserts to those who do wrong.
If I am destined to die by the doom of God,
I say that as my executor, senior to others,
To save my soul, you must distribute my estate
To mendicants and those made miserable by misfortune.
Take here the tally of my extensive treasure:
As I truly trust you, never betray me!
And as you will answer before the austere Judge   670
Who wields rule in the world as he deems wise,
Look that my last will be loyally executed!
You have complete power over what pertains to my
        crown –
All my worldly wealth and my wife as well.
Keep your soul clean so that no cavil is made
When I come back to this country, Christ permitting.
If you have grace to govern in a good way,
I shall crown you King,[1] cousin, with my own hands.'

    Then Sir Mordred himself softly answered,
Kneeling in denial to the noble Conqueror: 680
'I beg you, Sire, my blood brother and lord,
Choose another for this charge, for charity's sake!
If you appoint me to this post your people will be deceived;
I am too feeble to fulfil the function of a prince.
Where warriors wise in warfare are esteemed hereafter,
My talents, I truly say, will be attested as minor.
I intend to travel with your troops, my liege,
And my preparation is plain to my peerless knights.'

    'You are my nearest nephew, my nursling of old,

1. 678 Arthur will reward Mordred with a kingdom, but not Britain.

The child of my chamber whom I have cherished and
    praised.   690
Abandon not this service, for our blood tie's sake.
If you will not do my wish, you know what it means.'
  He lingered no longer, but took his leave
Of lords and liegemen to be left behind,
And then that worthy warrior went to his chamber
To comfort the crestfallen Queen awaiting him.
Softly sobbing, Guinevere kissed him,
Talked to him tenderly, her tears flowing:
'I could curse the man who caused this conflict,
Who severs me from service of my espoused lord.   700
All my life's delight leaves the land,
And I am left languishing, believe it, for ever!
Why do I not die, dear love, in your arms,
Before suffering this sad fate by myself alone?'
  'Grieve not, Guinevere, for love of God in heaven!
Grudge not my going, since good will come of it!
Your weeping and woe wound my heart;
I would not for the wide world see you suffer.
I have given you a guardian to be your own knight
And overlord of England under yourself.[1]   710
I mean Sir Mordred, whom you have much praised,
Who shall do as you direct, my dear, as your deputy.'
So lovingly he took leave of the ladies in the chamber,
Kissed them kindly and commended them to Christ.
She suddenly swooned when he asked for his sword,
And fell down fainting as if fated to die.
He hurried to his horse, his lords all round him,
Spurred from the palace with his princely knights,
That right royal company of the Round Table,
And sped towards Sandwich: she never saw him again.   720

---

1. 710 This provision contradicts Arthur's command to Mordred
(l. 649), which gives him ultimate power.

There the great ones, gathered with their glad-hearted
    knights,
Set forth on the field with their fine accoutrements,
Princely dukes and peers proudly riding,
And earls of England with a host of archers.
Sheriffs sharply shifted common soldiers about
With commands before the mighty men of the Round
    Table,
Apportioning each people to its particular lord
On the seashore in the south, to sail at his command.
Ships rigged and ready they rowed to the beach,
Brought battle-horses on board and fine helmets,   730
Safely stowing the steeds and their trappings,
The tents and siege tools and tested shields,
Marquees, sacks of clothes and noble coffers,
Pack-horses, palfreys and proud war-horses.
Thus they stowed the stores of the stalwart knights.

They delayed no longer when the loading was complete,
But quickly cast off on the crest of the tide.
Great craft and cutters squared their yards
At the King's command, crowding on sail
And heaving up anchors heartily on the gunwales,   740
All by wit of the watermen on the surging waves.
Yes, brave men in the bows coiled up the cables
Of freighters and frigates and Flemish vessels;
Some took sails to the top, some controlled the tillers,
And some stood on the starboard side – all strongly
    singing.
The principal ships from the port proved their draught,
Foaming with full sail over the varied waves;
Wholly without accident they hauled in the boats.
Shipmen sharply shut the portholes
And launched the lead over the luff, plumbing the depth.   750
They looked to the lode-star when the light failed,
And cast their course by craft when the sky was clouded

By knowledge of compass needle in the night currents.
In dread of the darkness they slowed down a little,
And all those stern seamen struck sail at once.
   King Arthur, on a huge vessel with a host of knights,
Was enclosed in a completely equipped cabin,
Resting on a richly arrayed bed,
And the swaying on the sea sent him to sleep.
He dreamed that a dragon dreadful to behold   760
Came driving over the deep to drown his people,
Ranging directly from the realms of the west
And soaring in spite over the surging sea.
His crown and neck were completely covered
With undulating azure in high enamel;
Scales of pure silver sheathed his shoulders,
Making the monster as if mantled with mail;
His wings and wide belly were wonderfully coloured,
And thus marvellously mailed he mounted aloft.
With tremendous tongues his tail was dagged;   769a[1]
Any contact would quickly kill a man!   770
His feet were flourished in finest black
And tipped with talons entirely of gold.   771a[1]
Such venomous flames flared from his lips
That the flood seemed on fire with the flying flecks.
   Then issuing out of the east against him
Came a bear fierce and black above in the clouds,
Each paw like a post, with prodigious pads
Culminating in cruel curling claws.
Hateful and horrid were his hair and the rest;
He was bow-legged and bristly and brutishly ugly,
With foully matted fell and foaming lips –   780
The vilest figure ever to be formed!

1. 769a and 771a: I follow Benson in accepting Gordon and Vinaver's
opinion that two lines of this sort have dropped out of the manuscript,
and accordingly include them with separate numbering.

He sprang about, scowled and snarled with menace,
And turned to attack with his terrible claws,
Roaring with a rage that rocked all the ground,
So savagely he struck as he stormed about.
    From afar the dragon flew furiously at him,
Sending him staggering off under the sky,
Hitting him like a hawk with high courage,
And fighting with feet and fiery breath together.
But in battle the bear seemed the bigger one   790
And boldly bit back with baleful fangs.
He struck so savagely with his spiked claws
That the dragon's breast and belly were bloody all over.
He ramped with such rage that he ripped open the ground,
Which ran with red blood like rain from heaven!
He'd have done down the dragon by dint of sheer strength
But for the wild fire the dragon wielded in defence.
Then the serpent soared to the very zenith
And dived down through the clouds with dreadful impact,
Attacking the bear with his talons and tearing his back   800
For ten feet between his tail and his crown,
Thus beating the bear down and battering out his life –
Let him fall in the sea-flood and float where he likes!
This bad dream so burdened the King aboard ship
He nearly burst with bitter pain on his bed there lying.
    When the wise King awoke, worn out with worry,
He took two of his attendant philosophers,
The subtlest scholars in the seven arts,
The cleverest clerics acclaimed in Christendom,
And told them of his time of torment in sleep.   810
'Beset by a serpent and such a savage beast,
I am desperately downcast: interpret my dream,
Or doomed by the dear Lord, I must die at once!'
    'Sire,' swiftly said those sage philosophers,
'The dragon you dreamed of, so dreadful to behold,
Who came driving over the deep to drown your people,

Is yourself, we swear with the certainty of truth,
Yourself sailing the sea with your staunch knights.
The colours coating his clear-shining wings
Stand for the realms you rule, having rightly won them;   820
And that tail dagged with tongues so tremendous
Means the fine host afloat in your fleet at sea.
The bear that was beaten above in the clouds
Betokens the tyrants who torture your people,
Or else a huge ogre whom you'll have to fight
Some day in single combat by yourself alone.
In that you will thrive, through Our Lord's help,
And gain victory as your vision vividly showed.
Your dreadful dream, Sire, dread it no longer,
Nor care, Sir Conqueror, but comfort yourself   830
And all who sail the sea with your steadfast knights!'

    They spread their sails to the sound of trumpets,
And over the surging sea the splendid company went.
They navigated to the noble coast of Normandy
    accurately,
And blithely at Barfleur the bold army landed,
Finding there a fleet of friends in hosts,
The flower and finest blossom of fifteen realms,
For kings and captains had kept waiting for him
According to his command given at Christmas in Carlisle.

    As soon as they stepped on land and set up tents,   840
A Templar[1] came in tumult to tell the King privily:
'A terrible tyrant here is torturing your people,
A huge Genoese giant engendered by devils.
He has feasted on fully five hundred people,
And as many infants, all high-born children.
Such has been his sustenance for seven winters,
Yet the sot is not sated, so strong is his pleasure in it!
In the country round Cotentin no clan has he spared

---

1. 841 The Order of the Templars was suppressed in 1312.

Outside kingly castles enclosed in walls,
But has murdered in masses all male children,   850
Carried them to the crags and completely devoured them.
This day he dragged off the Duchess of Brittany[1]
As she rode near Rennes with her royal escorts,
And haled her to the high summit of his habitation
To lie with him as long as her life should last.
We followed from afar, five hundred and more,
Bold men, burghers and bachelors of mettle,
But he got to his granite lair: with such grief she screamed,
That lady's lamentation will live with me for ever.
She was the flower of all France, indeed of five kingdoms,   860
And judged most gentle of jewels by lordly men
From Genoa to Gironne, by Jesu in heaven!
She was kin to your Queen, Sir King, as you know,
Derived of the most royal stock that reigns on earth;
So have pity on your people, as a just king should,
And try to avenge the villainies visited upon them!'

   'Alas to have lived so long!' said King Arthur,
'It would have been well had I been aware of this.
Not fair fortune but foul has befallen me   870
In the fate of this fair lady whom the fiend has ruined.
I'd have sacrificed fifteen years of France's revenues
To have set foot even a furlong from that fiend
When he haled the lady off to the heights above;
I'd have lost my life rather than let her suffer.
But take me to the tor the terrible being haunts,
And I'll penetrate the place and speak with him,
Treating with the tyrant who is treasonous in my realm,
Yes, take a truce till times are better.'

   'Sire, do you see that scarred steep with two fires?   880
That's the lair where he lurks, like it or not,

1. 852 The Duchess is the young wife of Arthur's cousin, King
Howell (see l. 1180).

On the crest of a crag beside a cold spring
Which covers the cliff with its clear streams.
You'll find many folk there, all foully dead,
More florins, in faith, than all France owns,
And more treasure by that traitor treacherously seized
Than was in Troy at the time it was taken, I swear.'

Then royal Arthur roared in grief for his people,
Strode to his tent in turmoil, not for rest,
And writhed about, wrestling with himself and wringing
    his hands: 890
No warrior in the world was aware of what he intended.
He called to him Sir Kay, his cup-bearer,
And Sir Bedivere the bold, who bore his great sword:
'After evensong come armed to the uttermost and
    mounted!
Be at that bush by the bubbling stream,
For when supper is served to the seated lords
I shall set out with speed on a secret pilgrimage
Beside the salt streams to seek out a saint
On the Mount of Saint Michael,[1] where miracles are
    performed.'

Then after evensong King Arthur on his own   900
Went to his wardrobe, swiftly undressed
And put on a padded jerkin piped in gold,
And over that an extra jacket of Acre leather,
And over that a hauberk, an excellent coat of mail,
And lastly a sleeveless tunic, loose and scalloped.
He put on a helmet of highly polished silver,
The very best from Basle, with borders of distinction.
The crest and the crown were kept in place
By grips of pure gold graced with jewels.
The visor and aventail were variously adorned   910

---

1. 899 Mont Saint Michel is sixty miles from Barfleur. It is still a place
of pilgrimage.

And devoid of defect, with vents of silver.
His gauntlets were brightly gilded and engraved at the hems
With seed-pearls and precious stones in superb colours.
He braced on his broad shield and bid bring his sword,
Strode to a bay steed, then stood for a second
Before leaping aloft with a lift from his stirrup,
Then reining him strongly and firmly directing him,
Spurred his bay steed and started for the wood.
 They rode by the river which ran swiftly ·   920
Where trees overreached it with branches in splendour.
There the roe and the reindeer ran free and careless
Among rose-bushes and shrubs, rioting in pleasure.
The forest was flourished with flowers in plenty,
With falcons and pheasants of fairy-like colours.
All the birds flashed brilliantly, beating their wings,
And the cuckoos clamorously cried in the groves,
All delighting gladly in their limitless joy.
The noise of the nightingales' notes was sweet:
Three hundred of them with thrushes debated!   930
The swift waters' singing and the warbling of birds
Might cure a man quite who was chronically ill!
 Then the fine trio fared forth, going forward on foot
After tethering their trusty mounts not too far off.
There the King keenly commanded his companions
To stay with the steeds and proceed no farther,
'For I shall seek out this saint by myself alone
And size up the sole possessor of this mount;
After which you may offer, each in turn,
Ceremoniously to Saint Michael, mighty in Christ's
     power.'   940
 The King ranged over the rock with its craggy ravines
And came climbing to the crest of the cliff,
Where he looked about livelily, having lifted his visor
And snatched breath in the sneaping wind to steady
     himself.

He found two fires there flaming high,
And fully a fourth of a furlong he paced between them,
Then walked by way of the welling water-springs
To find where the wicked warlock dwelt.
To the first fire he went and found beside it
A worn old woman woefully wringing her hands   950
And grieving with grim tears over a grave
Newly sunk in the soil since midday it seemed.
  He saluted that sorrowful one with suitable words,
And kindly inquired of her concerning the giant.
The woebegone woman weepingly greeted him,
Kneeling in courtesy, hands clasped, and called out softly,
'Mind, dear man, you make too much noise!
If the warlock becomes aware of you we shall be doomed.
Cursed be the caitiff who carried off your senses
And sent you searching by these savage waters!   960
I counsel you in courtesy: you crave only sorrow.
Whither do you wander, warrior unblest?
Do you seek to slay him with your splendid sword?
Were you worthier as a warrior than Wade[1] or Gawain,
No honour would you earn, as I have to warn you.
With no safety did you swear to search these crags.
Six of you would be too feeble to face him in fight,
For if you set eyes on him you'd have no heart
Even to cross yourselves, so huge he seems!
You are in the first flower of knighthood, fair and noble,   970
But you are fated to fall, which fills me with grief,
For if fifty of you faced him on the field of battle
That fearful being's fist would fell you as one!
Lo! the Duchess most dear – today she was taken –
Dug down, deeply buried in a ditch of earth,

1. 964 Wade: a hero of medieval romance twice mentioned by
Chaucer. Perhaps he and Gawain appear together here because Wade's
boat was called Guingelot, and Gawain's horse, Gringolet (Krishna,
p. 178).

A mild woman murdered before the midday bell
Meaninglessly, without mercy, on this domain of earth.
He forced her, defiled her, and fatal was her end,
Slain most savagely and slit to the navel!
I oiled her body here and afterwards buried her;   980
In anguish at her helplessness I shall be unhappy for ever.
No fellowly friend followed her here
But me, her foster-mother for more than fifteen winters.
I shall never seek to escape from this steep promontory,
But on the day that I die shall be discovered here.'
   Then King Arthur answered that ancient woman:
'I am come from the Conqueror most courteous and noble,
Being one of the best of Arthur's brave knights,
A messenger to this midden, to amend matters for the
     people
By parleying with the proud man who possesses this
     mount;   990
Yes, treating with the tyrant for the treasure of the land
By taking a truce until the times are better.'
'Your words are merely wasted,' the old woman said,
'He cares little for countries or clans of people,
And gives no regard to red gold or rents,
But lives outside the law as his liking determines,
Not empowered by the people as a prince with rights.
He is tricked out to his own taste in a tunic
Which was specially spun in Spain by maidens,
And soon after sewn most splendidly in Greece.   1000
It is all hide and hairy all over,
And bordered with the beards[1] of the best-ranked kings,
And crisped and curled so that inquirers may know
Each king and the country he comes from by the colour.
Here he farms the full revenues of fifteen realms:

---

1. 1002 The beard was the token of authority, cf. Gloucester's ''Tis
most ignobly done / To pluck me by the beard' (*King Lear* III, 6, 35).

Yes, every eve of Easter, however it falls,
For the peace of the people they dispatch it promptly,
Dead on the due date, by daring knights;
And he has asked for Arthur's beard each of these seven
    years.
So here he lurks hiding, to outrage Arthur's people   1010
Till the bold King of Britain has buffed his lips
And sent his best barons with his beard to that fierce one.
If you've brought no beard, then back off at once:
You'll get only grief if you give anything else,
For he takes more treasure totally unhindered
Than ever Arthur or any of his ancestors owned.
But if you've brought the beard, he'll be more happy
Than if you'd brought Burgundy or Britain the Greater.
But seal your lips close now, for the love of charity;
Let no sound escape in any circumstance.   1020
Put your present to him promptly, but don't press him,
For he's sitting at supper and soon annoyed.
Do as I direct: doff your armour,
Kneel in your gown and greet him as your lord.
All this season he sups on seven male children,
Chopped up on a charger of chalk-white silver,
With pickles and powders and precious spices
And plentiful piquant Portuguese wine.
Three mournful maidens make his spits turn;
They abide his bedtime to do his bidding then.   1030
Four such would fall dead within four hours
Before the foul lust of his flesh were fulfilled.'
   'That beard I have brought,' said he, 'and the better for
    me!
For, bearing the beard myself, I shall be ready.
But let me learn, dear lady, where that lord is now;
If I live, so the Lord help me, largesse shall be yours.'
'Go fast to the fire that flames high,' she said,
'There the fiend is filling himself. Venture if you wish,

But seek him from the side, going south a little,
For he can scent you himself from six miles off.'   1040
To the side where the smoke blew sped Arthur then,
Crossing himself soberly with sacred words,
And sidling to the spot he saw the man.
How ugly was that oaf hogging it there!
He was lying at full length, lolling uncouthly
With a human thigh held up by the haunch.
His back and his buttocks and his big loins
He was baking at the bale-fire, and bare-arsed he seemed.
Crude roasts and cruel cuts of meat
From boys and beasts were broached on spits together,   1050
And a cauldron was crammed with christened children,
Some skewered on spits turned by maidens.
   Then this comely king, on account of his subjects,
Bled at heart with bitter grief, on the bare ground
      standing.
Then no longer delaying, he lifted up his shield,
Brandished his broadsword by the bright hilt,
Faced the foul fellow with furious intent,
And hailed the hulk with these haughty words:
'Now may God great in power, to whom we give
      worship,
Strike you with sorrow, sot, spread out there,   1060
As the foulest fellow ever formed in nature!
You feed most filthily, the Fiend take your soul!
This is unclean cooking, you crude serf, I swear,
You outcast of all creatures, you accursed wretch!
Because you have killed these christened children
You have made them martyrs and murdered these
Who are spitted on this soil and smashed by your hands.
And so I shall assign you your deserts as reward,
Through the might of Saint Michael, this mount's true
      owner!
Because you did to death that duchess so beautiful   1070

After forcing her on the flat ground in your filthy lust,
Stand to fight, son of a dog, the Devil take your soul!
For you shall die this day from dire blows at my hand!'
   The glutton glared savagely, gaping with amazement,
And grinned like a greyhound with his grisly fangs.
He gaped and growled, glowered and grimaced,
Girding at the good king who greeted him so angrily.
All the hair on his head was hideously matted,
And stuck out from his skull six inches all round.
His face and his forehead were fretted all over   1080
Like the fell of a frog, with freckles it seemed.
Hook-billed like a hawk was he, with a hoary beard,
And hairy round the eyeholes were his beetling brows.
If you looked hard, harsh as a dogfish
Was the hide of that hulk from head to foot.
His ears were huge and ugly to look at
And his eyes were most horrible, hideously flaming.
He was flat-mouthed like a flounder, with fleering lips,
And the flesh round his fore-teeth stank foul as a bear.
His beard, black and bristly, on his breast hung down;   1090
His body bulged, as big as a porpoise's,
And the flesh of his foul lips fiercely quivered,
Each collop curling like a cruel wolf's head.
Bull-necked and broad in his brawny shoulders was he,
And badger-breasted with big bristles like a boar;
Ungainly arms had he, like an oak with ridged bark,
And his limbs and loins were loathsome, believe me.
His shanks were unshapely, shuffle-footed was he,
And gnarled and knock-kneed were his noisome legs;
He was thick at the thighs and thicker-haunched than a
     giant,   1100
And puffed with fat like a pig – repellent indeed.
Carefully counted, the creature's height
From forehead to foot was fully five fathoms.
   He started up sturdily on his two strong shanks

And quickly caught hold of a club of pure iron.
He'd have killed the King with his cruel weapon,
But through the craft of Christ the crude fellow failed;
Yet the crest and crown and clasps of silver
He hacked off Arthur's helmet with one heavy blow.
The King quickly covered himself with his shield   1110
And swung him a swingeing blow with his stately sword;
Full in the forehead of the foe he struck
And the burnished blade bore through to the brain.
But the fellow wiped his face with his foul hands
And countered with a quick blow at the King's head.
Arthur altered his stance and hopped back a bit;
Vice would have been victor had he not avoided the stroke.
Then he followed up fiercely and fetched a blow
High on the ogre's haunch with his hard weapon,
Burying the blade in his body six inches.   1120
To the hilt the hot blood of the hulk ran down,
For he had hit into the ogre's intestines
Straight to the genitals,[1] jaggedly severing them.
  The giant bellowed and bawled and battered fiercely
And hard at Arthur, but hit the ground;
A sword's length in the soil he struck his club.
The sound of his savage blows nearly stunned the King,
Yet he quickly came to the encounter again
And struck with his sword, slitting open the loins
So that the guts and the gore gushed out together,   1130
Making the grass greasy on the ground he trod.
Then the giant cast away his club and clutched the King
On the crest of the crag, clamping him in his arms
And enclosing him completely to crush his ribs,
Hugging him so hard his heart almost burst.
Then the grieving girls knelt on the ground,

1. 1123 Precise retribution for what the giant did to the Duchess (ll. 978–9).

Hands clasped, crying and exclaiming aloud,
'Christ comfort this knight and keep him from sorrow,
And foil that fiend who would fell him in death!'
   The sorcerer was still strong enough to roll on top,   1140
And wrathfully they writhed as they wrestled together,
Weltering and wallowing in the wild bushes,
Tumbling, fast turning and tearing their clothes.
They toppled down from the top in tumult together,
With Arthur over him and under by turns,
From the height of the hill to the hard rock below,
Not ceasing though they struggled at the sea's edge.
Then Arthur stabbed him savagely with a dagger,
Repeatedly hitting into the hulk to the very hilt.
So strongly the scoundrel squeezed him in death-throes,   1150
He broke three ribs in his royal breast.
   Then keen Sir Kay to the King leapt forward
Crying, 'Alas! We are lost! My lord is beaten,
Felled by a fiend. Foul fortune is ours!
In faith we are defeated and put to flight for ever!'
They heaved off his hauberk and felt his skin all over
From haunch and hip to the height of his shoulders,
His flanks and fine loins and fair waist,
His back and his breast and his bright arms.
Finding his flesh unflawed, full of joy   1160
These highborn knights were happy at the outcome of the
    day.
   'Now certainly,' said Sir Bedivere, 'it seems that my
    lord
Seeks fewer saints, the more sternly he hugs them,
Haling out this holy body from these high cliffs,
And lugging out this lout to lap him in silver.
By Michael, I'm much amazed that such a mean fellow
Is allowed by Our Lord in his lofty heaven.
If all saints are similar who serve Our Lord,
Beatified I shall never be, by my father's soul!'

Then the bold King bantered at Bedivere's words,   1170
'I have sought out this saint, so help me Lord,
And so draw your sword and spit him to the heart.
Be certain of this slave; he sorely hurt me.
I fought not such a fellow these fifteen winters;
But I met such a man on the mountain of Snowdon
More forceful by far than I had found before,
And my fortune being fair, I fell not in death.
So hack off his head at once and afterwards stake it;
Present it to your squire, whose steed serves him well;
Have it carried to King Howell, who is gripped in grief,   1180
And bid him have good heart: his enemy is destroyed.
Then bear it to Barfleur, brace it in iron
And set it on the central gate-tower, to display it to all.
My shining sword and shield surely still lie
On the crest of the crag where we clashed first,
And that terrible club, too, of tested iron,
Which has killed many Christians in Cotentin.
Go to the high ground and get me that weapon,
Then let us to our fleet that lies at sea.
If any treasure attracts you, take what you will;   1190
I claim the tunic and club: I covet nothing else.'
So they climbed to the crag, these comely knights,
And brought him his broad shield and bright sword;
Sir Kay himself carried the club and the tunic,
And accompanied the Conqueror to show to the kings
What the King had covertly kept for himself
As clear daylight climbed from the clouds about.

By then a clamouring crowd had come to court,
Who united in kneeling to the noble King:
'Welcome, liege lord! Too long you have been away.   1200
Our governor under God, great in splendid action,
To whom grace is granted and given at His will,
Your happy coming confers comfort on us all!
In your royalty, right revenge you render your people!

By act of your hand our enemy is destroyed
Who overran your ranked knights and robbed them of
    their children:
Never was realm in disarray so readily relieved!'
  Then in Christian style the Conqueror counselled his
    people,
'Thank God for this grace, and give none else credit,
For man could not manage it, only the Almighty's power,   1210
Or a miracle of his Mother, who is merciful to all.'
Then swiftly he summoned the sailors from the ships
To go with the shiremen and give the goods,
All the treasure taken by the treacherous creature,
To the country's common people, clergy and laity:
'See it divided and dealt out to my dear subjects
So that none complain of their portion, on pain of your
    lives.'
He commanded his cousin with courtly instruction
To build a church on the beetling crag where the body lay,
And to consecrate to Christ there a monastery   1220
In memory of that martyr in her mountain resting-place.
  King Arthur, having killed the cruel giant,
Merrily in the morning máde his way
From Barfleur in battle array by the bright rivers:
Choosing a champain way under chalky hills
To Castle Blank, he boldly bore onwards,
Then found a ford across the fresh waters
And crossed with his company in comely style.
There the stern man strode forth and set up his tents,
Making stronghold by a stream on a span of land.   1230
  Not long after midday, a little while after,
Two messengers, men of the far marches, came
From the Marshal of France and, making fair salutation,
Asked for his help in these words:
'Sire, your Marshal, your minister, begs that in mercy
Your mighty Majesty may save your subjects,

71

These men of the marches who have met misfortune
And been done much damage despite all defence.
I'd have you know the Emperor has entered France
With a huge host, hostile and fearsome.   1240
In Burgundy he is burning your beautiful cities
And dealing out death to your barons who dwell there.
He fiercely invades by force of arms
Countries and castles that your crown owns
And crushes your common subjects, clergy and laity.
Unless, King, you come to help they will never recover.
He is felling whole forests and plundering your farms,
And sanctioning no asylum as he assails the people.
He slaughters your subjects and seizes their goods.
The fair tongue of France by foreigners is destroyed.   1250
He scours[1] through sweet France, so the Germans say,
Driving under his dragon-banners,[2] a dreadful sight.
They do all to death with their deadly swords,
Even dukes and other dignitaries who dwell there;
So the lords of the land, the ladies and others,
Pray you for love of Peter, the apostle of Rome,
Since you are present in this place, to oppose
That princely oppressor as promptly as you can.
Under the high woods by yonder hills he lies,
Holding there his whole army of heathen kings.   1260
Help us for love of Him who sits in heaven above,
And speak sternly to those who destroy us thus!'
    The King called to Sir Boyce, 'Quickly, go!

1. 1251 Lucius conducts a *chevauchée*, that is, a series of mounted raids
in which plunder and destruction are carried out. Edward III's *che-
vauchées* during the Hundred Years War seriously depopulated Northern France.

2. 1252 Both Arthur and Lucius included dragon motifs in their
coats-of-arms. Here, banners in the shape of dragons, with long
floating bodies and tails, are probably indicated (Krishna, p. 180).

Bear with you Sir Berill and Bedivere the noble,
Sir Gawain and Sir Geryn, gallant chevaliers,
And go to those green woods to give my message.
Say to Sir Lucius that he proceeds too ignobly,
Thus unpardonably persecuting my people lawlessly.
I shall stop him very soon if I stay alive,
Or many he leads through our land shall lie dead.   1270
Command him immediately with menacing words
To retreat from my territories with his much-talked-of
    knights.
And if the vile fellow refuses to do so,
Let him come in his courtesy to encounter me but once,
Then swiftly we shall see the strength of his right
To ravage this realm and ransom the people!
Dire shall be the dealing with dreadful blows –
The dear Lord on Doomsday dispose as he will!'
    Now they got ready to go, these gallant knights,
All glittering in gold upon their great horses,   1280
With whetted weapons to the green wood shaping
To greet well the governor who would grieve before long.
They halted on a hill at the edge of the wood
And beheld the high tents of the heathen kings;
They listened to the loud din coming from the camp
And heard hundreds of elephants trumpeting.
The pavilions were pitched most proudly, and sumptuously
Palled with silk and purple cloth, with precious stones.
Pennons and pommels with princes' arms upon them
Were pitched in mid-plain for the people to see,   1290
For these regal Romans had ranged their tents
In rows by the river under the round hills,
With the Emperor's set for honour in the exact centre,
With eagles all over it, handsomely enamelled.
They saw him and the Sultan and senators numberless
Proceed to a stateroom with sixteen kings,
Softly and sweetly stepping forth in concert

To feast on fine rare foods with their sovereign.
   They went over the water, those worshipful knights,
Through the wood to the warrior's dwelling-place.   1300
When they had washed they went to the table,[1]
Where the worthy Gawain at once spoke out harshly:
'May the Might and the Majesty that graces us all
Who were moulded and made by His might alone,
Assail you with sorrow in your seats, you sultans
And others gathered here! Unhappy may you be!
And that hollow heretic who holds that he is Emperor,
Who occupies in error the Empire of Rome,
The heritage of Arthur, that honourable king,
Which all his ancestors but Uther owned,   1310
May the curse that came to Cain on account of his brother
Cleave to you, cuckold, couched there with your crown!
For you are the least noble lord I ever clapped eyes on.
My master much marvels, man, in truth,
Why you murder his men who merit no harm,
The common people of the country, clergy and laity,
Blameless beings who bear no arms.
So my seemly sovereign, splendid in courtesy,
Tells you sternly to retreat from his territory,
Or else offer fight for your honour as a knight.   1320
If you covet the crown, declare it openly!
I have done my duty here, dispute it who dares,
Before all your chivalry, chieftains and others.
Put your reply to us and palter no longer,
That we may go back at the gallop and give it to my lord.'
   The Emperor answered, austerely speaking:
'You hail from my enemy, King Arthur himself;
No honour should I have if I harmed his knights,
Though you are aggressive men who go on his errands.

1. 1301 As in Carlisle, when the Roman ambassadors demanded tribute, a challenge is conventionally issued at the start of a meal.

But for the reverence rightly owed to my royal table   1330
You would rapidly repent your rude words.
That a low fellow like you should belittle lords
Arrayed with their retinues, most royal and noble!
But say to your sovereign I send him these words:
As long as I like I shall linger here,
Then proceed along the Seine solacing myself,
And besiege every city by the salt strand,
Then ride by the Rhone which runs sweetly by,
And overwhelm the walls of his wealthy castles.
Let him prove it when he pleases, but in Paris I shall leave
          him   1340
Not a part of one penny, in process of time!'
   'I am certainly astonished,' said Sir Gawain,
'That a dolt like you should dare to deliver such a speech!
Rather than own all France, that finest of realms,
I'd deal with you in a duel to the death on the field.'
Then with haughty utterance answered Sir Gayous,
Uncle to the Emperor and an earl himself,
'These Britons have been braggarts always.
Lo, how he brawls, being bright in his armour,
As if he could destroy us all with his splendid sword!   1350
Some boast he barks out, that boy standing there!'
Sir Gawain, being grieved at his grandiose words,
Made towards the man with malice in his heart
And with his steely sword struck off his head,
Then bestrode his steed and spurred away with his men.
Through the guards they galloped, these glorious knights,
And found as they forged on foemen in plenty.
On their high-mettled horses they went over the water,
Then waited to get their wind back by the wood-margins.
Foemen on foot followed them in hosts   1360
And Romans on regal mounts richly arrayed
Through champain fields chased our chivalrous knights
On their chalk-white chargers to a lofty forest.

And a bold fellow in fine gold fretted with sable
In the forefront on a Friesian horse in flashing armour,
Set his splendid spear in his fewter[1]
And followed our knights fast, fiercely attacking.
Then Sir Gawain the Good upon his grey horse
Gripped his great spear and speedily skewered him.
Through the guts into the gore the well-ground steel   1370
Went sliding, then stuck straight through his heart.
That warrior fell weltering beside his huge horse,
Groaning on the ground with his grisly wounds.
Then rode in another rider, proudly arrayed,
With the badge on his buckler striped in purple and silver,
On his brown horse offering huge enmity;
It was a pagan from Persia that pursued him thus.
Sir Boyce, unabashed, bore at once against him
And with a savage spear-thrust stuck him through
So that bold man and broad shield lay battered on the
        ground.   1380
Then he jerked out his weapon and rejoined his fellows.
Next Sir Feltamour, a man of might much praised,
In high temper in turn, attacked swiftly
And galloped at Sir Gawain, going to work
In grief for Sir Gayous, on the ground left dead.
Sir Gawain was glad; against him he rode
And gave him a great blow with Galuth, his good sword.
That chevalier on a charger he chopped in two;
Cleanly from the crown he clove down the body,
Thus killing the knight with his renowned weapon.   1390
    Then a regal Roman rallied his men:
'We shall rue and regret it if we ride further.
Yon braggarts are bold who bring about such evil:
Ill fate befell him who first called them that!'
Then those royal Romans reined back their horses

1. 1366 Fewter: see Introduction, p. 31

And returned sad to their tents to tell the lords
How Sir Marshall de Mowne lay mouldering on the
    ground,
Outjousted for his giant japes in the day's fight.
But chevaliers still chose to chase our men,
Fully five thousand of them on fine horses,   1400
Riding fast to a forest across a foaming torrent
Which flowed from a fumid lake fifty miles off.
There the Britons laid an ambush with their best knights,
The chief of the chivalry from the chamber of the King.
These saw the enemy hunt our men, take their horses
And chop down the chief men they charged at.
   Then the Britons in ambush burst out suddenly
And boldly with their banners, all Bedivere's knights,
And ran down the Romans who rode by the wood,
Those noblest of knights acknowledging Rome's rule.   1410
The earls of England, hallooing, 'Arthur!'
Rushed out at their enemies and eagerly struck them.
Men's breasts through bright shields and mail-shirts they
    pierced,
Those boldest of Britons with their brilliant swords.
The Romans were overrun there and ravaged with
    wounds,
Caught like craven curs by courageous knights.
They stopped their pursuit suddenly, those Romans,
And rode away routed, in rank fear seemingly.
   A spokesman sped to the Senator Peter
And said, 'Sire, for certain your soldiers have been
    defeated!'   1420
Then swiftly he assembled ten thousand soldiers
And suddenly by the salt strand assaulted our men.
The Britons were shaken and shuddered a little,
But our boldest bannerets and bachelor knights
Yet broke the foes' battle-front with the breasts of their
    steeds;

Sir Boyce and his brave men dealt bitter pain.
Then the Romans rallied, their ranks in better order,
And freshly horsed flailed through our fellows,
Routing the bravest of the Round Table,
Yes, overrode our rearguard and gave us great grief. 1430
  Then the Britons on the battlefield fought back no
    more,
But fled to the forest, abandoning the field.
Sir Berill was borne down and Sir Boyce captured,
And the best of our brave men were badly wounded.
But some made a strong point which they sustained for a
    while,
Though stunned by the strokes of their stern enemies,
And sorrowing for their superior who had been seized
    there.
They sought God's succour: He would send it when He
    pleased.
  Then Sir Idrus arrived, armed at all points,
With five hundred fighters on fine horses, 1440
And eagerly asked our army at once
If their friends who had fled the field were far away.
Answered good Sir Gawain, 'So God help me,
We have been harried and hunted like hares today,
Routed by Romans riding noble steeds,
And we cowered under cover like craven wretches.
May I look no more on my lord while life lasts
If we serve so scurvily him who especially favoured us!'
Then sternly spurring their steeds again,
The Britons bravely bore to the battlefield afresh. 1450
All the fierce men in the forefront defiantly shouted,
Reviving their vigour as they advanced in the forest.
The Romans rapidly arranged their defence better
In one rank on a wide field, their weapons raised
And drawn up in good discipline by the dashing river;
Sir Boyce in bondage they bitterly held.

By the salt streams they savagely assaulted us,
Stalwart soldiers sternly striking their blows,
Their lovely lances clashing aloft together,
All in lordly trappings on their leaping warhorses.   1460
Chevaliers sheared through by sharpened weapons
Gasped and gaped, grisly their looks;
Great lords from Greece, grievously wounded,
Yet struck swiftly with their sweeping swords,
Dealing deadly blows at dying knights.
Many, struck senseless, swooned altogether
And died, cut down on the dark earth.
The gracious Sir Gawain got to work quickly,
Greeting the greatest with grisly wounds;
With Galuth he ground down the most gallant knights,   1470
In grief for the great lord grimly striking.
   In a rapid foray he then rushed royally
To where the brave Sir Boyce was bound captive,
Broke through the bright steel, battered to bits the
      hauberks,
Robbed them of their rich prize and rode back to his
      supporters.
The senator Peter swiftly pursued him
Through the press of the people with his princely knights,
For that prisoner promptly putting forth his strength
With the highest-mettled horsemen in the whole army.
He struck Sir Gawain savagely from the left,   1480
Hitting him a heavy blow with his hostile weapon,
And hacking the hauberk in half at the back
Of him who had unbound Sir Boyce despite baleful
      opponents!
   Then the Britons boldly blew on their trumpets
In bliss that Sir Boyce had been brought off free,
And bravely in battle they bore down knights;
With brands of burnished steel they battered chain mail,
Stabbed steeds with their steel weapons in the fight,

And struck down with strength all who stood against
    them.
Sir Idrus FitzEwan then cried out, 'Arthur!'   1490
And assaulted the Senator with sixteen knights,
The most stalwart soldiers our side possessed.
This tiny troop attacked at once,
On the first rank striking fell blows with flaming swords,
Then fiercely fighting the whole front next,
And felling not a few of the foe on the field
Who met their fates on the fair plain by the fresh waters.
    Then Sir Idrus FitzEwan sallied out alone,
Spurring in by himself and striking eagerly.
He sought out the Senator and seizing his bridle,   1500
He sternly spoke these most suitable words:
'Surrender, sir, speedily, if you desire to live!
Rendering ransom will rescue you perhaps,
But doubtless, delay or try devious tricks,
And you shall die this day, struck down by me!'
'I consent,' said the Senator, 'So save me Christ!
Let me be led safe to your liege king himself
And ransomed reasonably, since readily I can
From my Roman revenues raise what is needed.'
Then answered Sir Idrus with austere words,   1510
'The King shall conclude the conditions for you
When your case is called at the court place.
He may counsel that you be kept captive no longer,
But killed at his command before his concourse of
    knights.'
The soldiers escorted him, stripping him of his armour,
To leave him with the brothers Lionel and Lowell.
    Thus on land that lies low by the pleasant shore
Sir Lucius's liegemen were lost for ever!
The proud Senator Peter was taken prisoner;
Princely knights from Persia and the port of Jaffa   1520
And many other men met their ends;

Crowded by force at the ford, into the flood they leapt.
Behold! How heavily hurt were those Romans
Ridden down by the ranked knights of the Round Table!
On the river path our royal fellows set right their
    hauberks,
Ruddy with the red blood running over them.
Their rancorous Roman captives in the rearguard were
    held
For ransom by red gold and rarest warhorses.
They changed their chargers quickly to rest them,
Then rode to their royal king, ranged in order.   1530
   A fine knight rode before them to inform the King:
'Sire, your messengers come merrily from the mountains.
They have been matched with men of the marches today
And been mangled in the morass by marvellous knights.
In faith we have fought beside the fresh waters
With the boldest battlers your baleful foe has;
Fifty thousand on the field, fierce warriors all,
Were fatally felled, and in a furlong's span lie dead.
The Lord doomed our destiny, delivering us from defeat
By the splendid soldiers who assaulted your subjects.   1540
The chief chancellor of Rome, a chieftain most noble,
Will plead for peace and petition you for charity.
We have snatched as a prisoner Peter, the Senator;
Pagans in plenty from Persia and the port of Jaffa
Ride in the ranks of your unrivalled knights
To your prisons, pain and poverty to undergo.
I beseech you, Sire, state your will,
Whether you propose them peace or prompt death.
For the Senator you may receive sixty horses loaded
With silver, paid for certain by Saturday,   1550
And for the chief chancellor, that chevalier so noble,
Chariots charged chock-full with gold.
Let the rest of the Romans remain under arrest
Till their revenues in Rome be correctly determined.

I beseech you, Sire, signify to these lords
Whether you will send them over the sea or yourself detain
    them.
All your high henchmen remain hale and whole
But Sir Ewain Fitz Henry, who is hurt in the side.'
  'To Christ the credit,' cried the King, 'and his pure
     Mother!
He heartened and helped you with his holy skill.   1560
Deserved discomfiture God disposes as he pleases;
No wrongdoer can run from him or wriggle out of his
    grip.
All fortune and valour in fierce warfare
Are rewarded as he wishes by the will of God.
For your coming, which comforts us, I commend and
     thank you.
So Christ save me, Sir Knight,' said the Conqueror,
'For these tidings I bestow on you Toulouse the splendid,
Its tolls and attached revenues from taverns and other
     sources,
The town, its tenements and towers so lofty,
All that is temporal in title, during the time of my life.   1570
But say to the Senator, I send him these words:
No silver shall save him, except if Ewain survive.
I would sooner the Senator sank dead on the salt shore
Than see my staunch knight stay sick from his wounds.
I shall break up that band by Christ's help,
And send them, each solitary, into separate kings' lands.
Never again shall he know his nobles in Rome,
Nor sit in the assembly in sight of his compeers,
For no king known as Conqueror would count it
     becoming
To palter with a prisoner out of a passion for silver.   1580
It never goes with knighthood, let him know it or not,
To raise questions of commerce when captives are taken,
Nor is it proper for prisoners to put pressure on lords,

Or appear in princes' presence when public business is
    done.
Command the Constable, the castle's governor,
To keep him securely in close confinement.
By tomorrow's midday bell my command shall advise him
To what land they must go, to languish in despite.'
  This captive was conveyed by competent guards
To the care of the Constable, as the King had commanded, 1590
And afterwards they eagerly informed Arthur
Of the answer of the Emperor, angry in his actions.
Then Arthur, highest-mettled of earthly kings,
At evening at his own table uttered this praise of his lords:
'I must honour above all on earth those
Who when I was away waged my battles.
I shall love them while I live, with Our Lord's help,
And allot them the spacious lands they like best.
Those who suffered wounds for my sake by these soft
    waters
Shall gain from this game if I am granted life.'   1600
As day brightly dawned the dread King himself
Commanded Sir Cador, with his accomplished knights,
Sir Cleremus, Sir Cleremond and their comely
    co-warriors,
Sir Clowdmur and Sir Cleges, to convoy those captives,
And Sir Boyce and Sir Berill, with their banners displayed,
Sir Baldwin, Sir Brian and Sir Bedivere most noble,
Sir Ronald and Sir Richard, Roland's sons,
To ride with the Romans, trooped with their comrades.
'Spur secretly to the fair city of Paris
With the prisoner Peter and his peerless knights,   1610
And pass them to the Provost in the presence of lords
On pain and on peril – and all that appends thereto –
That they be carefully controlled and closely guarded
By wardens of warrant, sworn-in knights.
Hire hardy men for him; don't hesitate to spend.

I have warned that worthy, let him beware if he will!'
At the King's bidding the Britons busily prepared
Their battle gear and flying banners, and as a body moved
    off,
Pushing on towards prison, peerless chevaliers
Showing well in the shining Champagne country.   1620
  Now the powerful Emperor had himself ordered
Sir Utolf and Sir Evander, two honourable nobles,
Earls of the orient commanding awesome knights,
The most enterprising in all his host of warriors,
The Libyan Sir Sextynour and several senators,
The Syrian king himself with his Saracen forces,
And the Senator of Sutri with his huge armies,
– Given that governorship by agreement of his peers –
All to travel towards Troyes on treason bent,
To trap with a trick our travelling knights,   1630
Having perceived that Peter was on the path to Paris
And prison under the Provost to suffer his penalty.
This force set forth with unfurled banners
And planted themselves by the path with their powers
    drawn up
In the bushes round about on their big battle-steeds,
To pluck back the prisoners from our peerless knights.
  Sir Cador of Cornwall then commanded his peers,
Sir Gleges, Sir Cleremus and Sir Cleremond most noble:
'Here is the chasm of Clyme with its cliffs rearing up:
Clear the country, for cover is plentiful.   1640
Scrupulously search the scrub and bushes
For enemies in the undergrowth who might harm us.
Lest damage be done to us, dutifully perform this,
For no onslaught from ambush is ever repelled.'
So they hurried to the holt-wood, these hot-blooded
    knights,
Ears open for the haughty men, thus to help their lords,
And found them fully armed and fairly mounted

Waiting by the wayside on the wood's outskirts.
   Courtly of countenance, Sir Cleges himself
Called across to that company in these words: 1650
'Will any renowned knight, a noble or royal man,[1]
Prosecute the craft of arms for his king's love?
We have come from the King of this fine country,
Who is called the Conqueror, crowned over the world.
All the regal retinue of his Round Table
Are ready to ride with that royal man at his request.
If any will offer it, we hope for a deadly duel
Between two intrepid men esteemed by lords.
So is there any man, an earl or other,
Who for the Emperor's love will offer to fight?'   1660
   An earl then in anger answered him quickly:
'I am angry with Arthur, with his high-born warriors,
Who in error occupies these kingdoms,
Thus outraging the Emperor, his earthly lord.
The proud array and royal show of the Round Table
Are commented on with contumely in countries far and
     wide,
For he revels on the revenues which are rightly due to
     Rome.
He will be quickly called to account if our right triumphs,
For a great many will regret they galloped in his war-band,
So rashly rules that ruffian king!'   1670
Then countered Sir Cleges, 'May Christ save me,
But you seem to speak like a sort of cashier,
Yet whether auditor or earl or emperor yourself,
On Arthur's behalf I answer you at once.

1. 1651 Cleges exceeds orders by issuing a personal challenge when he is meant to be simply reconnoitring. His action leads eventually to a greater disobedience, by Cador, whose remit is to deliver his prisoners safely to Paris, not engage a superior Roman force. This whole action earns Arthur's reasoned rebuke (ll. 1922 ff.) when Arthur laments the casualties suffered.

That knightly man so noble we acknowledge, all of us
Fierce and famous fighters of the Round Table.
He has made clear his account and conned his records,
And will give a right reckoning that you will rue
    afterwards.
Yes, all lords shall lament who belong to Rome
Before the arrears of rightful revenues are returned to him.   1680
We crave of your courtesy three courses of joust,
The winner to take the weapons as well as the loser's
    horse.
You merely trick us today with trifling words;
That betokens treachery from you tiresome men!
Assign and send out some serious knights,
Or simply surrender. But speak with certainty.'
   Then said the King of Syria, 'So save me Our Lord,
You won't have your wish if you wait all day
Unless you first inform me before all true knights
That your crest and coat of arms carry weight with nobles,   1690
And the ancestry of your arms carries ownership of lands.'
   'Sir King,' said Sir Cleges, 'that's courtly indeed;
I conclude such a question comes out of cowardice.
The ancestry of my arms all nobles acknowledge:
They have been borne on my banner since Brutus's days.
At the time that the towered city of Troy was besieged,
It was often seen in assaults made by sterling knights.
Hence Brutus brought us with our brave ancestors
To Britain the Greater on board his ships.'
   'Sir,' said Sir Sextynor, 'say what you like,   1700
And we shall bear with you as seems best to us.
So truss up your trumpets and trifle no longer,
For though you delay all day, you'll do no better.
No Roman that rides in my ranks shall ever
Be rebuked by ribalds while I rule here!'
   Then Sir Cleges inclined to the King with a bow
And came back to Sir Cador with this courtly account:

'We have found in that forest with its rich foliage
The flower of the fairest of your foeman's army,
Fifty thousand fellows, fierce warriors,   1710
Their spears set in fewter under those sweet branches.
They are in ambush on their horses, all their banners out,
By yonder beechwood, on its borders by the path.
They have blockaded the crossing of the clear stream,
So that in faith we are forced to fight them there.
So doubtless our destiny today, to be brief,
Is to attack, or retreat: tell us what you wish.'
   'No, may Christ comfort me!' Cador replied,
'If we should for so little shun battle it would shame us.
Sir Lancelot[1] shall never laugh, where he loiters with the
       King,   1720
That I can be put off my path by any opponent on earth.
I would rather be dead and quite undone than draw back
       here
In dread of any dog's son in those dim bushes!'
Sir Cador then encouraged his cohorts in noble style,
Heartening them all with his high spirit:[2]
'Ponder the proud prince who makes presents to us
Of land and lordships where we like best to live;
Who has dealt us dukedoms and dubbed us knights,
And given us gifts of gold and many rewards,
Greyhounds, great horses and gladness unstinting   1730
That would profit any person prospering under God.
Remember the rich renown of the Round Table!
Let us never be robbed of it by any Roman alive.
Do not strike softly, or spare your weapons,

1. 1720 Lancelot: this is the only reference in the poem to Lancelot's
activities as a carpet-knight, and it is indirect at that, seeming only to
note his favour with the King.

2. 1725 One of several speeches of exhortation with the flavour of
Anglo-Saxon epic.

But fight fiercely like the faithful fellows you are.
Better I should be boiled alive and my body quartered
Than fail in this fight, feeling such fury.'
    Then this doughty duke dubbed new knights,
Ioneke and Askanere, Aladuke and others,
Who were heirs to Essex and all the eastern marches,   1740
Howell and Hardolf happy in armed fortune,
And Sir Heryll and Sir Herygall, hot-blooded knights.
Then stalwart knights were set aside by Cador –
Sir Baldwin, Sir Bedivere the brave and Sir Uriel,
And Ronald and Richard, Roland's offspring:
'Guard well this great prince with your peerless knights!
And if fortune in the fight should fall to us,
Then stay standing here, and stir no farther.
But if in evil fortune we are overridden,
Escape to some castle and keep in safety,   1750
Or if respite allows, ride back to royal Arthur,
And urge him to hurry to the aid of his army.'
    Then the Britons boldly braced their shields,
Put on their helmets and held their lances ready.
So Cador arranged his ranks and they rode to the field,
A front of five hundred, their lances facing forward,
On steeds with trappings, to trumpets' sounds
And calls from cornets and clarions skilfully played.
Shattering was the shock; they shunned nothing
Where the shrubs brightly shone under the shimmering
        trees.   1760
The Roman ranks retreated a little,
Giving ground in their rearguard's direction.
So rapidly they rode there that the air rang
With the sound of steel and spikes and splendid gold mail.
Then showers of shield-bearers shot out of the woods,
With their weapons of war at once sharply shooting.
The Lybian king led the leading line
And all his loyal liegemen loudly shouted.

The cruel king then couched his spear,
And mounted on a mailed horse made his charge,   1770
Bearing down on Sir Berill and battering him fiercely,
Gashing him through the gullet and the gorge-piece
    accurately.
Warrior and warhorse wavered to the ground,
And he called gravely on God and gave up his soul.
Thus was Berill the bold knight borne out of life,
And abode his burial as best befitted him.
Sir Cador of Cornwall, cold with heart-sorrow
Because his kinsman had come to grief,
Clasped the corpse and kissed it repeatedly,
And gave orders that he be guarded by good knights.   1780
    Then the Lybian king laughed and loudly exclaimed,
'That man has dismounted! It much pleases me.
He won't do us harm today, devil take his bones!'
'Yonder king,' cried Sir Cador, 'cracks a big boast
Because he killed this keen knight – Christ take your soul!
That king shall cough up his corn,[1] with Christ's help.
Before I flee this field, we shall fight together.
As the wind turns the wheel, I shall well requite him,
By fall of night felling him or some of his followers!'
    Then the keen Sir Cador comported himself as a knight,   1790
Called out, 'A Cornwall!' and couching his spear,
Spurred his splendid horse straight through the
    battle-throng,
Striking many stern men by his own main strength.
When his spear snapped he surged on furiously,
Slashing with his sword that never failed him

1. 1786 ME 'corne-boute': payment, especially when the price of corn
is high, hence requital (Krishna, p. 183). Hamel (p. 311) suggests,
correctly I think, that Cador is punning on his name as Duke of
Cornwall: a novel way of calling on one's own name while riding into
battle.

And cutting wide swathes through, wounding knights,
Dealing deadly pain as he drove through men's bodies,
And hacking the hardiest enemies' necks asunder
So that blood splashed wherever his steed galloped.
Many men's lives the mighty warrior ended,   1800
Hitting those harsh tyrants and emptying their saddles,
Then turned away from that toil when the time seemed
    right.
Then the Lybian king loudly let fly
At Sir Cador the keen these cruel words:
'You have earned much honour and hurt many knights,
And suppose for your prowess that you possess the whole
    world.
By my troth, I tarry till you turn on me;
I have warned you well, fellow; beware if you will!'
   With horn-calls and clarions our new-created knights
Responded to the sound, set spears in fewters,   1810
And rode at the Roman front rank on iron-grey horses,
Felling at the first shock fifty at once.
They shot through the shield-wall, their spear-shafts
    shivering,
And hurled down in a heap their high-born enemies.
Thus nobly our new-made knights used their strength.
But now came a new matter which annoyed me greatly:
The Libyan king laid hold of a steed he liked,
And lordlily spurred in, silver lions on his shield,
Surrounding the group and driving them apart,
And with his lance letting out the life of many.   1820
Thus the squires of the King's chamber he chased about,
In the champain country chopping down chivalrous
    knights
And hacking down a host of men with his hunting spear.
Sir Aladuke was slain, Achinour wounded,
Sir Origge and Sir Ermyngall hewn all to pieces.
Sir Lewin was seized and so was his brother

By the lords of Libya and led to their strongholds.
Had Sir Cleges not come with Clement the noble
Our new men would have been annihilated, and not only
    them.
  Then Sir Cador the keen couched his spear,   1830
And careering at the king with his cruel weapon,
Hit him high on the helmet with the point
So that all the hot blood ran down to his hand.
On the earth lay the hot-hearted heathen king,
Not ever to be healed of that mortal hurt.
Then Sir Cador the keen cried out loudly,
'You have coughed up your corn, King, in penance,
For killing my cousin. Now my cares are less.
Cool yourself in clay now and comfort yourself!
For long you levelled scorn at us with low insults;   1840
All the harm you now have is your own doing.
Hold what you have; it'll hurt you but little,
For hateful scorn homes back on whoever uses it!'
  The Sultan of Syria was then sorrowful at heart
For the sake of this sovereign, so suddenly destroyed.
He assembled his Saracens and scores of senators
And furiously they fell on our scattered forces.
Sir Cador of Cornwall quickly countered them,
Forming up his fine fighters in a group
In front of the forest where the path came forth.   1850
Fifty thousand were felled in the fight at once
As many stalwarts in the stern struggle there
On both sides swiftly received savage wounds.
The stoutest Saracens on the side of the Romans
From their saddles were struck six feet backwards
As our chivalry sheared through their shielded knights,
Piercing the plated mail of powerful men
And hitting through hauberks to the hearted breasts.
Burnished arm-braces they burst asunder;
At bloodied bucklers and battle-horses they hacked,   1860

Slashing with shining steel at the prancing steeds.
The Britons boldly beat down so many of them
That blood bubbled all over the broad field.
By then keen Sir Cador had captured a captain,
And Sir Cleges had cut in and clutched another,
The Captain of Corneto, the King's deputy,
Corneto, key to that country's whole rich coast.
Ioneke had in hand Utolf and Evander,
With the Earl of Africa and other great lords.
The Sultan of Syria had surrendered to Sir Cador   1870
And the Seneschal of Sutri to Sagramour himself.
When that company saw their captains captured
They fled to the forest as fast as they could,
Feeling so faint that they fell among trees
And ferns of the forest for fear of our people.
See our mighty men with their mounts in the
          undergrowth,
Ripping to bits the Romans already rent with wounds!
Yes, our hot-hearted heroes hallooed after the heathens,
Hewing them down in hundreds at the edge of the wood.
Thus our fine fellows hunted the flying foe,   1880
And the ones that got away went to a castle.
    Then the troops of the Round Table rallied,
And in the wood where the Duke was they searched,
Tracking among the trees to take up their comrades
Who had fatally fallen in the fighting before.
Sir Cador had them carted, covered sumptuously,
And carried to the King by his best knights,
Then pressed on to Paris with the prisoners himself,
Put them in the Provost's hands, princes and all,
Dined briefly in the barbican, and biding no longer,   1890
Came back quickly to the King with this account:
    'Sire,' said Sir Cador, 'such was our chance:
We have dealt today in this delightful country
With kings and commanders most cruel and noble,

Keen and fully equipped knights and men.
By that wood they waited for us, blocking our way
At the ford in the forest with fierce warriors.
There, by God, we battled, brandishing spears
Against your foes on the field, felling them in death.
The Libyan King is laid low and left on the field   1900
And many liegemen loyal to him are laid low too.
And more lords were made prisoner by men I can't name;
We have led them along here, to live if you so please.
Sir Utolf and Sir Evander, honourable knights,
In an armed onslaught Ioneke captured,
With earls of the Orient and hard-hearted knights
Of ancestry the highest our enemies owned.
Noble knights seized the Senator Carous,
The Captain of Corneto, for cruelty renowned,
The Seneschal of Sutri, savage in intent,   1910
And the Sultan of Syria himself, with his Saracens.
But fatally felled on the field were fourteen of our knights,
I faithfully inform you, not failing to report it:
Sir Berill, that brave banneret, for one,
Was killed at first encounter by a great king;
And Sir Aladuke of Tintagel with his true knights
Was destroyed among the Turks and in time found dead;
Good Sir Mawrell of Maunces and Mawren his brother too,
And Sir Meneduke of Mentoche with his marvellous
     knights.'

   The worthy King wept, in woe and tears writhing,   1920
And said to his cousin Sir Cador these words:
'Sir Cador, your courage confounds us all!
Coward! You have cast away the crown of my
     knighthood.
To put men in peril is not prized greatly
Unless the parties are prepared and powerfully armed.
Being established in a stronghold, you should have stayed
     there,

Not sought to destroy all my stalwarts at once!'
'Sire,' said Sir Cador, 'you yourself must know
You are King in this country and may carp as you wish,
But no baron who boards with you shall ever upbraid me   1930
That his vaunting prevented me advancing your purposes.
Any fighting force setting forth must be fully supported
Lest it be struck and destroyed in this stern country.
I did my duty today – may lords judge me! –
With danger of death from many doughty knights,
But I get no goodwill grace from you, only great words:
If I heave out my heart in words, I'll have no better luck.'
    Though King Arthur was angry, he answered fairly:
'You have done doughtily, Sir Duke, with your handling,
And done your duty with my dauntless knights,   1940
And so you are esteemed by senior dukes and earls
One of the most courageous ever to be ranked as knight.
On this earth no issue has sprung from me,
Hence you are my heir apparent, or your offspring are,
You being my sister's son. Forsake you, I never shall.'
Then in his own tent he ordered a table laid,
Had trumpeted an invitation to his tired warriors,
And served them ceremoniously with seldom-seen dishes
On silver salvers splendid to behold.
    When they heard of these happenings, to the Emperor
        went   1950
The senators and said, 'Your soldiers have lost.
King Arthur, your enemy, has overthrown your lords
Who rode to rescue those high-ranking knights.
Your time is ill-taken in so torturing your people;
You are betrayed by the troops you trusted most,
Which will give you great pain and grief for ever!'
Angry-hearted, the Emperor raged
That our valiant fellows had the victors' prowess.
With King and Kaiser to council they went
With Saracen sovereigns and many senators.   1960

He swiftly summoned his staunch nobles
And spoke this speech to the assembled company:
'My heart is hard set, if you agree,
To set out for Val-Suzon with my stalwart knights
To fight against my foemen, if Fortune permit me
To find those fellows in earth's four corners.
If not, I shall enter Autun adventuring,
And stay with my stalwarts in that splendid city,
Resting and revelling with right jollity
In leisurely delight among those lordly lands,   1970
Till Sir Leo lights in with all his loyal knights
And lords of Lombardy to block Arthur's way.'

    But our wily King was wary and watched for this force,
And wisely withdrew his warriors from the woods,
But had the fires fed so that they flamed up high
As they trussed up their trappings and stole away.
He sped off to Val-Suzon[1] as swiftly as possible,
And as soon as the sun rose he split up his knights
Into seven great sections, and speedily sent them
To stop access to the city from any direction,   1980
But in the valley placed a vanguard in vigilant ambush.
    Then on Sir Valiant the Welsh King with his valiant
        warriors,
Who before the face of the King had professed a vow
To vanquish by victory the Viscount of Rome,
The King conferred, come what may,
Chieftainship of the chivalry in the initial charge.
He gave orders to others whom he held in most trust,
But took command of the main force in his own mighty
        honour,
Setting forth his foot-soldiers in the fairest order,
And the flower of his knights in front, in the first rank.   1990

1. 1977 Val-Suzon: it used to be agreed that the great battle took place at Soissons; the newly proposed site is about a hundred miles south-south-east of Soissons. See Hamel, p. 314.

He ordered his archers on each flank next
To shove forward in a shield-wall and shoot at will.
In the rearguard he arranged his most royal-hearted
    knights,
The noblest, the most renowned of the Round Table:
Sir Ronald and Sir Richard who were recreant never,
And the regal Duke of Rouen, with riders in hosts.
Sir Kay and Sir Cleges, with competent warriors,
The King charged to keep watch by the clear streams.
Sir Lot and Sir Lancelot, lordly knights,
Were to lie on his left flank with legions in plenty,   2000
To move in the morning if need emerged.
Sir Cador of Cornwall with his keen knights
Was to keep watch at the crossroads, close to them.
He put at such places princes and earls
So that no power could pass by a hidden path.
    Soon the Emperor came on with his host of nobles
And valiant earls adventuring into the valley,
And found King Arthur with his army drawn up,
And as he came on, to add to his sorrow,
Our brave and bold King, on the battlefield waiting,   2010
Had his broad banners flying and battalions deployed.
He had stopped access to the city from all sides;
The cliffs and chasms were covered by armed men,
The high mountains and marshes and mossy lands too
By masses of men to maul the marching enemy.
    When Sir Lucius saw him, he said to his lords,
'This traitor has travelled here on treason bent.
He has sealed off the city on all sides
And covered the cliffs and chasms with warriors.
Our only course here – there is no other advice –   2020
Is to fight with our foes, since flee we never can!'
Then the royal man rapidly arranged his battle order,
Drawing up his Romans and regal knights,
Placed in the vanguard the Viscount of Rome

And valiant knights from Viterbo to Venice,
And drew up to our dread their gold dragon banner,
With eagles all over it edged with sable.
They broached wine bountifully and drank it together,
Dukes, distinguished peers and newly dubbed knights;
With the dancing of Germans and the din of piping 2030
The vale reverberated as the valiant men waited.
Then Sir Lucius spoke aloud with lofty words:
'Ponder the prowess of your proud forefathers,
Those Roman ravagers ruling through their lords,
Who overran all earth's regnant powers,
Conquering all Christendom by craft of arms;
Every expedition was hailed a victory.
In seven seasons the Saracens were beaten
In all the parts from Port Jaffa to Paradise Gates.
We little care if a land launches revolt: 2040
It is reason and right that rebels be restrained!
So let us address that deed, delaying no longer,
Since doubtless the day shall be deemed ours!'
    When these words were said, the Welsh King himself
Was aware of this warrior who had made war on his
        knights,
And valiantly in the vale he voiced his challenge:
'Viscount of Valence, envious of deeds,
That adventure at Viterbo shall be avenged today;
I shall never fly unvanquished from this field of battle!'
    Then the Viscount valiantly voiced a command, 2050
And advanced from the vanguard, veering on his horse.
He held up his hateful shield edged with sable
On which a dragon ghastly to see with its gaping maw
Was devouring a dolphin of doleful aspect
As a sign that our sovereign would be destroyed
And done out of his days with dread sword–strokes;
For death alone is due when the dragon is raised.
Then our splendid sovereign set spear in fewter

And pitilessly with its point pierced him exactly
A hand's-breadth above the waist, between the short ribs,   2060
So that steel plate and spleen stuck on his spear.
Blood spurted and spattered as his horse sprang up,
And he sprawled, struck down swiftly, to speak no more.
Thus did Sir Valiant's vows avail
To vanquish the Viscount who was victor before.
    Then Sir Ewain fitz Urien eagerly rode
Up to the Emperor to seize his eagle,
Spurring swiftly through the soldiers' phalanx.
He drew his deadly sword in dreadless mood,
Suddenly snatched the standard and sped away,   2070
Bearing the bird-banner back in his hands,
And scot-free joined his fellows in the front rank.
Now rapidly riding with raised weapon,
Sir Lancelot struck the Lord Lucius[1] fiercely,
Putting his point through paunch-guard and mail
So that the proud pennon stuck in his stomach.
The head came out behind half a foot,
As through hauberk and hip went the hard weapon.
Thus he smote stern man and steed to the ground,
Struck down a standard and sallied back to his men.   2080
'I like it,' said Sir Lot, 'that those lords are dispatched!
If my lord gives me leave, the lot[2] now falls to me.
Today my name shall be annihilated and not known
        hereafter
Unless some leap from life who linger on this land.'
The stern man stood in his stirrups and strained at the
        bridle,

1. 2074 Lucius survives this serious wound, to be killed by Arthur at
l. 2255.

2. 2082 Following Cador in the matter, Lot also puns on his own name
as he invokes it.

Spurred to the assault on his splendid steed
And, joining fight with a giant, jabbed him right through.
In jocund mood this noble knight outjousted another,
Cut a wide swathe through as he warred with enemies,
And woefully wounded all who stood in his way.   2090
For a furlong's length he fought the whole fierce troop,
Felling many on the field with his fine weapon
As in victory he vanquished valiant knights,
Then rode round the whole area and retreated unscathed.
   Then the bowmen of Britain bitterly next
Fought against foot-soldiers from afar in that place,
Fiercely firing off flighted arrows at them,
The feathered shafts flying through the fine mail.
Such archery is hateful that so harms the flesh,
Flying from far into the flanks of warhorses.   2100
With missiles the Germans menaced us in return,
Casting them so cruelly that they cut through our shields;
Crossbow bolts cunningly skewered through knights,
The iron so fast hurtling they had no time to flinch.
So shrank men from the shots of sharp arrows
That the shield-wall was shattered, and shuddering they
    scattered.
Big horses bucked, bridles dragged on arms,
Till a whole hundred were lying on the heath.
But the highest-hearted nobles, heathens and others,
Yet furiously rushed forth to do fearsome deeds.   2110
All the fiend-engendered giants fighting at the front
Joined battle with Sir Jonathal and his gentle knights,
With their solid steel clubs stoving in helmets,
Crashing through crests and crushing skulls.
They killed cavalry and armour-clad horses,
And chopped through chevaliers on chalk-white chargers.
No steel, no steed, could stand against them
As they stunned and struck down our still-resisting band,
Until the Conqueror came with his keen knights

And with cruel countenance, cried aloud,   2120
'I believe no Briton would be daunted by so little
As these bare-legged boys who brave this battlefield!'
   He brandished Excalibur the brightly burnished,
Got close to Golopas, who had done greatest harm,
And cut him in two clean through the knees.
'Come down!' said the King, 'And account for it to your
      fellows!
You are too high by half, I have to tell you.
You'll be even handsomer soon, with Our Lord's help!'
And with his steely sword he struck off his head.
Sternly in that assault he struck another,   2130
And set on seven more with his stalwart knights:
Till sixty giants had been so served, they never ceased.
So this assay saw the destruction of the giants,
Outjousted by gentle knights in the doings of the day.
   Then both Romans and ranked knights of the Round
      Table
Drew up afresh their rearguards and the rest,
And hacked at helmets with hardy war weapons,
Slashing with strong steel through splendid mail.
Yes, they did things duly, those daring warriors,
Fixing lances in fewters freely on their iron-grey horses,   2140
With their skewering spears savagely duelling,
And shearing off shields their shining goldwork.
Felled on the field of that fight were left so many
That every runnel ran with red blood in the forest.
By then life-blood lay in pools on the lovely grassland;
Swords were smashed in two, dying knights
Giddily lurched guardless on galloping steeds.
Gashes grieved the bodies of gallant men;
Their faces, disfigured under the foaming waters,
Were smashed by the stamping of steeds in armour.   2150
It was the fairest field of fight ever to be described;
There fell over a furlong's length fully a thousand.

By then the Romans had been beaten back a little,
And in dread withdrew, enduring no more.
Our prince with his powers pressed after them,
Spurring at the proudest with his peerless knights.
Sir Kay, Sir Cleges and Sir Cleremont the bold
Caught them by the cliff with a company of heroes,
Fought furiously in the forest, sparing no weapon,
And felled in the first assault five hundred at once.   2160
When our foemen found that our fierce knights had
        trapped them
And fought the more fiercely, being few to their many,
They took on the whole troop, attacking with spears
In battle with the bravest of all bold men in France.
    Then fearless Sir Kay fewtered his weapon,
Spurred on his steed straight up to a king,
And with his Lithuanian lance split his side
So that liver and lungs from the lance-point dangled.
Yes, the shaft shot shuddering into the shining warrior,
Stuck through the shield and stayed in the man.   2170
But as Kay drove in, came an unfair lunge
From a cowardly knight of the country of Rome:
As he turned in the attack the traitor speared him
Low in the loins and through the flanks as well,
The harsh head hitting through the bowels,
Bursting them with the blow, then breaking in two.
Sir Kay, well aware that a wound of such extent
Had dealt him his death-blow and that he must die,
Got himself together and galloped at the enemy,
Raging for revenge against the recreant fellow.   2180
'On guard, you great coward!' he girded at him,
And with his stainless sword he sliced him in two.
'Had you with your hands offered a fair blow,
I'd have forgiven you, by God, for giving me my death!'
    Then he came to the wise King and calmly greeted him:
'I have been dealt my death-blow and will never recover.

Accomplish your courtesy as required by the world
And bring me to burial; no better thing I ask.
Greet well the Queen my lady if the world so fortune you,
And all those lovely ladies belonging to her bower,   2190
And my noble wife who never annoyed me.
Ask her for honour's sake to offer prayers for my soul.'
The King's confessor came, carrying the Host,
And uttered the words of extreme unction to console him.
The knight then knelt up with nerveless courage
And received his Creator, who comforts us all.
The great Conqueror cried out, clamorous in pity,
Then rode into the rout to get revenge for the deed.
He thrust into the throng and there met a prince
Who was heir of all Egypt in those eastern parts,   2200
And cut him clean in two with Excalibur.
He spitted that swordsman and split his saddle,
Ripping through the rump and bursting the beast's
        bowels.
Then, fierce in his frenzy, he fell on another;
At the middle of the mighty man who much angered him
He hewed through his armour and hacked him in two,
So that the man's main part toppled to the turf
While the other half, the haunches, stayed upright on the
        horse.
He would never be healed, I imagine, of that hurt.
Arthur shot through the shield-wall with his sharp
        weapon,   2210
Shearing through the chivalry, shattering their armour,
Bearing down their banners and battering to bits their
        shields,
And wreaking his wrath on their ranks with his sword.
He twisted and turned in his towering strength,
Angrily harming the adversaries he attacked,
And thrust through the throng thirteen times,
Powerfully pressing, and pushed right through.

Then Sir Gawain the Good with his gallant knights,
Spurring in a sortie by the skirts of the wood,
Was aware of Sir Lucius lurking in a glade   2220
With the lords and liegemen belonging to his service.
The Emperor eagerly asked him quickly,
'What do you want, Gawain? Work for your weapon?
I can see by your stirring that you are searching for sorrow.
I shall be avenged on you, varlet, for your vainglorious
        words!'
He seized his long sword and slashed with it,
Loosing at Sir Lionel a lordly blow
Which hit him on the head, hewing through the helmet,
And broke into his brain-pan a hand's-breadth deep.
Thus he attacked that troop like a true noble,   2230
And dealt deadly wounds to distinguished knights,
Fighting with Florent, that finest of swordsmen,
Till the foaming blood flowed down to his fist.
   Then the Romans who had been routed rallied their
        forces
And scattered our soldiers with their spirited steeds.
Seeing their sovereign so sternly engaged,
They chased and chopped down our chivalrous knights.
Sir Bedivere took a blow; his breast was pierced
By a big sword broad at the hilt;
The stark noble steel struck him to the heart   2240
And he hurtled to the earth: O heavy the woe!
The Conqueror took cognizance: he came with his force
To rescue the royal knights of the Round Table,
And overthrow the Emperor if opportunity offered.
They rode up to the eagle with 'Arthur!' on their lips.
The Emperor eagerly struck at Arthur
A bitter backward blow that broke his visor,
The naked sword severely scraping his nose.
Down his breast ran the blood of the brave king,
Bloodying his broad shield and bright mail-coat.   2250

Arthur turned his horse with the brilliant bridle
And with his splendid sword struck him a stroke,
The hard blow hitting through hauberk and chest
Slantwise from the slot of the throat, slitting him open.
So ended the Emperor at Arthur's hands,
Which made the stern men of Rome much afraid.

   The few still on the field fled to the forest
For fear of our fellows, by the fresh water;
The flower of our fierce men followed boldly
On their iron-grey horses that never-before-frightened
   host.   2260
Then the acclaimed Conqueror cried loudly,
'Cousin of Cornwall, keep this command:
Save none for the sake of silver ransom
Till the killing of Sir Kay is cruelly avenged!'
'No, Christ help me!' Sir Cador quickly answered,
'There is no kaiser or king under Christ's rule
Whom I shall not kill stone-cold by craft of my hands!'
Now behold warlords and warriors on white horses
Chasing and chopping down noble chivalry,
The richest and most royal of Roman kings,   2270
With strong steel smashing their ribs asunder.
Their brains burst out through burnished helmets,
Split by swords and scattered about the field.
They hewed down the heathens with their hilted swords
Absolutely by the hundred at the edge of the wood.
No silver ransom could succour them or save their lives,
Not Sultan, nor Saracen, nor Senator of Rome.

   Then they rallied, those royal knights of the Round
     Table,
By the sumptuous stream that sweetly flowed by,
Relaxing in pleasure by the lovely shore,   2280
On its grassy ground, those great lordly fighters.
They trotted to the baggage train and took what they
   liked –

Camels and crocodiles and coffers crammed full,
Warhorses, hackneys and hacks as well,
And the high tents and awnings of infidel kings.
They led away large numbers of lords' dromedaries,
Milk-white mules and marvellous creatures,
Noble elephants, Arab horses and camels
Of oriental habitat, owned by high monarchs.
   But King Arthur hurried in haste directly   2290
To the Emperor with an escort of honourable kings,
Had him lifted up lovingly by lordly knights
And carried to the couch in his own quarters.
Then heralds at hasty behest of the lords
Hunted for the heathens on the heath lying dead,
The Sultan of Syria and staunch kings,
And sixty of the senior senators of Rome.
They laid out and oiled those honoured bodies,
Lapping them in sixty layers of linen
And enclosing them in lead lest they decompose   2300
Or rot before arriving in Rome safe
In their coffins, complete and undecayed,
With their banners above and their badges below,
So that everywhere they went warriors could tell
Each king by his colours, according to his nation.
   Straight away on the second day, as soon as it dawned,
Two senators with their staunch knights stepped forth
From the heath bare-headed, by the edge of the wood,
Barefoot over the fields, with their fine swords,
And prostrate before the peerless King, proferred him the
     hilts: 2310
Would he hang or behead them, or let them hold on to life?
Girt only in their gowns, to the great victor they knelt,
And with sad expressions spoke these words:
'Two senators are we, your subjects from Rome,
Who by these salt strands have saved our lives
By hiding in the high forest with the help of Christ.

We beseech you, give us succour as our sovereign and
    lord,
Granting us life and limb with a liberal heart
For love of Him who lent you your lordship on earth!'
  'I grant it by my grace,' the good king replied,   2320
'I allow you life and limb and leave to depart
If you take my terms trustily to Rome,
Exactly as I now state them before my senior knights.'
'Yes,' said the senators, 'we certainly shall
Affirm our faith thereto and fulfil your order,
Not wavering from it for anyone in the world:
Not for Pope, or noble prince or potentate
Loth to proclaim your letters loyally through the land;
Not for princely duke or peer, on pain of death.'
Then the bannerets of Britain brought them to tents   2330
Where barbers with basins borne aloft were ready.
With warm water they wet them quickly, I assure you,
And shaved those chivalrous men to show most suitably
That the Romans were reckoned recreant, and had
    surrendered;
For the shaving would show forth the shame of Rome.[1]
  The coffins were quickly corded on camels,
Asses and Arab horses, all holding famed kings,
But the Emperor in honour was all on his own,
High on an elephant, his eagle banner above.
The King committed them to the captives himself,   2340
And before his fine men spoke forth as follows:
'Here to take home over the hills are chests
Measured full of the money you mightily yearned for,
The tax and the tribute of ten score winters
Which was lamentably lost during the lordship of our
    ancestors.

1. 2335 Following the Giant's precedent, Arthur has his enemies'
facial hair, their token of power, removed.

Say to the senator who presides over the city
That I send him the right sum, assess it how he will.
But bid them never be so bold while my blood rules
As to trouble themselves to attack my territories,
Nor demand tribute or tax by any entitlement   2350
But like treasure to this, while my life lasts.'
   Now they rode back to Rome the readiest way,
Then called the Commons to the capital by ringing bells,
Assembled the city's senators and chieftains,
And gave them the goods, great chests and all
As the Conqueror had commanded with cruel words:
'We have truly toiled to fetch this tribute,
The taxes and takings of ten score winters
From England, Ireland and the outer isles,
Over all of which Arthur holds sway in the west.   2360
He bids you never be so bold while his blood rules
As to do battle for Britain or his other broad lands,
Nor demand tribute or tax by any entitlement
But like treasure to this, while his life lasts.
We have fought in France and had foul fortune,
And our fine fighters on the field are left dead.
Neither our nobles nor our knights escaped,
But were chopped down in the chase, as chance would
     have it.
We say, store up stone and strengthen your walls!
You have awoken woe and war: beware if you will!'   2370
   This case came about in the kalends of May:
That renowned royal King with his Round Table
In the province of Burgundy with its bright waters
Had routed the great Romans, trouncing them for ever.
When he had fought in France, and won that field,
Fiercely felling his foemen in death,
He gave orders for the burial of his brave knights
Who in the assault of swords had been struck out of life.
At Bayeux he had buried Sir Bedivere the noble,

And at Caen the corpse of brave Sir Kay was left   2380
Completely covered in clear rock crystal
Because that country had been conquered by his father.
He ordered burial in Burgundy for other knights –
Sir Berade and Baldwin, and Sir Bedwar the magnificent;
But good Sir Cayous[1] at Caen, at his kinship required.
  After that, from Autun, King Arthur at once
With his armed hosts entered Germany,
Lingering first in Luxemburg with his loyal knights
To heal his wounded henchmen, as lord in his own right,
Then called a council on St Christopher's Day   2390
Of kings and kaisers, clerics and laymen,
And ordered them to exercise their ingenuity
In counselling him how to conquer the country he
    claimed.
The kingly Conqueror, courteous and bold,
Himself spoke these splendid words in council:
'In this cliff country closed in by hills
Lives a knight I must know, his renown is so great:
The liege lord of Lorraine, let me not hide it!
Beautiful is his bailiwick, so bold men tell me.
I shall parcel out that province, apportioning it as I please,   2400
And then deal with the duke, if destiny permit.
He has been a rebel to my Round Table,
Ever ready with the Romans to ravage my lands.
We shall quickly give account according to reason
Who has right to those revenues, by Our Ruler in heaven.
Then in Lombardy, land lovely to look on,
I shall lay down laws that shall last for ever,
And trouble the tyrants of Tuscany somewhat,
Tackling only matters temporal in my time of rule.

1. 2371–85 In this passage, the names of knights and places make little
sense. See Krishna, pp. 187–8. I follow Hamel in amending Thornton's
'Cador' to 'Cayous'. Cador is killed in the last battle.

I shall proffer my protection to all Papal domains,   2410
Showing my people my proud pennant of peace;
It is folly to offend our Father under God,[1]
Or Peter or Paul, those apostles of Rome.
If we cherish the Church, we shall achieve our aims better:
Its holdings shall be unharmed while I have my say.'
   They spurred off at speed, saying no more,
This manly company, to the marches of Metz,
Which is lauded in Lorraine as London is here,
A city esteemed the most splendid in the kingdom.
On his comely horse cantering, the King advanced   2420
With Ferrar and Ferraunt and four other knights,
The seven men circling the city closely
In search of a serviceable site for their siege engines.
In the besieged town they bent their crossbows
And aimed at brave Arthur with hostile intent;
At the King the crossbowmen keenly shot
To harm him or his horse with their hurtful weapons.
But he shrank from no shot and asked for no shield
As he brilliantly braved them in his bright clothes,
Lingering at leisure and looking at the walls   2430
For a low place to launch an attack on the townsmen.
   'Sire,' said Sir Ferrar, 'it is folly thus to go
Naked in your noble garb so near to the walls,
Proceeding to the city in your surcoat only,
And showing yourself to the citizens, thus to destroy us
    all.
Let us hurry hence lest ill hap befall us,
For if they hit you or your horse, we are undone for ever!'
'If you are craven,' said the King, 'I counsel you, ride back
Lest they harm you with their harsh hurtling weapons.
No surprise, but you seem to be but a baby   2440
Who would be frightened if a fly alit on his flesh.

---

1. 2412 Arthur fails to follow his own advice: see ll. 3176ff.

I feel no fear, so favour me God.
If those low fellows are furious, I fear them not at all.
They gain no glory from me, thus wasting their shots.
They shall lose all equipment before I leave, my head on it.
Such louts shall not be so lucky, by the Lord's grace,
As to kill a crowned and anointed king.'
    Then out at our head surged hot-blooded knights,
The whole following host urging them on with shouts,
And our furious foragers forged forward on all sides,   2450
Hurtling ahead on their iron-grey horses,
Advancing in formation, all famous warriors
Renowned as the retinue of the Round Table.
All the fierce men of France followed next
And, finely fitted out, on the field lined up.
Then swiftly the men swung their steeds round,
Displaying in style their splendid accoutrements,
In battle formation with banners unfurled,
High helmets on and broad shields braced,
And the pennants and pennons bearing each prince's arms   2460
Were spangled with pearls and precious stones;
The lances with floating pennons, the shimmering shields,
Flashed like lightning, gleaming all over.
Then those princely men spurred to prove their horses,
Closing in on the city from all sides.
First they scoured the suburbs, searching carefully,
Hunting out the archers, having small skirmishes
And scaring out the shield-bearers and sentinels,
Then battering their barricades with bright weapons,
Beating down a barbican and gaining a bridge.   2470
Had the garrison not been good at the great gates,
They would have won their way in by sheer force.
Then our brave men drew back, the better to concentrate,
In dread of the drawbridge being dashed asunder,
And cantered back to camp where the King was waiting
With his main might of warriors, mounted on horses.

When the Prince was provided for, places were allotted
And silk pavilions pitched in preparation for a siege.
In lordly style they lay there as long as seemed good,
Keeping watch every way as war requires,   2480
And speedily set up stout siege engines.
    On Sunday when the sun spread its brightness
The King called to Florent, flower of knights:
'The Frenchmen grow feeble; I am far from surprised,
For as troops they are untried in this fair territory.
The food and flesh they are fond of are lacking.
Here on every hand are ample forests
Where herdsmen have hurried with their excellent cattle.
You must go up to the heights and hunt in the mountains:
Sir Ferraunt and Sir Floridas shall follow your lead.   2490
We must revitalize our fighters with the fresh meat
Which feeds in the forest on fruits of the earth.
The good Sir Gawain shall go on this quest,
Lordliest leader, if his liking so determines,
And Sir Wichard and Sir Walter, worthiest knights,
With the greatest warriors of the western marches –
Sir Cleges, Sir Claribald, Sir Cleremond the noble
And the Commandant of Cardiff, equipped perfectly.
Go, warn all the watch, Gawain and the rest,
And set forth on foray without further discussion.'   2500
    Now forth to the forest went these fine fighters,
Doughty and daring, to the dappled mountains,
Through valleys, forest verges, fells and the like,
Past holts and hoar woods with hazel copses,
Across marsh and wet moors and massive hills;
And in the misty morning to a meadow they came
Where the hay was mown but not harvested or even
        stooked,
But still in swaths and full of sweet flowers.
There these bold men unbridled their beasts and grazed
        them

In the grey dawn glimmer, with birds beginning to sing   2510
As the sun was ascending, sign of Christ
That solaces all sinners who can see it on earth.
     Then Sir Gawain, warrior chief, went off alone,
Being both sage and strong, in search of adventure.
He was aware of a wonderfully well-armed man
By a woodside stream, his steed grazing,
Clad in a coruscating corslet and carrying
A broad buckler; beautiful was his horse.
No other men had he, only a squire
On a steed standing beside him, holding his spear.   2520
His arms bore three black greyhounds backed with
          glittering gold,
With collar-chains and scabbards of chalkwhite silver;
Shimmering as its hues shifted, a carbuncle crowned all:
A chivalrous chief was he, challenge him who would.
     Gladly Sir Gawain gazed on the man:
He grasped from his groom a great spear,
Spurred his fine steed straight over the stream
And strode in his strength to that strong warlord,
Crying eagerly in English, 'Arthur!'
Angrily the other answered him at once   2530
In the language of Lorraine in a loud voice,
That men might hear a full mile away:
'Where are you riding, robber, with your rash challenge?
You'll pick up no plunder here, however proudly you
          vaunt.
Either in battle be a better warrior than me,
Or be my prisoner despite your pompous look!'
'Sir,' said Sir Gawain, 'so save me God,
But such blathering boys bother me little!
So get your fighting gear ready, and grief shall come to
          you
Before you go from this grove, for all your great words!'   2540
     Then they levelled their lances, these lordly warriors,

Laying them full length on their grey mounts,
And striking with skill in a spate of spear-thrusts
Till both savage spears snapped at once.
They shot through shields and sheared through
    chain-mail,
Hitting through shoulders a hand-span deep.
Thus both heroes were hurt with honourable wounds;
Till they had wreaked all their rage, neither would retreat.
Then they wrenched their reins and rode to attack again,
Two hurrying men eagerly heaving out swords,   2550
And hit each other's helmets with heavy blows,
And hacked at hauberks with hard-edged weapons.
Stoutly they struck, these stern knights,
Stabbing at the stomach with their steel points.
They fought, flourishing fiery swords
Till flurries of fire flashed on their helmets.
   Then Sir Gawain grew furious and greatly enraged:
Grimly with his good sword Galuth he struck
And cleft the knight's shield cleanly in two.
Looking at his left side as his horse leapt,   2560
By the light of the sun men might see his liver.
That gallant groaned in grief at his wounds
And struck at Sir Gawain as he swept past,
Slashing slantwise as he smote furiously;
He sheared through an enamelled shoulder-plate,
Breaking the rerebrace[1] with his brilliant sword-edge,
And hacking it off at the elbow-piece,
By the forearm plate fretted with silver.
Through the vesture of velvet rich and doubled
His venomous sword severed a vein   2570
Which spurted so violently Gawain's senses were dimmed,
And his visor, lower face-guard and fine vesture

1. 2566 Rerebrace: a plate of armour on the upper arm, protecting it
from shoulder to elbow.

Were all sprayed with spots of the staunch man's blood.
    In no time the tyrant turned his bridle
And talking untenderly, 'You are touched!' he said,
'Better have a bandage lest you blench in pallor,
For no barber-surgeon in Britain can staunch the blood,
Since one struck by this sword can never stop bleeding.'
'So!' said Sir Gawain, 'You disturb me but little,
Trusting to terrify me with your tremendous words;   2580
You expect such piffle to perplex my heart.
But trouble shall trip you before you turn hence
Unless you tell me at once, not tarrying at all,
What will staunch this swiftly flowing stream of blood.'
'I shall tell you truly, and you may trust my word –
No surgeon from Salerno could save you better –
Provided you vouchsafe me for the sake of your Christ[1]
How to gain forgiveness of sin as I get ready for death.'
'Yes,' said Sir Gawain, 'so God help me,
I grant you grace, though you have given me grief,   2590
If you will tell me truly upon what quest
You proceed thus singly, yourself alone,
And what religion you believe in – let it not be hid! –
And what land you are lord of, what allegiance you owe.'
    'My name is Sir Priamus; a prince is my father
Who is lauded in his lands by well-acclaimed kings;
In Rome where he rules he is rated as royal,
But he rebelled against Rome and rode over its territory,
Waging war for winters on end
With wit and wisdom and his warrior's strength,   2600
And by honourable action achieved independence.
He is of Alexander's blood, overlord of kings;

1. 2587 The yearning of a good pagan to become a Christian is a
common theme in medieval literature: cf. *Sir Ferumbras* and the dead
judge in *St Erkenwald* (in *The Owl and the Nightingale, Cleanness, St
Erkenwald*, trans. Brian Stone, Penguin, 2nd ed. 1987).

His ancestor was Hector of Troy, his uncle's grandfather,
And in the kindred I come from I count also
Judas Maccabaeus and Joshua, noble knights.
I am his heir apparent, eldest of his kin.
I possess and wield plenary power
Over Alexandria and Africa and other foreign lands.
To me shall truly come the treasure and territories
Of all the princely cities the port possesses,   2610
And the tribute and taxes during my time of life.
While at home so haughty of heart I lived,
That as high as my hip I accounted none under heaven;
And so I was sent here with seven score knights
To try my fortune in this fight with my father's
    permission;
And I for my arrogance am ingloriously captured,
By hazard of arms everlastingly damaged!
Now that I have recounted the kindred I come of,
Let me know your name, for your knighthood's sake!'
   'By Christ,' said Sir Gawain, 'I never was a knight,[1]   2620
But as a household helot of Arthur the Conqueror
I have worked at his wardrobe for winters on end
On the full armour he favoured for fighting.
I pitched proud tents for his personal use,
Dressed in their doublets his dukes and earls,
And Arthur himself in the excellent aketoun[2]
That he has used all of eight years in battle.
At Christmas he created me yeoman and gave me great
    gifts,
A hundred pounds, a horse and armour of quality.

1. 2620 A constant theme in all chivalric literature. Gawain is playing a
trick on Priamus, who wants to be sure that his opponent is of noble
rank like himself.

2. 2626 Aketoun: a padded jacket worn under armour to soften the
effect of the metal.

If my hap is to be healed that hero to serve,   2630
I shall immediately be elevated, have my word for it!'
  'His knights must be noble if his knaves are such as you;
No king under Christ could counter him alone!
He will be heir to Alexander whom the whole world
      bowed to,
More able than ever was Sir Hector of Troy.
By the holy oil used at your christening,
Make known to me now whether you are knight or
      knave!'
  'My name is Sir Gawain, I grant you truly,
Cousin to the Conqueror who acknowledges my kinship:
In his records I am reckoned rightly a knight of his
      chamber,   2640
Enrolled as the most reputable of all the Round Table.
I am a duke of the dozen best he dubbed himself
One day with all dignity before his dearest knights.
Grudge not, good sir, that such grace favours me;
It is the gift of God, whose good will grants it.'
'By St Peter!' said Priamus, 'that pleases me better
Than if I were Prince of Provence and prosperous Paris.
For I'd sooner be secretly stabbed to the heart
Than that any ordinary man should have such a prize.
But harbouring at hand in the high woods yonder   2650
Is a whole huge army, heed that if you will!
The dread Duke of Lorraine with his daring knights,
The doughtiest in the Dauphiné and many Germans,
The lords of Lombardy, of leadership renowned,
The garrison of Mount Gothard grandly armed,
Warriors from Westphalia, worthy fighters,
Saxons, and Saracens from Syria are all there.
Their known number as they are named on the roll
Is sixty thousand and ten, I say, staunch soldiers.
Unless you hurry from this heath we shall both be harmed, 2660
And I shall never be whole if my hurts are not tended.

See that your squire does not sound his horn
Lest in utmost haste you be hacked to pieces,
For here on hand are a hundred good knights.
They are my retinue and ride where I direct them;
No loyaller liegemen live on earth.
If you are caught by that company you will campaign no
     more,
And earth's richest ransom will never rescue you!'
  Before that woe came, Gawain went to where he wished
With that worshipful and sorely wounded man,   2670
Making for the mountain where our men were encamped,
Grazing their grey steeds in the goodly meadowland.
There lords were leaning low on their gleaming shields,
And lifting light laughter for love of the birds,
The larks and linnets with their lovely song;
And some slipped into sleep ensorcelled by them
As they sang at that season in the sparkling shrubland,
Lurking low with their lulling tunes in the glades.
Then Sir Wicher was aware that their leader was wounded,
And went to him weeping and wringing his hands.   2680
Sir Wicher, Sir Walter, warriors sagacious,
In concern for Sir Gawain went straight to him,
Met him midway and marvelled greatly
That he had mastered that man so mighty in strength.
By all the world's wealth, more woeful were they never:
'For all our honour on earth is declining!'
  'Grieve not,' said Gawain, 'for love of God in heaven,
For this gash is but gossamer such as is given as a foretaste.
Though my shield was shot through and my shoulder cut
     deep,
And the movement of my arm makes some pain for me,   2690
This prisoner, Sir Priamus, who is perilously wounded,
Says he has salves which can save us both.'
Then stern knights stood to his stirrup to help,
And he alit in lordly style, relinquishing his bridle,

117

Let his highly bred beast browse on the flowers,
Drew off his helmet and fine armour,
Leant on his large shield and inclined to the ground:
In the bold man's whole body no blood was left!
Then to Sir Priamus pressed princely knights,
Eased him anxiously off his horse,   2700
And took off his helmet and hauberk next.
But at once his wounds made his heart waver,
So they laid him down in that dale and undressed him,
And he lay stretched at length, which brought him relief.
They found a fine gold flask at his girdle
Filled with the fragrance of the four magic springs
Which at full of the flood flow from Paradise,
Giving form to the plenteous fruit that feeds us all.
If flesh is fretted with it when sinews are severed,
In four hours the sufferer is as fit as a fish.   2710
With utterly clean hands they uncovered their bodies
And a knight cleansed their cuts with that clear liquid,
Cooling them kindly and comforting their hearts.
When their cuts were cured, they clothed them again.
Then they broached barrels and brought them wine,
Best roasts and brawn and bread of quality;
And after eating they armed themselves at once.
    'To arms!' was those intrepid men's stentorian cry,
And a clear clarion called together
The company for counsel to consider their case.   2720
'A host of armed men is harbouring yonder,
All in fine fettle in that forest of oaks,
Yes, fighters from foreign parts full of determination,
So says Sir Priamus, St Peter help us!
Go, men,' said Gawain, 'and engage your minds:
Who will go to that grove and greet those great lords?
If we go home empty-handed King Arthur will be angry,
And say we are scoundrels scared of almost nothing.
By today's fair fortune, Sir Florent is with us,

The flower of France, who never fled from foe: 2730
In the King's chamber he was chosen and charged
    solemnly
To head this day's exploit, by our highest chivalry.
Whether he fight or flee, we must follow him,
But in fear of yonder force I shall never forsake him.'
  'Sir,' said Sir Florent, 'you speak well.
But I am but an infant, in arms untested;
If misfortune befall us, the fault will be ours,
And like foreigners we shall be forced out of France for ever.
Let your honour not be hurt; I have but simple wits.
You are certainly our senior: the decision is yours.'   2740
Sir Priamus spoke: 'You are scarcely five hundred,
Too few by far to fight with them all,
For your serfs and scullions, being of scant service,
Will hurry off hence for all their brave words.
I suggest you scheme like subtle warriors,
And get away guilefully like the great knights you are.'
  Said Gawain, 'I agree, God help me!
But these are fine fellows, most fit to be rewarded,
The most cruel in combat of the King's chamber,
Who with their wine can waft knightly words: 2750
Today we can test who can take the trophy!'
So forth to the forest rode a fierce vanguard,
Took to the fair field and then went forward on foot.
Florent and Floridas with five score knights
Spurred after their prey, princely armed men
Following in the forest, finding their way
Forward at a fast trot, towards their foes driving on.
Then five hundred advanced towards our force,
Fighters on fresh horses coming to the forest.
In front was one Sir Feraunt,[1] on a fine charger,   2760

1. 2760 Another confusion of names. A knight called Ferraunt is with
King Arthur at l. 2421.

Who had been fostered in Famagusta; the Fiend was his
    father.
He rode fast at Sir Florent and flung him these words:
'Why flee, false knight? The Fiend take your soul!'
Sir Florent, keen to fight, set spear in fewter,
And on Fawnell of Friesland[1] at Feraunt he rode,
Wrenching the rein of his right noble steed,
Urging it at the host, no pauser he!
Flush in the forehead he transfixed his foe,
Disfiguring his face with his fell weapon;
In through bright helmet he hit to the brain,   2770
Broke the neck-bone and stopped his breath.
    Feraunt's cousin saw it and cried out, calling loudly,
'You have killed cold-dead the king of all knights,
Who has been confirmed on the field in fifteen kingdoms,
And never found a foe to fight in single combat!
For his death you shall die by my deadly weapon,
And so shall the chivalry shirking fight in yonder valley.'
'Fie!' said Sir Floridas, 'You fleering wretch!
You fluke-mouthed fellow, frighten me, would you?'
And suddenly as he slipped by, with his sword Floridas   2780
He flapped free all the flesh on the flank of the other,
Whose intestines tumbled out and trailed with their filth
In the hooves of his horse as onward he rode.
    A knight rode rapidly to rescue the man.
It was Raynold of Rhodes, a rebel to Christ,
Persuaded by pagans to persecute Christians,
Who pressed forward, proudly pursuing his quarry,
For in Prussia his prowess had been praised highly –
Hence his boldly boastful battle offer here.
But Sir Richard, a right warrior of the Round Table,   2790
Spurred straight at him on his splendid steed
And thereupon thrust clean through his red shield,

1. 2765 Friesland was famous for its horses.

And the blood-stained spear sped to his heart.
Raynold reeled around and sprawled to earth
Roaring most crudely, but never rode again.
   Now the hale and the whole left of the five hundred
Fell on Sir Florent and his five score knights
On a level plain between flood and marshy land.
Our fighters stood firm and fought against them.
   Then loudly aloft was cried, 'Lorraine!'   2800
As the long spears were launched in the clash of armies,
And 'Arthur!' on our side when ill hap threatened.
Sir Florent and Floridas set spear in fewter,
Rushed fiercely at the foe, frightening their knights,
And felled five at the front in their first assault,
And before going farther, not a few more.
They burst braided hauberks and battered shields,
Beating and bearing down the best that stood against
      them.
All the great ones in that group galloped away,
So ferociously they drove back those royal knights.   2810
   Then Sir Priamus, that prince, perceiving the sport,
Not daring to do battle, and downcast in pity,
Went to Gawain and spoke these words:
'In your assault your splendid men stand disadvantaged,
For Saracens swamp them, seven hundred and more
Of the Sultan's soldiers from several countries.
Suffer me, sir, for the sake of your Christ,
To lead some of your liegemen and lend you support.'
'I grudge you not,' said Gawain, 'the guerdon will be
      theirs,
For great gifts shall be given them by my lord.   2820
But let the fighters of France fairly prove themselves;
They have not fought their fill these fifteen winters!
I'll not stir with my soldiers half a steed's length
Till they are beset by stronger forces than stand on that
      plain.'

   Then Gawain was aware that at the wood's edge
Westphalian warriors on stalwart steeds
Were tearing along the track at them tumultuously
With all the weapons, I warrant, that warfare needs.
The old earl, Antele, headed the vanguard
With on either hand eight thousand knights,   2830
And bowmen and shield-bearers in bigger numbers
Than any other prince on earth had ever equipped.
Next the Duke of Lorraine came dashing along
With twice as many Germans, justly judged brave,
While pagans from Prussia, proud cavalrymen,
Pressed forward prancing with Priamus's knights.
   Then said Earl Antele to Algere his brother,
'I am utterly angry with Arthur's knights
For thus eagerly taking on such a host unaided.
They'll be utterly outfought by early mid-morning   2840
Thus fighting on the field foolhardily against us;
If they are not trounced, in truth I'd take it as a wonder!
If they'd turn from their intention and retreat elsewhere,
Give up their aim and ride home to their prince,
They might lengthen their lives and lose but little.
That would lighten my heart, the Lord help me!'
'Sir,' said Sir Algere, 'they're scarcely accustomed
To being beaten in battle, which makes me boil more.
The finest fighters in our forces shall fall dead,
Few as our foes are, before they flee the field.'   2850
   Then the good Gawain, gracious and noble,
With glorious good heart gladdened his knights:
'Fear not, my fine fellows, the flashing of shields
As those rotten men revel on their great rearing horses!
Bannerets of Britain, brace your spirits!
Be not abashed by those brightly clad knaves!
We shall abate their boasting for all their bold vaunts,
Till they're as obedient as bedded bride is to lord.
If we fight the foe today, the field shall be ours.

Their foul faith shall fail and falseness be destroyed.   2860
Those fellows in their front rank look frail and untested;
Their faith is in fealty to the Fiend himself.
We shall be warranted as winners in this war
And vaunted by the voices of valiant men;
Yes, praised by princes in the presence of nobles
And loved by ladies in lands a-plenty.
Our ancestors never had such high honour,
Not Unwin or Absalom or any of those others.
We must have Mary in mind when most in distress,
That sign of our sovereign[1] that he especially trusts,   2870
Which speaks of the sweet Queen who so favours us all –
Who magnifies that Maiden shall never miscarry!'
     That speech being spoken, so close were they
That a field's length from them the foe cried, 'Lorraine!'
Such a fearful day's fighting was never fought,
Not in the vale of Jehosaphat, as history records,
When Julius and Joatell met judgement in death,
As when the worthy warriors of the Round Table
Rushed at the Roman rout on their regal steeds,
For so swiftly did they assault with their gory spears   2880
That their base foemen were frightened and fled to the
          woods,
Careening back to court to be called craven for ever!
'By Peter,' said Gawain, 'it gladdens my heart
That those good-for-nothings have gone for all their great
          number!
I reckon such riff-raff will wreak little harm on us,
For they will hurry to hide at the edge of the wood.
They are fewer on the field than when first they were
          counted
By forty thousand, i'faith, for all their fine army.'
     But one Johan of Genoa, a huge giant,

1. 2870 'That sign of our sovereign'. The reference is to Arthur's
shield, on which the Virgin and Child figured.

Joined combat with Sir Gerard, a judge from Wales   2890
Who, shearing his chequered shield, stabbed him
Through his coat of mail of incomparable quality.
He cut clean through clasps and joints!
On a swift steed that sally he made.
Thus was the giant, that vagrant Jew, outjousted,
And Gerard was happy at heart and rejoiced greatly.
Then Genoese on jennets joined battle as one
With fully five hundred pressing forward.
A fighter called Sir Frederick and not a few others
Rode forward in a rush, eagerly raising their war-cry,   2900
To fight with our foragers who held the field;
And then the royal ranks of the Round Table
Charged forward furiously and fiercely rode at them,
Massing against their middle-guard. How ill-matched
The mighty multitude was, it was marvellous to see.
In the onslaught the Saracens soon discovered
That the Sovereign of Saxony was hard beset,
For his giants were outjousted by gentle knights
And hit in their hearts through their Genoese hauberks.
Our heroes hacked the helmets of haughty warriors,   2910
Their swords stuck deep in hearts to the hilts.
The renowned knights of the Round Table
Carved through and cut down those craven heretics,
Thus driving to death their dukes and earls
By their dread deeds all that day's length.
   Then the Prince Priamus, in the presence of the lords,
Spurred to his standard and seized it openly,
Reversed it vigorously and veered away
To the royal ranks of the Round Table,
And his whole host hurried after him   2920
In assent to the signal on his splendid shield.
Forth from the phalanx like sheep from the fold
They streamed towards the struggle and stood by their
   lord.

That done, to the Duke they delivered this message:
'We have served you as paid soldiers these six years and
    more;
We forsake you forthwith as feudaries to our true master.
We shall follow our feudal lord to foreign kings' lands.
Four winters you have defaulted, failing to pay us:
You are feeble and false, nothing but fair words!
Our pay has petered out; your campaign is finished.   2930
We can go wherever we wish with honour.
Why not treat for a truce and trifle no longer? –
Or ten thousand of your troops shall be destroyed by
    nightfall.'
'Damn you!' cursed the Duke. 'Devil take your bones!
I shall never dread danger from those dogs yonder.
This day we shall deal by deeds of arms
With my doom, my dukedom and my dauntless knights.
I set little store on such mercenaries as you,
Who suddenly forsake and desert their lord!'
    The Duke did not dawdle with his troops,   2940
But picked a dromedary and some dread knights
And galloped at Gawain with his great host
Of fierce and famous fighters from Granada.
Those freshly horsed men forged to the front
And felled forty of our foremost men at one sweep.
These had fought against five hundred just before that;
No wonder they waxed weary and faint, in faith!
Then Sir Gawain grew angry, gripped his spear,
And galloping in again with his gallant knights,
Met the Marquis of Metz and smote him dead –   2950
The man on middle-earth who most enraged him.
Then Chastelayne, a squire of the King's chamber,
Who was ward to Sir Gawain in the western marches,
Charged at Sir Cheldrik, a chief of degree,
And with a hunting-spear hit him right through.
He got that great success by good fortune in war.

But they pursued the assailant so that he could never
    escape,
And Swyan of Swecy with his sword's edge
Severed our squire's spine at the neck.
On the greensward sprawling, he swooned in death,   2960
Dying at once, and was a warrior no more.
    From the grey eyes of Sir Gawain great tears fell:
The boy, a mere beginner in battle, had been virtuous.
For that cherished child Gawain's cheer so changed
That the chill tears ran in channels down his cheeks.
'Woe is me,' he wailed, 'that I was not watching!
For him I offer all I own in pledge
If I fail to take revenge on the villain who felled him!'
Sadly he armed himself and spurred up to the Duke,
But one Sir Dolphin the Dauntless drove against him,   2970
And Sir Gawain struck him with a grim spear
So that the ground point glided through to his heart.
Hastily he hauled it out and hit another,
Hardolf, a heathen high-fortuned in arms,
Thrusting right through his throat cleverly,
And the slippery spear slid from his hand.
There slain on that slope by his skill in arms
Lay sixty splendid warriors! And they slung them into a
    swamp.
Though Sir Gawain was woeful, he watched with care,
And when he saw that Swyan who had killed the squire,   2980
With his sword he speedily slashed him through;
In swift death Swyan sank to the ground.
Gawain rushed at their ranks and thrust at helmets,
Hacked through fine hauberks and shattered shields.
He kept to his course as he quickly galloped
Right through the rearguard, still riding on,
Then reined in abruptly, this royal noble,
And rejoined the ranks of the Round Table.
    Then our chivalrous men changed their horses,

And chased and chopped down noble chieftains,   2990
Hacking heartily at helmets and shields,
Hurting and hewing down heathen knights
And cleaving kettle-helmets clean down to the shoulders.
Never had earth known nobles in such disorder!
Kings' sons were captured, courteous and of quality;
And knights of the country, noble in fame,
Lords of Lorraine and Lombardy as well,
Were laid hold of and led in by our loyal knights.
Fairer fortune had those who fled the field that day –
Such a defeat never befell them, flying as they did.   3000
 When Sir Florent had fought and won the field,
He forged further forward with his five score knights;
The spoils and prisoners presently followed
With shield-bearers, bowmen and brave men-at-arms.
The good Sir Gawain guided his men,
Spurring the swiftest way, as his scouts told him,
For fear that a group of very great lords
Might latch on to his loot or do like mischief.
So he placed guards at passes and paused with his company
Till his goods had gone past the paths he thought perilous.   3010
When they saw the city the King was besieging,
Which, to tell the truth, was to be taken that very day,
A herald hurried ahead on the orders of the lords
Out of the high lands right into the encampment,
Turned at once to the royal tent and told the King
In true terms of the triumph they had won:
'Your soldiers are all safe whom you sent foraging,
Sir Florent and Sir Floridas and all your fierce knights.
They have forayed and fought with huge forces
And relieved of their lives large numbers of your enemies.   3020
Our worshipful warden has done wonderfully well,
Gaining today great glory for ever:
He is the Dauphin's deathsman and the Duke's captor,
And many dauntless men are dead by deeds of his hands.

Prisoners of price, princes and earls has he
Of the bluest blood that bears rule on earth.
All your chivalry have achieved choice victories
Except the squire Chastelayne, whom mischance struck.'
    'High-spirited herald,' said Arthur, 'by Christ
You have healed my heart, I would have you know: 3030
A hundred-pound holding in Hampton I freely give you!'
The King then assembled his knights for the assault,
Setting up on all sides siege-towers and sows,[1]
Disposing his shield-bearers to scale the walls,
While every sentinel stood guard with soldiers on the alert.
Then boldly and busily they braced their mangonels,
Loading them with large missiles and letting them fly.
Holy buildings and hospitals they hammered to the
      ground,
Churches and chapels painted chalk-white;
Very strong stone steeples were strewn in the streets,   3040
Also many fine inns and houses with chimneys,
And they battered and broke to bits plastered walls.
To hear the inhabitants' anguish was pitiful.
    The Duchess, drawn up with her damsels of honour,
And the Countess of Crasine, with her comely maidens,
Bowed the knee on the battlements where the brave King
      was stationed
On a splendid steed stylishly caparisoned.
They knew him by his countenance and cried loudly:
'Rightly crowned king, take account of our words!
We beseech you, Sire, as sovereign and lord,   3050
To save us today for the sake of your Christ.
Lend us your support and make peace with the people,
Lest in sudden assault the city be destroyed!'
    With a gentle gesture he just raised his visor,

---

1. 3033 Sow: a portable strong roof under which sappers worked to undermine walls of besieged cities.

And with visage full of virtue the valiant hero
Said softly to the Duchess these conciliatory words:
'None of my men, madam, shall maltreat you.
I promise my peace to you and your peerless maidens,
To children, chaste holy men and chivalrous knights.
But your Duke is in danger – do not doubt that!   3060
His doom shall be truly dealt him, dread nothing else.'
Then to each sector he sent steadfast lords
To stop the assault, for the city had submitted,
The Earl's eldest son having handed over the keys
And surrendered the same night with consent of his lords.
The Duke was sent to Dover with all his dauntless knights
To dwell in dire bondage all the days of his life.
When King Arthur had consummated his conquest
By seizing the citadel of the splendid city
By soldierly skill, all its stern and keen men,   3070
Its captains and constables, acclaimed him as lord.
He devised and divided among various nobles
An endowment for the Duchess and her dear children,
And wisely made wardens to wield rule
In all the countries he had conquered with his skilled
        warriors.
Thus in Lorraine he lingered, lord in his own right,
Making laws for the land exactly as he liked.
    Then on Lammas Day to Lucerne he moved,
Where he lingered at leisure in delight unceasing,
And where his galleys were gathered in great numbers,   3080
All glittering like glass under the green hills,
With canopied cabins for anointed kings,
And high quality cloth-of-gold covers for knights.
Swiftly they stowed their gear and stabled their horses,
Then struck straight over Lake Lucerne into narrow
        passes.
Now merry-hearted, he moved his mighty army
Over immense mountains by marvellous paths,

Struck through St Gothard and seized the watch-tower,
Giving the garrison grievous wounds.
As he came over the crest, the King paused   3090
And with his whole army eyeing the prospect,
Looked down on Lombardy and loudly announced,
'Of this lovely land I intend to be lord!'
   With crowned kings they came then to Como,
Which was accounted the key to the country round about.
Sir Florent and Sir Floridas went forward there
With fully five hundred brave French fighters
To seek out secretly the swiftest way to the city
And set up an ambush, as they intended.
Then soon after sunrise from the city there rode   3100
Crafty scouts who controlled their coursers,
Scouring the hill-crests in careful reconnaissance
To flush out ambushes and so avoid harm.
Poor people and shepherds pressed after them
To pasture their pigs by the princely gates,
And servants in the suburbs laughed loudly
As a lone boar went loping off to the plains.
   Then our bold men broke ambush, took the bridge,
Sallied into the city with streaming banners,
Slashing and stabbing whoever withstood them,   3110
And destroyed four streets before they stopped.
From the far gate then folk fled in crowds
In fear of Sir Florent and his fierce knights.
They fled the fair city, to the forest running
With their victuals and vessels and very fine clothing.
Above the broad gates the victors raised a banner,
And Sir Florent, in faith, was happier than ever he had
    been.
Arthur, halted on a hill and eying the walls,
Said, 'I see by that sign that the city is ours.'
Then he entered with his army in order at once,   3120
Meaning to maintain them till midday there.

The King loudly proclaimed to each company
That on pain of life and limb and loss of land
No loyal liegeman belonging to his forces
Should lie with a lady or her loyal maids,
Or debauch a burgess's wife, or a better or worse woman,
Or mistreat any man among the citizens.
Now the Conqueror was in Como and held court there
With crowned kings in the castle of high fame,
And placated the common people of the country,   3130
Comforting the careworn with kingly words.
He conferred the captaincy of Como on a knight of his
    own,
And he and the inhabitants were in harmony at once.
   The Sire of Milan learned of the collapse of Como
And sent to our sovereign staunch lords
With sixty horses saddle-bagged with huge sums of gold.
He prayed him to pity the people as their master,
And said he would truly serve him as his subject for ever,
Offering him homage for all the lands he held:
For Piacenza, Ponte and Pontremoli,   3140
Pisa and Pavia, he plentifully proffered
Precious stones, purple dye and pure silk,
Palfreys fit for princes and proven warhorses,
And for Milan an annual million in gold
To be humbly handed over on St Martin's Day.[1]
And he and his heirs, for ever and unquestioningly,
Would pay homage to Arthur throughout his life.
The King in council accorded him safe-conduct,
And he came to Como and acclaimed him as lord.
   Arthur turned into Tuscany when the time seemed
    ripe,[2]   3150

1. 3145 St Martin's Day is 11 November. He is the patron saint of
innkeepers and drunkards.

2. 3150 Arthur's *chevauchée* in Tuscany is the cruellest in the poem.

And tumultuously took its high-towered towns,
Welting down walls, wounding knights,
Overturning towers and tormenting the people.
Worshipful widows he made wail in woe,
Cursing and crying and clasping their hands.
Wherever he went he laid waste with war
Their wealth and their dwellings, working misery.
They spread their surging assaults, sparing few,
Pitilessly plundering and despoiling their vines,
Consuming without stint what had been saved with care,   3160
Then sped on to Spoleto with spears in plenty.
From Spain to Prussia word spread about him,
With talk of his extravagance; and terrible was the
    bitterness.
Towards Viterbo then he turned his horse,
And in that vale victualled his valiant men prudently
With various vintages and baked venison,
Intending to stay in the territory of the Viscount:
Very soon the vanguard let free their horses
In that virtuous vale among the vines.
There sojourned the Sovereign in solace of heart   3170
To see if the senators would send any message,
Carousing with rich wine and revelling joyously,
This royal king with regal members of his Round Table,
With mirth and melody and many amusements.
Men were never made merrier on this earth.
  But at noon one Saturday, seven nights later,[1]
The cleverest cardinal from the court of Rome
Came kneeling to the Conqueror, carrying this proposal:
He pleaded for peace and the promise of Arthur
To pity the Pope, now put under stress,   3180
Seeking for him a safe truce for the sake of Our Lord
For seven days, so that they could all assemble

---

1. 3176 See note to l. 2412.

And see Arthur for sure on the Sunday following
In the city of Rome as their sovereign and lord,
And crown him as true king with consecrated hands
With his sceptre and sword, as their sovereign and lord.
Hostages were offered for this undertaking:
Eight score scions, sweet noble children,
Attired in tunics of rich Turkestan silk,
Who were handed over to Arthur and his high-born
    knights.   3190
This truce attested, to trumpets' fanfare
To a tent with trestle tables they proceeded.
The King himself was seated with steadfast lords
Under a silken awning, happy at the festive board.
All the senators were seated separately and apart,
And were solemnly served with seldom-seen foods.
Jocund in his joy and gentle in his words,
Arthur at his high table hosted the Romans,
And courteously comforted the Cardinal himself.
Thus this royal ruler, as the romances say,   3200
Honoured the Romans at his rich table.

    These learned and clever men at length, as was fitting,
Took leave of the King and left for Rome.
They sought the swiftest way to the city that night,
Leaving with Arthur the hostages of Rome.

    Then this splendid sovereign said these words:
'Now we can revel and rest, for Rome is ours!
Put our hostages at ease, these high-born children,
And look after everyone I have in my army.
As Emperor of Germany and all the eastern marches,   3210
We shall be overlord of everything on earth.
Ascension Day shall see us sovereign of these lands,
And come Christmas Day, we shall be crowned thereafter
And rule in royal style, keeping my Round Table,
With revenues from Rome, as is right and proper,
Then go over the great sea with goodly men-at-arms

To avenge that valiant One who died on the Cross.'
   Then according to the chronicle, this comely king
Went briskly to bed with a blithe heart.
He hurriedly undressed and undid his girdle   3220
And languid with sleep slipped into slumber.
But by an hour after midnight his mood quite changed;
Towards morning he met most marvellous dreams.
When his dreadful dream had driven to its end,
Arthur quaked with horror as if he would die,
And sent for his sages to tell them of his terror:
'In faith since I was formed I never felt such fright!
So search swiftly to make sense of my dream,
And I shall readily and rightly recount it truly.
It seemed I was in a wood, wandering alone,   3230
Bewildered as to which way I should go,
For wolves and wild boars and wicked beasts
Stalked that sterile land slavering for prey;
Loathsome lions were licking their fangs
And longing to lap the blood of my loyal knights.
I fled through the forest to where flowers grew high,
In horror at those hideous things, to hide from them,
And emerged in a meadow by mountains enclosed,
The happiest place on earth men ever could see.
The enclosure was covered in its entire compass   3240
With clover and clerewort which clothed it completely.
The vale was environed with silvery vines
Bearing golden grapes, the greatest ever,
And edged with arbours and all kinds of trees
Fair of foliage with flocks feeding under them.
All fruits earth provides were flourishing there,
Harmoniously hedged in, hanging on noble boughs.
No dank dewfall there could damage anything,
For in the heat of the day, all dry were the flowers.
   'Then descended to that dale, down from the clouds,   3250
A duchess richly dressed in decorated robes,

134

A surcoat of silk exotically coloured
All overlaid with otter fur right to the hems,
And ladylike lappets at least a yard long,
And revers all trimmed with ribbons of gold,
With brooches and besants and other bright jewels.
Her back and her breast were embroidered all over,
And she carried her caul and coronet perfectly.
On lovelier looks no light ever fell.
She whirled a wheel about with her white hands,   3260
Turning it intrepidly as she was tasked to do.
This round was red gold, set with royal gems
And richly arrayed with rubies in plenty.
The spokes were all plated with slats of silver,
Their splendid span a spear's length from the hub.
A seat of sparkling silver was set on top,
Chequered with carbuncle rubies of changing colours.
On the circumference clung kings in succession,
Their crowns of clear gold all cracking to pieces.
From that seat six of them had suddenly fallen,   3270
Each sovereign separately, saying these words:
   '"How I regret that I ever ruled on this round wheel!
Never was royal king so rich, reigning on earth!
When horsed at the head of all I had no thought
But hunting, having pleasure and holding folk to ransom.
Thus did I with my days, enduring while I could,
And so to dire perdition I am damned for ever."
The lowest was a little man, lying below:
Lean were his loins and loathsome to look at,
His locks a yard long, and lank and grey,   3280
And his features were foul, his frame crippled.
One brilliant eye blazed as bright as silver;
The other was yellower than the yolk of an egg.
"I was lord of limitless lands," said he,
"And low in allegiance to me all living men bowed,
But now I've not a rag to nurture my body

And I am swiftly struck down – let all see the truth!"
 'The second lord, I say, who was strung next after,
Seemed to me much stronger and stalwart for fighting,
But often sighing in his suffering he spoke these words: 3290
"I have sat on that seat as sovereign and lord,
And ladies most loving clasped me in their arms,
But now lost are my lordships, laid low for ever!"
 'The third was a thrustful man with thickset shoulders,
So thoroughly fierce that thirty would scarcely threaten
  him.
His diadem, indented with diamonds all over
And adorned and decorated with jewels, had slipped
  down.
"I was dreaded in my day in different kingdoms:
Now I am doomed to be damned in death," grieved he.
 'The fourth was a fair man, forceful in arms,   3300
His figure the finest ever framed on earth.
Said he, "I firmly defended my faith when king;
I won fame in far lands and was flower of all kings.
Now my face is faded and foul fate has struck me,
For I have fallen far, and am friendless abandoned."
 'The fifth was yet finer than the four others,
A fiery and forceful fellow who foamed at the lips.
He crooked his arms round the rim, gripping it grimly,
Yet he faltered and fell fully fifty feet.
Still he sprang up sprinting and spread his arms,   3310
And from the spear's-length spokes spat out these words:
"I was a sovereign in Syria, and sole in eminence
As monarch and master of many kings' lands.
Now sunk from that sweetness, I have suddenly fallen,
Struck from that seat for the sins I committed."
 'The sixth held a psalter sumptuously bound
With a silk cover sewn in a stylish way,
And a harp and a handsling with hard flint stones;
The disasters he had suffered, he spoke of at once:

"In my days I was deemed, for deeds of arms,   3320
One of the doughtiest who ever dwelt on earth.
But my martial might was marred and spoiled
By this maiden so meek who moves us all."
   'Two kings[1] were clambering, clawing their way up,
Craving to come to the crest of the wheel.
"This ruby throne," they ranted, "we shall rightly claim
As two of the noblest ever known on earth."
Both warriors went white, wan-cheeked with the effort,
But they were never to attain that topmost throne.
The foremost made a noble figure, with his fine forehead,   3330
The fairest of face who was ever formed,
And he was clothed in the colour of courtly blue,
Flourished all over with fleur-de-lys in gold.
His co-peer was clad in a coat of pure silver
Engraved in gold with a graceful cross,
And so I could see that the king was a Christian.
   'I went to the lovely woman and warmly greeted her.
"Welcome!" was her word, "it is well that you have come.
Were you wise enough, my wishes you should respect   3340
Above all heroes who were ever on earth,
For all your war honours you have won through me.
I have befriended you, fine Sir, and been a foe to others.
In faith you have so found it, and not a few of your men,
For I felled Sir Frollo[2] and his fierce knights,
Whence the foison of France is all freely yours.
You shall achieve this chair, I choose you myself,

---

1. 3324–9 These last two worthies, Charlemagne and Godfrey de Bouillon, are represented as future subjects of Fortune, because historically Arthur antedates them. The sage refers to them in the future tense (ll. 3422–37).

2. 3345 Sir Frollo was the ruler of Gaul under the Emperor Leo. In a previous campaign, Arthur had won France by killing Frollo in single combat, so Geoffrey of Monmouth recorded (ix. 12).

Over all the emperors honoured on earth."
   'Then she lifted me lightly in her slender hands
And set me softly on the seat, sceptre in my grasp,   3350
And skilfully with a comb she combed my hair
So that the crisping locks curled up to my crown.
Then she dressed me in a diadem decorated most
      beautifully
And offered me an orb set full of fine stones,
And enamelled in azure, with the earth painted on it,
Encircled with the salt sea on all sides
As a certain sign that I was Sovereign of the World.
Then she handed me a sword with scintillating hilts
And bade me, "Brandish this blade! The sword is my own;
Many have lost their life-blood with the slash of it,   3360
And while you work with this weapon it will never fail
      you."
   'Then peacefully she departed to rest at her pleasure
In the fringes of that forest of foison unparalleled.
No orchard on earth was ever so planted for prince,
Or apparelled so proudly but in Paradise itself.
She bade the branches bend down and bring to my hands
The best fruit they bore on the boughs above,
And they held to her behest, all together,
The greatest in each grove, I give you my word.
She told me to stint not, and take what fruit tempted me.   3370
"Make free with the finest, noble fighting man!
Reach for the ripest, and revel in it.
Now rest, royal king, for Rome is your own,
And I shall willingly whirl the wheel at once
And bring you rich wine in rinsed goblets."
Then she went to the well by the wood's edge,
Where the wine welled up, wondrously flowing,
Caught up a cupful and cleverly raised it
And tenderly told me to take some, toasting her.
In such style she solaced me for the space of an hour   3380

With all the liking and love a man could long for.
But at midday exactly her mood quite changed,
And she menaced me much with marvellous words.
When I beseeched her, she bent her brows on me:
"King, you can claim nothing, by Christ who made
    me!
For you shall lose this pleasure, and your life later:
You have delighted long enough in lands and lordliness!"
Then she whirled the wheel about, whipping me
    downwards,
Which promptly pounded to pieces all my limbs,
And by that seat my spine was smashed asunder.   3390
And I have shivered with chill since that ill-chance befell
    me;
Thus weary with wild dreaming, I awoke, truly.
You understand my distress now, so speak as you wish.'
   'Sire,' said the sage, 'Fortune is finished with you.
You shall find she is your foe, force it how you will.
You are at the height, have it truly from me.
Chance and challenge as you will, you will achieve no
    more.
You have destroyed sinless men and spilled much blood
In vainglory in your victories in various kings' lands.
Take shrift for your shames and shape up for death!   3400
Be advised by the vision vouchsafed you, Sir King,
For fearsome shall be your fall within five winters.
Found abbeys in France – the fruits shall be yours –
For Frollo and Feraunt and their fierce knights
To whom you dealt dreadful death in France.
Think of those other kings and ask your heart about them,
Who were acclaimed as conquerors and crowned on earth.
The most ancient was Alexander, to whom all the world
    bowed;
Next in time was Troy's Hector, sweet-tempered knight;
Julius Caesar, who was judged a knight, was third,   3410

Well-bred and bold in battle, as barons agree;
Sir Judas, a jouster of gentle birth, was fourth,
A masterful Maccabee, mightiest in strength;
Joshua, who made joy for Jerusalem's host,
Was the fifth, and a fine fighter was he;
The sixth, dauntless David, was deemed by kings
One of the worthiest warriors ever to wear knighthood,
For he slew with a sling by sleight of hand
The great man Goliath, grimmest in the world,
Then spent his time composing all the precious psalms   3420
Which are set down in the Psalter in striking words.
One of the kings clambering, I can truly tell,
Shall be called Charlemagne, son of the French king;
He shall be accounted a conqueror cruel and keen,
Who will acquire by conquest countries in plenty;
He will capture the crown that Christ himself wore,
And the very same spear that struck to his heart
When He was crucified on the Cross; and all the cruel
    nails
He will recover with courage for Christian men to keep.
The other will be Godfrey, who will avenge God   3430
On Good Friday, going to it with gallant knights;
He will be Lord of Lorraine by leave of his father,
And revel in rapture in Jerusalem later,
For he will recover the Cross by skill in battle
And then be crowned king with consecrated oil.
Such destiny no other duke in his day shall have,
Nor undergo such harm when the whole truth is told.
So Fortune has fetched you to fulfil the number
Of nine for the noblest ever named on earth.
This shall be read in romance by royal knights: 3440
By acclaim you shall be accounted among conquering
    kings,
And on Doomsday deemed, for your deeds of arms,
One of the worthiest warriors ever to dwell on earth.

Accordingly many clerics and kings shall recount your
    exploits
And keep your conquests in the chronicles for ever.
But the wolves in the woods and the wild beasts in your
    dream
Are the wicked men who wage war on your realm,
Having entered in your absence to harry the people
With hosts of aliens from uncouth lands.
You will have tidings, I tell you, within ten days,   3450
Of the trouble that has overtaken you since you turned
    from home.
I advise you to confess your flagrant misdeeds,
Or most promptly you will repent your pitiless acts.
Amend your mood, man, before misfortune strikes,
And meekly beg mercy for the merit of your soul.'
  Then the royal king rose and reached for his clothes:
A red jerkin with roses, the richest of flowers,
A neck-piece, a paunch protector and a precious girdle,
And put on a hood of exquisite scarlet,
And over it a fur hat ornamented beautifully   3460
With pearls from the orient and precious stones.
His gloves were gaily gilded and engraved round the
    borders
With miniature rubies much to be admired.
Then taking only a hunting hound and his sword,
With anger in his heart he hurried over a broad field,
Taking a track by the still edge of a wood
To a highway, where he halted, abstractedly musing.
As the sun was ascending he saw approaching,
Walking the swiftest of ways towards Rome,
A man in a capacious cloak and clothes all baggy,   3470
With hat and high boots of homely style.
The fellow was adorned with flat farthings all over,
And shaggy shredded ends showed at his skirts.
With his money-bag and mantle and many scallop shells,

And staff and palm, he seemed a pilgrim.
   He hailed Arthur with a hearty, 'Good morning!'
And the King answered loftily in the language of Rome,
A Latin somewhat loose, but polite to a degree,
'Where do you want to go, walking by yourself?
While the world is at war, I would think it dangerous.   3480
An enemy with an army is hiding in that vineyard;
I can say that if they see you, you will suffer sorrow.
Unless you can come by a safe-conduct from the King,
Slaves will slay you and steal your possessions.
And if you hold to the highway, they'll have you there
    too,
Unless you have prompt help from his high-born knights.'
   Then said Sir Craddock to King Arthur,
'I shall forgive for my death, God help me,
Any fellow who foots the fair earth under God.
If the keenest knight the King has comes to me,   3490
I shall combat him in courtesy, Christ take my soul!
For you yourself cannot seize me or stop me in my way
For all your rich array and robes of splendour.
No war shall make me waver from going where I like,
Nor any knight who has been nurtured on this earth.
But I shall proceed by this path to pilgrimage in Rome
To purchase a pardon from the Pope himself,
And of the pains of Purgatory to be perfectly absolved.
Then I shall strenuously seek my sovereign lord,
King Arthur of England, that honourable man.   3500
For he is in this empire, as honest men say,
Battling in these eastern borders with his bold knights.'
   'Where do you come from, keen man,' the King then
    asked,
'You who know King Arthur and also his knights?
Were you ever at court when he was in his home country?
The familiar way of your words warms my heart.
You have proceeded soundly, and search wisely,

Being a British knight, as your speech reveals.'
  'I should know the King, who is my acknowledged lord;
I was named in his noble court a knight of his chamber.   3510
In his courtly company I was called Sir Craddock,
Keeper of Caerleon after the King himself.
Now I am hunted from my homeland, with heavy heart,
And that castle has been captured by uncouth people.'
  Then the comely King clasped him in his arms,
Cast off his kettle-hat[1] and kissed him forthwith,
Saying, 'Welcome, Sir Craddock, Christ save me!
Dear kinsman and cousin, you make my heart cold:
How goes it in Great Britain with my gallant knights?
Are they cut to bits, or burnt, or banished from life?   3520
Tell me truly your terrible tidings:
I press for no proof; your probity I know.'
  'Sire, your regent is recreant and rancorous in his
      actions,
For he has done dire deeds since your departure.
He has captured your castles and crowned himself,
And raked in all the revenues due to the Round Table.
He has carved up the kingdom and conferred it at will,
Dubbing men from Denmark dukes and earls,
Who dispersed, destroying cities far and wide.
With Saracens and Saxons in his soldiery everywhere,   3530
He collected legions of loathsome foreigners,
Sovereigns of Surgenale and many mercenaries,
Picts and pagans and practised knights
From Ireland and Argyll, outlawed men.
All those knaves are now knights, nobodies from the
      mountains,
Who have leadership and lordship to use as they like.
And there Sir Childrik is now called a chieftain –

---

1. 3516 Kettle-hat: a close-fitting cap made of skin. At l. 3995 Arthur
catches the dead Gawain's blood in one.

A pitiless man who oppresses your people.
They rob your religious folk and rape your nuns,
And he rides with his rout ready to rob the poor.   3540
From the Humber to Hawick he holds as his own land;
All the country of Kent he has covenanted to himself,
All its comely castles which the crown possessed,
Holts, hoary woods and hard sea-shores –
Yes, all that Hengist and Horsa once occupied.
On the sea at Southampton are seven score ships
Full of fierce fighters from foreign countries
Whose task is to take on your troops when you attack.
But one word more yet: the worst you have not heard.
He has wedded Guinevere and calls her his wife,   3550
And dwells in the wild parts of the western marches,
And has got her with child, so goes the word.
Of all men in the world, woe be to him,
Warden unworthy to watch over women!
In this manner has Sir Mordred done mischief to us all.
Hence I made my way over the mountains to make it
      known to you.'
   Then the mighty monarch was maddened at heart
At this fortune most fell, his face death-pale:
'By the Rood!' the royal man raged, 'Revenge shall be
      mine!
He shall promptly repent all his pitiless acts.'   3560
So, woefully weeping he went to his tents.
Without joy this wise king woke his men,
Called kings and others with clarion trumpets,
And in council recounted the case to them.
'I am betrayed by treason, though I have dealt truly,
And all my work is wasted; the worse is my state.
Misfortune shall befall the faithless traitor
If I can get hold of him, as I am a true lord!
It is Mordred, the man I most trusted,
Who has captured my castles and crowned himself king,   3570

With the revenue and riches of the Round Table.
Renegade wretches he has recruited for his retinue,
And divided my fair realm among various lords,
Mere Saracens and mercenaries from many lands.
He has wedded Guinevere and calls her his wife,
And if a baby is born, no better is the luck.
They have assembled on the sea seven score ships
Full of foreign warriors only to fight me.
So back to Great Britain we are bound to hurry
To deal death to the dastard who has done this harm.   3580
No fighter shall go forward except on fresh horses,
And only my best knights who have been blooded in
    battle.
Sir Howell and Sir Hardolf shall here remain
To rule the realms I have rightly acquired.
Look that in Lombardy no allegiance is changed,
And attend truly to Tuscany, as I tell you.
Receive the revenue from Rome when it is reckoned,
Possessing it the same day that we assigned recently,
Or else all the hostages[1] who are outside the walls
Must be hanged on high, all together.'   3590
   Now the bold King bustled with his best knights,
Ordered his liegemen to load and leave at once.
He returned through Tuscany, tarrying but little,
Not lingering in Lombardy except when light failed,
Marched over the mountains by marvellous paths,
Struck the straight way swiftly through Germany,
And forged his way into Flanders with his fierce knights.
His fleet was fitted up in fifteen days,
And he shaped up to take ship with the shortest delay
Before shearing over the shining water with a sharp wind.   3600
Moored with ropes by the rocky cliffs then he rode at
    anchor

---

1. 3589 The only hostages mentioned are the 160 children.

Where those foul villains were afloat on the flood waiting,
Their ships chocked together with great chariot chains,
And all full of fierce fighting men;
Under the hatches were hidden heathen troops.
High at the sterns were helmets and crests
Proudly pictured on painted cloths
Sewn piece by piece upon each other
With thrums doubly thick on the heavy friezes.
Thus the dreaded Danes had decorated their ships,   3610
So that no hurtling arrow could harm them.
Then the kingly ruler with ranked men of the Round Table
Right royally in red[1] arrayed his ships.
That day he dealt out dukedoms and dubbed knights,
Got barges and galleys together loaded with stones,
To his satisfaction set slings on the topcastles,
And had the crossbows cruelly bent in readiness.
The slingers sedulously straightened their tackle
And put broad heads of bronze on their big missiles.
Gallant men got ready gear for strongpoints,   3620
Grim steel spikes and great iron grapnels.
On stern after stern stout warriors were massed;
Many a splendid spear stood upright,
And on the lee side were set strong lords and others
Who placed on that port side painted shields,
While high on the hindcastle were helmeted knights
To guard against shots across the glittering water,
Each bold man in battle garb most brightly clad.
    The brave King rowed about in a barge,
Bare-headed in the bustle, his beaver locks waving,   3630
A servant bearing his sword and a splendid helmet
Matched with a mantlet of silver mail
And ringed with a coronal richly arrayed.

---

1. 3613 The red means that no quarter would be given in the coming battle.

To cheer on his chivalry, to each ship he went:
To Cleges and Cleremond he cried aloud,
To Gawain and Galyran, those good strong men;
To Lot and Lionel he lovingly spoke,
And to Sir Lancelot du Lake these lordly words:
'Let us recover our country – its coasts are our own –
And make them bitterly blench, those bloodhounds there,   3640
Butcher them on board and burn them afterwards!
Yes, heartily hack down those heathen dogs.
They are harlots' offspring, my hand upon it!'
  Then he went back to his war-galley and weighed
    anchor,
Put on his fine helmet with the handsome mail,
And spread broadly his banners of brilliant scarlet,
With their coruscating crowns of clear gold.
But in chief place on his shield was a shining white maiden,
With a child on her arm who is chieftain in heaven;
Such was the chief device, never changed in the chase   3650
Of honourable Arthur, while on earth he lived.
Then mariners shouted, and shipmasters too,
And each man merrily urged on his mate,
In seamen's slang discussing the state of things.
They tugged on the trusses, tautened the mainsails,
Set small sails and secured hatches,
Brandished bright steel and blared on trumpets,
Then stood sturdily in the bows or steered from the stern,
Striking over the sea to where the strife would start.
When a squally wind from the west arose,   3660
Its fierce gusts filled the fighters' sails,
And it tossed stout ships stern against stem
So that bilge and beam burst apart.
Stem and stern struck each other with such force
That the starboard side timbers were splintered.
Then galley after galley, and gigs as well,
Cast grappling hooks across with crafty skill,

And men hacked through the head-ropes that held up the
    masts;
Most stern was the strife and the splitting of ships.
Great war-galleys were ground to bits, 3670
Many cabins cleft through and cables destroyed.
   Men of courage keenly killed warriors;
Topcastles were cut down by keen weapons,
Stately turrets with their striking colours.
They sliced sideways at the mainstays next,
And the slash of the swords made the masts sway
And with the first blow fall on the fighters and others,
So that many a man on the main deck was mangled to
    death;
Thus they fought furiously with fearsome weapons.
Barons in mail boldly boarded ships 3680
From boats nearby and were bombarded with stones,
Yet beat down the best men and burst open the hatches.
Some men, struck through by spikes of iron,
Well-clad warriors, made the weapons slimy.
So eagerly the archers of England shot,
Their darts dealing death-blows through durable steel,
That heathen knights in the hold in agony jerked,
So hurt through hard steel they would never be whole
    again.
Then our fellows surged forward, fighting with spears,
In front those famed as fiercest in battle, 3690
Each fighter freshly testing his fame,
Warring on the waves with weapons of death.
So they dealt that day, these newly dubbed knights,
Till all the Danes were dead and dumped in the deep.
Next with broadswords our Britons bitterly hacked,
Leaping aloft at their lordly foes.
When the outlandish louts leapt in the water,
All our lords fell to laughing at once.
By then timbers were shivered, ships were shattered,

And the Spaniards speedily sprang overboard;   3700
All those armed men, high-born and low,
Were killed cold and dead and cast overboard.
There squires swiftly spilled their life-blood;
Heathens heaving on the hatches rose in horror
And sank in the salt sea, seven hundred at once.
Thus Sir Gawain the Good gained the victory,
And all the great galleys he gave to his knights,
Sir Gavin, Sir Griswold and other great lords.
He had all prisoners' heads hacked off by Galuth.
That was what befell the false fleet on the sea,   3710
And thus the foreigners fell fated to die.
   Yet the traitor was still there with tried knights on land,
And they trotted up in their trappings to the trumpets'
    blare,
Showing up on the shining shore behind their shields.
Mordred shrank not for shame, but showed himself
    proudly.
Turning together towards them, Arthur and Gawain
Saw the sixty thousand soldiers advancing.
The high tide had ebbed after the slaughter,
Leaving such slack pools and slush lying everywhere
That the King was loth to make land across the low water. 3720
So he stayed at sea to save his steed being bogged,
And looked after his liegemen and loyal knights
So that any lamed or lost should live if possible.
   Then Sir Gawain the Good took a galley
And glided up an inlet with his admirable troops.
Landing in his spleen he leapt into the water,
Going in girdle-deep in his golden garments,
Strode up the sand in sight of the lords,
Single with his small troop, I sorrow to say it.
With banners bearing his badges, and his best arms,   3730
He forged up the foreshore in his fine armour
And bade his banner-bearer, 'Be quick!

Hurry to that huge army drawn up on the bank,
And I tell you in truth I shall attend you closely.
See you shun no sharp sword or shining weapon,
But beat down the most dauntless, denying them daylight.
Let not their boasts abash you, but bravely stand firm:
You have borne my banners in great battles before.
We shall fell those false men, the Fiend take their souls!
Fight that force furiously, and the field shall be ours.   3740
Ill hap to him if I lay hands on the traitor
Who struck with such treason against my true lord!
From such bad beginning little bliss can follow,
As shall well be warranted in our warfare today.'
   Now the tiny troop attacked across the beach,
Making for the mercenaries with smashing blows,
Shearing through shining shields at the enemy,
Their shafts shivering to shreds their bright lances.
Dreadful strokes they dealt with their deadly spears.
In the dankness of the dew the dead lay in crowds,   3750
Dukes of the best dozen and newly dubbed knights,
The doughtiest men of Denmark undone for ever.
In their high rage our heroes hacked open corslets,
Battering the boldest with baleful blows,
Thronging in the thick of it and thrusting to the ground
Three hundred of the hardiest enemies at once.
But Gawain, hugely angry, could not hold back,
And seizing a spear rode straight at a man
Whose standard was bright scarlet with spots of silver,
And thrust through his throat the grim weapon.   3760
The spike of the ground spear-point splintered;
Down went the man in death at the deadly thrust.
He was the King of Gotland, a great warrior.
Their vanguard then voided the field at once,
As if vanquished by a victory of our valiant men,
Who now met the middle ranks commanded by Mordred.
Unfortunately our fellows advanced at them,

For had Gawain been graced to hold the green hill,
Take my word, he would have won glory for ever.
    But Gawain watchfully awaited his chance   3770
To take revenge on the warlock who had awoken this war,
And made for Sir Mordred among all his men –
The Montagues and many other mighty lords.
Sir Gawain, incensed and stern of will,
Set his fine spear in fewter and furiously cried,
'False to him who fostered you, the Fiend take your bones!
Fie on you, felon, and your false actions!
You shall be dead and undone for your dire deeds,
Or I shall die this day, if destiny wills it.'
    Then the enemy with his host of outlaw warriors   3780
Cornered our company of incomparable knights.
That was the trick of the treacherous traitor:
Dukes from Denmark he quickly detailed,
And leaders from Lithuania with their legions massed,
And mercenaries and mighty Saracens from many lands,
All with their steely spears surrounded our men.
Sixty thousand soldiers in splendid array
Swarmed solidly round our seven score knights
By sudden deceit beside the salt sea.
Great tears from his grey eyes Sir Gawain wept   3790
In grief for the good men whose guardian he was.
Aware that they were wounded and weary with fighting
And wonderfully woeful himself, his wits failed him
And he said, with sighs and streaming tears,
'On all sides we are beset by encircling Saracens;
I sigh not for myself, so help me Our Lord,
But in sorrow at seeing us surprised and caught.
Be dauntless this day, and yon dukes shall yield to you!
Dread no dire weapon today, for our dear Lord's sake!
We shall end this hour as we ought, excellent knights   3800
Moving to immortal bliss with immaculate angels;
Though we have unwittingly wasted ourselves,

We shall gain much good for the glory of Christ.
Yonder Saracens shall see to it, I solemnly promise you,
That we sup with Our Saviour solemnly in heaven,
In presence of that precious Prince of the world,
With prophets and patriarchs and apostles most noble,
Before the kingly countenance of the Creator of us all.
If any of you should yield to yonder mares' sons
While he is still sound and not struck down,   3810
May he never be saved nor succoured by Christ,
But may Satan sink his soul into hell!'
     Then grimly Sir Gawain gripped his weapon,
And against that great force girded himself.
He rapidly set right his rich sword-chains,
Shoved forward his shield, shunning nothing,
And spurred to the assault, berserk and reckless,
Striking with savage strokes at the foe
So that the blood burst out where he battered past them.
Full of woe as he was, he wavered but little,   3820
But wreaked Arthur's wrath to his rightful glory.
He speared stalwart knights and steeds in the battle
So that strong men stood stone-dead in their stirrups.
He severed strong steel, slashed through mail,
Unstoppable by any, being out of his mind,
And fallen in frenzy out of fury of heart;
He fought and felled whoever stood before him!
Such fortune in fight never befell a fated man:
Headlong he hurtled at the whole host,
Dealing dire wounds to the doughtiest dwellers on earth.   3830
In exploit like a lion he lanced them through,
Lords and leaders on that land drawn up.
And still he would not stop in his savage grief,
But with bloody blows battered the enemy
As if he were hankering for his own death,
His wits astray with woe and wilfulness
As he went like a wild beast at the warriors nearest.

Wherever he went all wallowed in blood;
Each dread foe smelled danger from the death of one near
    him.
  Then he moved towards Sir Mordred among all his
    knights,   3840
Met him mid-shield and smote him through.
But the shuffler slightly shrank from the sharp sword
And sheared him on the short ribs a hand's-breadth deep.
The shaft shuddered as it shot into the shining warrior
So that the gore gushed out, gleaming on his legs
And showing on the shinguard which shone with its
    burnish.
As they struggled and strove, Mordred, struck to the
    ground
By the lunge of the lance, landed on his shoulders
On the field a furlong off, fearfully wounded.
Gawain flew after him and fell face down;   3850
His grief being great, no good fate graced him,
For when he drew a short knife sheathed in silver
To cut his kinsman's throat, the close mail held;
His hand slipped and slid aslant on the steel,
And his enemy heaved him underneath craftily.
With a deadly dagger the dastard stabbed him then
Through helmet into the head, and up into the brain.
And thus Sir Gawain was gone, the good warrior,
Unhelped by any, and heavy was the pity.
Yes, Gawain was gone, who guided many men.   3860
From Gower to Guernsey all the great lords
Of Glamorgan and Wales, gallant knights,
Struck with horror at that stroke, would never again see
    happiness.
  Then King Frederick of Friesland in good faith
Asked the false fellow about our fierce knight:
'Did you ever know this knight in your noble country?
Declare truly the kin that he comes of now.

What hero was he, with his armour so splendid,
With this gryphon in gold, on the ground now sprawling?
Heavy harm he handed us, so help me God,   3870
Striking down our stalwarts and sorely grieving us.
He was the bravest in battle who ever bore steel,
For he stunned our troop and destroyed it for ever.'
    Then Sir Mordred made this memorial speech:
'He was unmatched on middle-earth, I must affirm, Sire.
This was Sir Gawain the Good, the greatest of all
Of men who go under God, the most gracious knight,
Hardiest of hand-stroke, highest-fortuned in war,
Most courteous in court under the kingdom of heaven,
And the lordliest leader as long as he lived.   3880
In many lands his lion-like lustre was praised.
Had you encountered him in the country he came from,
    Sir King,
And known his knighthood, his noble acts and wisdom,
His manners, his might and his marvellous deeds in war,
You would deeply mourn his death all the days of your
    life.'
    The traitor let fall his tears freely at that,
Spurred off suddenly and spoke no more,
Went away weeping and bewailing the hour
His destiny doomed him to deal such woe.
The thought of the thing burned through his heart,   3890
And he sighed for kinship's sake as sadly he rode.
When that mutinous man called to mind
The royal honour and revels of the Round Table,
He groaned and regretted all his disgraceful deeds,
Then rode off with his armour, delaying no longer,
In awe of our high King, should he hurry forward.
    Heavy of heart, he hastened to Cornwall
Because of his kinsman lying killed on the shore.
There he tarried, ever trembling, attentive for news.
The next Tuesday the traitor took his departure,   3900

Determined to work treason by trickery again,
And this time by the Tamar his tents he pitched,
And meanwhile commanded a messenger to go
To Guinevere to warn her how the world was changed
Since the King had come to the coast of England
And fought his fleet and felled his forces in death.
He told her to fly far, fleeing with her children
Until he could steal away and succeed in speaking to her;
To hurry to Ireland, to its outermost mountains,
And dwell there in the wilderness, in its waste lands.   3910
Guinevere sobbed and groaned in her great room in York,
Weeping and wailing with welling tears,
And pressed from the palacc with her peerless maidens,
Who escorted her in a coach across to Chester,
Dressed as for death in dolefulness of heart.
To Caerleon she came, and took the veil,
Asking for the habit for the honour of Christ –
All in falseness and fraud, in fear of her lord!
    When our wise King was aware that Gawain had landed,
He writhed about in grief, wringing his hands,   3920
And bade men launch his boats in the low water.
He landed like a lion with his lordly knights,
Slid slantwise in the scum, slopping himself to the girdle,
Waded swiftly through the water waving his sword,
Then drew up his army, raised high his banners,
Sped across the wide sand in savage rage,
And fiercely went forward to the field where the dead lay.
Of the traitor's troops, on steeds with their trappings,
To tell you truly, ten thousand were killed,
And but seven score knights on our side, I swear,   3930
Were left lifeless, along with their leader.
Courteously the King turned over knights and others,
Earls from Africa and Austrian men,
Argyll and Orkney men, Irish kings,
The noblest from Norway in enormous numbers,

Dukes and Denmarkers and newly dubbed knights,
And in his garish gear the King of Gotland,
Who lay groaning on the ground, gashed right through.
Our great sovereign searched in sadness of heart,
Looking for the lords of the Round Table,   3940
And saw them huddled in a heap all together,
With the slaughtered Saracens surrounding them,
And Sir Gawain the Good in his glittering armour
Fallen on his face, fingers clutching the grass,
His banner of brilliant scarlet beaten down,
His blade and broad shield bloodied all over.
Such sorrow our splendid sovereign never knew,
Nor was his spirit ever sunk as by that single sight.
    The good King gazed, gripped with horror,
Groaned gruesomely, wept gouts of tears,   3950
Bent kneeling to the body, embraced it,
Cast up his visor, quickly kissed Gawain,
Looked at his eyelids, now locked fast shut,
His lips like lead and his complexion pallid,
And then, crowned king, cried aloud:
'Dear cousin and kinsman, in care I am left,
For now my glory is gone, and my great wars finished.
I hold here my hope of joy and armed success;
Wholly on him depended my heart and strength!
O my counsellor, my comfort, keeper of my heart,   3960
Renowned king of all knights ever known under Christ!
Worthy to be king, though I wore the crown!
Throughout the wide world my wealth and my glory
Were won by Gawain, through his wisdom alone.
Alas!' cried the King, 'my grief grows now;
I am utterly undone in my own country.
Ah, dire and dreadful death, you delay too long!
Why spin out so slowly? You smother my heart!'
    Then the sweet King sweated and sank in a faint,
But staggered up suddenly and solemnly kissed Gawain   3970

Till the blood bespattered his stately beard
As if he had been battering beasts to death.
Had not Sir Ewain and other great lords come up,
His brave heart would have burst then in bitter woe.
'Stop!' these stern men said, 'You are bloodying yourself!
Your cause of grief is cureless and cannot be remedied.
You reap no respect when you wring your hands:
To weep like a woman is not judged wise.
Be manly in demeanour, as a monarch should,
And leave off your clamour, for love of Christ in heaven!' 3980
  'Because of blood,' said the bold King, 'abate my grief
Before brain or breast burst, I never shall!
Sorrow so searing never sank to my heart;
It is close kin to me, which increases my grief.
So sorrowful a sight my eyes never saw.
Spotless, he is destroyed by sins[1] of my doing!'
Down knelt the King, and cried aloud,
With careworn countenance calling out:
'Gaze on this grief, O God most righteous!
See this royal red blood running upon the earth! 3990
Worthily should it be shrouded and enshrined in gold,
For it is unsullied by sin, so help me, Lord!'
Down knelt the King, great care at his heart,
Caught up the blood carefully with his clean hands,
Cast it into a kettle-hat and covered it neatly,
Then brought the body to the birthplace of Gawain.
  'I pledge my promise,' then prayed the King,
'To the Messiah and to Mary, merciful Queen of Heaven,
I shall never hunt again or unleash hounds
At roe or reindeer ranging on earth, 4000
Never let greyhound glide or goshawk fly,

1. 3986 Arthur's only expression of sin in the poem is touched off by
his grief over Gawain. But perhaps it was a battle-sin of caution, in that
but for being 'loth to make land across the low water' (l. 3720) Arthur
would have been at Gawain's side in the battle.

Never see bird brought down that beats its wings,
Nor falcon nor formel[1] handle on my fist,
Nor gain great joy with a gier-falcon,
Nor reign in royal state, nor hold my Round Table,
Till your death, my dear one, be duly avenged!
But shall languish woe-laden as long as I live
Till God and dread death have done that just doom!'
   Then with anguish in their hearts they took up the body,
And carried it on a courser beside the King himself   4010
The shortest way there was to Winchester,
With their wounded knights, wearily and falteringly.
The prior of the place and his pious monks came out,
Pacing in procession to greet the Prince,
Who commended to them the corpse of the courteous
     knight:
'Care for it well,' he commanded, 'and keep it in the
     chapel,
And as is done for the dead, have dirges sung,
And garner good for his soul by gracing it with masses.
Let it lack nothing of lit candles and honour,
And have the body embalmed and kept above ground   4020
If you care that your convent may claim reward
When I come here again, should Christ allow it.
But for his burial, bide the time till they are beaten
Who have given us this grief and begun this war.'
   Then Sir Wichard, a warrior most wise, said,
'I warn you, go warily; that way is best.
Stay in this city and assemble your forces;
Stop with your stalwarts in this strong town.
Call from their countries your knights who keep castles,
And get from great garrisons their good soldiers,   4030
For in faith we are too few to fight with all those
We saw assembled in his service by the sea.'

---

1. 4003 Formel: female of the falcon (or eagle or hawk).

With a stern expression the King spoke these words:[1]
'Fear no misfortune, and fret not, sir knight.
If myself were the sole man under the sun,
And could have him in view or under my hands,
Even among all his men I would smite him to death
Before I stirred from the spot half a steed's length.
I shall attack him among his troops and destroy him for
    ever:
That vengeance I vow devoutly to Christ,   4040
And to his mother Mary, merciful Queen of Heaven.
I shall never rest easy or have peace of heart
In any city or suburb set upon earth,
Never slumber nor sleep though my eyes sink in
    weariness,
Till he is killed who killed Gawain, if my craft prevail,
But shall ever hunt down the heathen who hurt my people,
Until I pen them and imprison them where I please.'
    None dared to disagree of all the Round Table,
Nor pacify that Prince with placatory words,
Nor did his loyal liegemen look him in the eye,   4050
So lordly he loured at the loss of his knights.
Delaying no longer, he left for Dorset,
Woeful, I warrant, eyes welling with tears,
And came into Cornwall comfortless of heart.
The track of the traitor he trailed unerringly,
And turning by the Tamar in search of that trickster,
Found him in a forest the Friday after.
Alighting, the King let out a loud war-cry,
And with his fearless fighters took the field.
    Now his enemy issued from under the wood's edge   4060
With his alien host, hideous to behold.

---

1. 4033 Arthur, who has exercised due caution as a general throughout, now determines on rash action, the death of his beloved Gawain
having clouded his judgement.

Sir Mordred the Malebranche[1] with his mighty force
Came forth from the forest, moving forward everywhere,
In seven great battle groups geared for combat:
Sixty thousand soldiers – a stupendous sight! –
All fighting folk from far countries
Forming a strong front beside the fresh streams.
And in Arthur's whole army, the knights' tally
Was but eighteen hundred in all, entered in the rolls: –
A match without measure, but for the might of Christ,   4070
To take on that titanic force in that territory!
   Then the royal King of the Round Table
Rode upon his rich steed arranging his men,
And set forth his vanguard as he favoured it.
Sir Ewain and Sir Eric and other great lords
Commanded the middle-guard manfully next
With Merrak and Meneduke, mighty in strength;
Idrus and Alymer, intrepid young men,
And seven score knights, stayed with Arthur.
He readily arranged the rearguard next,   4080
The most active henchmen of the Round Table.
His force thus formed up, he flung out his war-cry
And then kindled his company with kingly words:
'I beseech you, sirs, for the sake of Our Lord
To do well today, and dread no weapon.
Fight fiercely now, and defend yourselves!
Fell those foredoomed fellows and the field shall be ours.
They are Saracens, that set; may they soon be destroyed!
Hew at them hard, for the honour of Our Lord!
If we are fated to fall on this field today,   4090
Before we are half cold we shall be heaved up to heaven.
Let no man limit the lordliness of your actions!

1. 4062 Malebranche: a medieval northern nickname meaning
'wicked offspring', not meaning 'bastard' or 'misbegotten', as was
once thought (Hamel, p. 387).

Lay those louts low by the end of the game!
Neither attend nor protect me, nor take account of me,
But be busy about my banners with your bright weapons,
Ensuring that strong knights sternly defend them
And hold them nobly high for our army to see.
If some caitiff captures them, quickly rescue them:
Uphold my honour now, for today ends my war.
You know what graces or grieves me: grant which you
    like.   4100
May the fitly crowned Christ comfort you all
As the loyalest lords ever led by a king!
With a happy heart I give you all my blessing,
And to all brave Britons: may bliss be your lot!'
   At prime morning they piped up and approached the
     enemy,
Peerless men prompt at proving their prowess.
Boldly men blew for the trumpets to blare
And the horns to sound sweetly as the stalwarts assembled.
Then joyfully those gentle knights joined battle;
They judged it the most justified jousting day ever,   4110
As Britons boldly buckled on their shields,
Crossed themselves as Christians and couched their spears.
   Then Sir Arthur's army set eyes on the enemy,
Shoved forward their shields and shunned further delay,
Shooting forward at the foe with fierce high shouts,
And battering through the bright bucklers at the warriors.
Readily the ruthless men of the Round Table
Struck with strong steel through chain-mail,
Cut through corslets and crushed bright helmets,
Hacking down heathens and hewing necks asunder.   4120
In the fighting with fine steel fated blood flowed;
The foremost foes fell defeated, fierce no more.
But heathens from Argyll and Irish kings
Surrounded our vanguard with venomous knights;
Picts and pagans with perilous weapons

Speared with grim spite and destroyed our knights,
Struck down the sturdiest with savage blows.
Through our whole army they held their course,
Fighting our force most fiercely everywhere
So that from the bold Britons much blood spilled. 4130
None dared ride to the rescue for all the riches on earth,
So powerful was support for the implacable foe.
Arthur stirred not a step, but simply stood his ground
Till three separate sallies were destroyed by his strength
　　alone.
　　'Idrus,' said Arthur, 'you must hurry there now;
I see savage Saracens are assailing Sir Ewain.
Get ready to rescue them: draw up your men!
Hurry there with hardy knights to help your father!
Spur at them from the side and save those nobles!
Till they are safe and sound I shall sorrow ceaselessly.' 4140
　　Earnestly then Idrus answered him:
'In faith he is my father: I shall never forsake him,
For he has fostered and fed me and my fine brothers.
But I must give up going there, God help me,
And abandon every blood-tie but what binds me to you.
I never disobeyed his bidding for anybody on earth,
But blindly obeyed him like a beast always.
He commanded me nobly, in knightly words,
To latch my loyalty on you, and be lieger to no other –
A command I shall keep to, if Christ permit. 4150
He is older than I, but both of us must end;
He will fall first, and I shall follow after.
If he is destined to die today on this field,
May the fitly crowned Christ take care of his soul!'
　　Then the noble King cried out, comfortless at heart,
Lifting his hands aloft and looking up to heaven:
'Why has God not granted it me through his great will
That He doom me today to die for you all?
I should like that more than being lifelong lord

Of all that Alexander had in his earthly life.'   4160
   Then Sir Ewain and Sir Eric, excellent warriors,
Attacked the enemy troops, striking intrepidly.
They chopped down with sharp swords the chief men
Of the Orcadian heathens and Irish kings,
Hacking those hulks of men with their hardened weapons,
Felling to earth those fighters with fearsome blows.
Shoulders and shields they shredded down to the
     haunches,
And grinding through mail, they gashed gizzards asunder.
Earthly king never had such honour in battle
On his ending day except Arthur alone.   4170
But the drought of the day dried up their hearts,
So that drinkless both died – dread pity it was!
   Now Sir Mordred the Malebranche and his mighty host
Moved against our middle-guard and mingled with them.
He had hidden behind at the edge of the wood,
His troops on the ground intact, to our distress.
He had studied the struggle from start to finish,
And the achievement of our chivalry by chance of arms,
And knowing our folk were fight-weary and fated to die,
He swiftly decided to assault the King.   4180
But the churlish chicken changed his device:
Instead of his scalloped saltire,[1] which he forsook,
He bore aloft three lions all in glittering silver,
Passant, on purple cloth, with precious stones,
So that the King should not know him, cunning wretch.
Because of his cowardice he had cast off his own device,
But the splendid sovereign straight away recognized him,
And called out to Sir Cador these characteristic words:
'Here comes the traitor, eagerly cantering forward;
That lad with the lions looks just like him.   4190
If I once get hold of him, he shall suffer hardship

1. 4182 Saltire: shaped like the cross of St Andrew.

163

For all his treason and trickery, as I am a true lord.
Today Clarent and Excalibur shall clearly show in conflict
Which cuts the more cleanly or has the keener edge.
We shall try tested steel against tested armour.
I kept Clarent as my clean darling, accounted it precious,
And kept it for crowning consecrated kings.
On days when I dubbed dukes and earls
It was bravely borne by its bright hilts.
I never dared to damage it in deeds of arms,   4200
But always kept it clean because of my purposes.
Now I see Clarent unscabbarded, crown of all swords.
I am aware that my wardrobe at Wallingford is plundered;
No one knew where it was but Guinevere alone;
She herself had safekeeping of that sword of high renown,
And the close-locked coffers belonging to the crown,
With the rings and relics and regalia of France
That were found on Sir Frollo when he was felled and left
    dead.'
   Then Sir Merrak met Mordred in maddened mood
And smote him mightily with a battered mace.   4210
The edge of his helmet he hacked off
And the bright red blood bubbled down his corslet.
Mordred faltered under the fierce pain, and his face went
    pale,
But he gave battle like a cornered boar and struck back.
He shook out a bright sword shining like silver,
Which was Arthur's own, and had been Uther his father's,
Which was wont to be kept at Wallingford in the armoury,
And with it the dread dog dealt such dire blows
That the other drew back some distance, daring nothing
    more,
For Sir Merrak was a man undermined by age,   4220
And Sir Mordred was mighty and in his utmost strength.
Neither knight nor any other could come within the
    compass

Of that sword's swing without spilling his lifeblood.
  Our Prince perceived it, and pressed fast forward,
Hurtling through the host with his whole strength.
There he met Mordred and with full malice said,
'Turn, untrue traitor, your time is up!
By the great God I shall give you your death-blow,
And no rescue or ransom shall reach you from any man!'
The sovereign struck him staunchly with Excalibur,   4230
Shearing off the corner of the shining shield
And hitting a hand's-breadth deep into the shoulder,
So that the bright red blood blazoned the mail.
Mordred shuddered and shivered, but shrank back little,
Rather shot forward sharply in his shining gear,
And the felon struck fiercely with that fine sword,
Ripping through the rib-plates on Arthur's right side.
Through surcoat and hauberk of armoured steel
The hilding hacked off a half-foot of flesh.
That deadly blow brought his death, and dread pity it was   4240
That the dauntless man should die but by God's deeming!
Yet still with his sword Excalibur he struck nobly,
Guarding himself guilefully with his glittering shield,
And slashed off Mordred's sword hand as he surged past.
An inch from the elbow he hacked it clean off,
So that Mordred sank down and swooned in the dust;
Yes, through brassard of bright steel and brilliant mail,
And hilt and hand upon the heath were left lying.
Then deftly he dragged that devil upright again
And broached him with the blade to the bright hilts,   4250
So that he squirmed on the sword-point in his
      death-struggle.
  'In faith,' said the fated king, 'it fills me with grief
That such a false felon should have so fair a death.'
That fight being finished, the field was won,
And the false folk on the field were left to their fate.
They fled to the forest and fell in the thickets

As our fierce fighters followed after them,
Hunting and hacking down the heathen dogs,
And smiting dead in the mountains Sir Mordred's knights.
Not one man got away, warrior or chieftain;   4260
All were chopped down in the chase, and cheap was the
      cost.
But when the King came to the corpses of Sir Ewain
And Eric most honourable, and other great lords,
He caught up Sir Cador, consumed with grief,
And Sir Cleges and Sir Clermond, keen warriors,
Sir Lot and Sir Lionel, Sir Lancelot and Lowes,
Merrak and Meneduke, ever mighty in battle,
And grieved as he laid them together on the ground,
Loudly lamenting as he looked on their bodies,
Like a man hating life and lost to joy.   4270
    Then in a stupor he staggered, and his strength failed.
He looked up to heaven, and all his face changed;
He swayed and sank down, suddenly swooning.
Then he clambered to his knees, crying and calling:
'O King rightly crowned, in care I am left!
All my lordship is laid low to the ground.
Those who gave me gifts through the grace of God,
Maintained my majesty by their might in battle
And set me up in honour as Earth's master,
In a terrible time this trouble has come to them,   4280
That through a traitor all my true lords are taken in death.
Here rests the rich blood of the Round Table,
Squandered by a scoundrel, which is scalding sadness.
Helpless on the heath I must house alone
Like a woebegone widow bewailing her man.
I may curse and cry and clasp my hands in grief,
For my strength and prestige are stopped for ever.
I take leave of all lordship till my life ends.
Here the blood of the Britons is borne out of life,
Here all my happiness ends today.'   4290

Then the Round Tablers rallied their ranks,
And to their royal ruler they rode all together.
Swiftly were assembled seven score knights
In sight of their sovereign sinking in death.
The crowned King knelt, crying aloud:
'With goodwill, God, I give thanks for thy grace
In vouchsafing us the virtue to vanquish our enemy,
And granting us glorious victory over those great lords.
You never stained us with dishonour or disgrace,
But always handed us overlordship of all other kings.   4300
To look for our lords we have no leisure now,
For that craven caitiff has quite crippled me.
Let us go now to Glastonbury – it is our only good
          course –
To repose in peace and repair our wounds.
For this precious day's process, praised be the Lord,
Who has destined us the doom of dying in our own land.'
     They wholeheartedly then held to his behest,
And went the swiftest way to Glastonbury.
They entered the Isle of Avalon, where Arthur dismounted
And made his way to a manor: he could move no farther.   4310
A surgeon from Salerno searched his wound,
But the King could tell that he would never recover,
And straight away he said to his staunch followers:
'Call me a confessor with Christ in his hands,
For I must speedily receive the sacrament, come what
          may.
My cousin Constantine shall wear the crown,
As becomes a kinsman, if Christ permit.
Bear my blessing, men, in burying these lords
Who were slaughtered by sword in the struggle today.
Then be stern and see that the offspring of Mordred   4320
Are secretly slain and slung into the sea:
Let no wicked weed wax twisting on this earth!
I urge you, for your honour's sake, do all as I bid.

167

All offences I forgive, for heavenly Christ's love;
And if Guinevere has done well, well may she prosper!'
He strongly said 'In manus' as he lay stretched out,
And so passed his spirit: he spoke no more.
   Then the baronage of Britain, bishops and others,
Shaped with shuddering hearts to go to Glastonbury
To bury their brave sovereign, bearing him to earth   4330
With all the honour and high ceremony any man could
    have.
They had the bells rung and chanted the Requiem,
And sang masses and matins in mournful tones.
Religious men arrayed in their rich capes,
Pontiffs and prelates in precious robes,
All the dukes and dignitaries dressed in mourning,
Countesses kneeling and clasping their hands,
Ladies languishing and looking forlorn,
And girls too, all garbed in garments of black,
Surrounded the sepulchre with their tears streaming down; 4340
So sorrowful a sight was never seen in their time.
   Thus ended King Arthur, as old authors affirm.
Of Hector's blood was he, son of the Trojan king,
And kin to Sir Priamus, a prince praised the world over.
From Troy the Britons brought all his brave ancestors
To Britain the Greater, as the Brut records.

   [1]Here lies Arthur, king once and king to be
   Here ends Morte Arthure written by Robert of Thornton   4348
   May the said R. Thornton, who wrote this, be blessed. Amen

1. 4347–9 These three lines are not by the poet. The first, in Latin,
which is the inscription on Arthur's tomb, is in a hand different from
the scribe's. Then there is Thornton's line, in English. The last line,
again in Latin, was written by a late-fifteenth-century reader.

LE MORTE ARTHUR

The Manuscript, and Translator's Sources

The poem survives in a single manuscript, MS Harleian 2252, which is a late-fifteenth-century copy by two scribes of a work which was probably written in about 1350. The first scribe was from the West Midlands and the second from the Northeast Midlands, and it is suggested that both men were transcribing from a manuscript written in the dialect of the Northwest Midlands which has not survived. At line 1181 one leaf of the manuscript is missing; while versifying the relevant narrative material from the source in about sixty lines, I have nevertheless followed Benson in using the line-numbering of Bruce. The editions of the poem that I have used in translating it are those of Bruce, Benson and Hissinger (see Bibliography). I have relied most on Benson.

The Poet's Source

The source is the French prose *Mort Artu*, which is five times as long as the poem. The poet achieves his brilliant and almost naturalistic compression by several means. First of all, anything like a subsidiary episode is either omitted or treated briefly and causally related to his main single story; this means that the medieval narrative technique which Vinaver identified as 'inter-lace', the weaving together of stories and themes by starting them, leaving them for a while, and then returning to them to make a sophisticated integration, is hardly used. When the poet starts what seems to be a new section by telling his listeners that he is leaving court, or leaving Lancelot, his new episode is rapidly integrated, and the experience of having the scene shifted is no more to the modern reader than that of suspense when reading a novel.

Then, the chivalric debate, which in the French is conducted in detail at almost every point of the action, and most often in a spirit of detachment, is shortened and brought as irresistible motivation into decisive speech or action. And lastly, much of the mystery and magic, though a little of it may be detected as almost sub-textual, is excised. The result is a powerful expression of an immortal story for a popular audience.

The Metre

The poem is written in eight-line stanzas which run together without division on the manuscript. They consist of four-stress lines, in which the strict syllabic rules of the octosyllabic line which was standard in French romance are taken lightly, in deference to the natural stress characteristics of the English language. Another kind of four-stress line had been standard in early English alliterative poetry, and in that, the strict counting of syllables had no part. Popular poets of both England and Scotland during the great period of medieval ballad and drama took this syllabic freedom into their style of composition, while those literary poets who followed the new French rules slavishly, such as Chaucer's contemporary Gower, fell into monotony. Byron was right to note 'the fatal facility of the octosyllabic metre', which works better for short poems and satire than for sustained narrative.

But the poet of *Le Morte Arthur* shouldered a heavy burden in opting to have only two rhyme sounds in each stanza, the rhyme pattern being *abababab*. This led him into several resorts, not all of which commended themselves to me as translator. One resort is reliance on sets of stock rhymes. Such combinations as the following are repeatedly used: lay, play, say, away, day, may, alway; lake (Sir Lancelot du Lake), take, sake, wake, make. And readers of the original surely tire of meeting the filler word 'bydene' (vaguely meaning 'in one body', or 'continuously', or 'as well'), which the poet requires to complete his rhyming set with any three of queen, mene, wene, seen, beene. Two other resorts are assonance, which is the rhyming of vowel sound only, and deliberate imperfect rhyming, in which the vowels or consonants involved do not quite match. Since the poem was written, the English language has become further restricted in its potential for rhyme, owing to changes in pronunciation, accentuation and inflection.

My resort in the face of all this has been to translate the poem into eight-line stanzas of double ballad form which have four- and three-stress lines alternating, with a minimum rhyme scheme of *xaxaxbxb*. The main effects of this decision are three: by reducing the incidence of rhyme, I gain some freedom of vocabulary; I also gain elbow room to keep a more natural word order, so that when I invert the order of words, I can often do it deliberately for rhetorical effect, and not because I am forced into it by the exigencies of rhyme scheme or dominant rhythm; and the saving of four whole poetic feet in each eight-line stanza gives me opportunities for compression and force because I have less need of line-fillers and rhyme-makers than the original poet. The formulaic phrases, stock epithets and conventional exaggerations of the original, which contribute greatly to its strength, present few problems in the finding of modern equivalents.

The poet is quite masterly in his use of the old English poetic adornment of alliteration; its unobtrusive insistence, in that it is used in 42 per cent of the lines, gives a formal driving force to the narrative, whether its effect is to intensify a dramatic moment, or to emphasize a spoken plea, or to make music in a beautiful description. I probably exceed that 42 per cent in my translation.

The Story

Lines 1–833. After the conclusion of the Grail Quest, Queen Guinevere suggests that King Arthur holds a tournament at Winchester, which Lancelot attends in disguise. In it he distinguishes himself but is wounded, and takes refuge with the Earl of

Ascolot, whose daughter nurses him and falls in love with him. When he recovers, he leaves his armour with her, and when knights from Camelot, searching for him, recognize the armour, Gawain reports to Guinevere that Lancelot is in love with the Maid of Ascolot. When Lancelot returns to court, Guinevere in jealousy sends him away, and a second search for him fails.

Lines 834–1671. At a feast Guinevere inadvertently kills a knight with a poisoned apple, and his brother, Sir Mador, demands justice. Guinevere is sentenced to death, and is given forty days to find a defender. Meanwhile, the Maid of Ascolot dies of her unrequited love for Lancelot, and her funeral boat floats into Camelot, bearing a letter in which she reviles Lancelot for refusing her love. Guinevere understands from it that Lancelot remains faithful to her. Several knights refuse to defend her in her coming trial, and she laments that, having sent him away, she cannot now call on Lancelot. News reaches Lancelot of Guinevere's predicament, and he arrives in court in time to defeat Mador and prove the Queen innocent. The real poisoner is discovered and tortured to death.

Lines 1672–2459. Agravain, one of Gawain's brothers, tells King Arthur that Guinevere and Sir Lancelot are lovers, and a plot is laid to catch them in the act. Lancelot is caught in Guinevere's bedroom, but kills all the ambush party except Mordred, who escapes to inform King Arthur. Lancelot leaves court with his hundred knights and Guinevere is sentenced to be burnt to death. Lancelot interrupts the burning at the last moment, and in the slaughter Gawain's two remaining brothers are killed by Lancelot's men. Lancelot takes the Queen to his castle Joyous Gard, and Gawain and the King swear vengeance. They besiege Lancelot, who sues for peace but is eventually forced to fight. A Papal nuncio requires Lancelot to return Guinevere to Arthur, and Arthur and Gawain to make peace with Lancelot. Lancelot agrees, and takes Guinevere back to court in a peace procession. The King would agree to a truce, but falls in with Gawain's insistence on continuing his feud with Lancelot. Lancelot leaves England for his French dominion of Benwick.

Lines 2460–2945. Arthur leaves Mordred in charge as regent, and he and Gawain, with the main force of the Round Table, besiege Lancelot in Benwick. Lancelot again makes peace overtures, but at length is forced to fight several battles as well as two single combats against Sir Gawain, which he wins. On both occasions Gawain receives serious wounds, but Lancelot spares his life.

Lines 2946–3969. News reaches Arthur that Mordred has usurped the kingdom. Arthur and Gawain lead their forces back to England, and in the disembarkation fight at Dover, Gawain dies from a tap on the old head-wound inflicted on him by Lancelot. Arthur wins the Battle of Barlam Down, and Mordred retreats to Salisbury Plain. A peace conference between them is broken when a knight draws his sword to kill an adder, and the last battle begins. Arthur kills Mordred, but receives his death-wound in the process. The dying Arthur is tended by Bedivere and Lucan. Bedivere returns the sword Excalibur to the lake, and Arthur is taken by ship to the Isle of Avalon. Bedivere finds Arthur's tomb at Glastonbury. Guinevere takes the veil at Amesbury, and Lancelot returns to England to search for her. They meet; she repents their joint guilt for the death of Arthur and the destruction of the Round Table, and refuses to give him a farewell kiss. Lancelot becomes a monk and serves at Arthur's tomb at Glastonbury while his searching brother and knights slowly gather together with him. He dies and goes to heaven. Guinevere dies and is entombed with Arthur.

The Poem

That summary of the story, and the previous discussion of the kind of romance that *Le Morte Arthur* is, give an initial idea of the poem, in which each of the limitations the poet worked by contributes to the force, movement and characterization. For example, his minor use of 'interlace' may be seen in the way that he makes the stories of the Poisoned Apple and the Maid of Ascolot, which are formally separate in Malory, into closely related parts of his main love story. And his treatment of the niceties of 'fine amour' usually appears as strongly motivated action and especially speech. Then, the virtual absence of magic is remarkable. Here there is no giant, no enchanted castle or other supernatural machinery, no equivocal Morgan la Fay who schemes against the Round Table but at the last receives the dying Arthur. The forces at work are human desires for glory, power or love, operating within a community in which group and personal loyalty is conceived as the highest single value, and in which the true values of religion, though given the usual lip-service, take over only when worldly values have brought disaster. That seems to me all very modern.

Continuous chivalric demonstration of knightly prowess in tournament or single combat, which some romancers including Malory use as their main narrative procedure, is much reduced. It is true that the poem's first series of events is centred on a royal tournament, but thereafter the single combats are entered and concluded as events in deadly feuds or trials, the motives for which have little to do with idealistic aspects of chivalry. In this poem, knights do not ride out in search of adventure, and when they are away from their bases, it is on the business of the single plot.

Accordingly the vast forest of Romance with its magical potency, in which knights-errant look for adventure, here exists for utilitarian purposes only. Lancelot takes refuge there when dismissed by Guinevere, and again after being discovered in her bedroom. But certain formal elements from Romance remain, some of them being residual products of anthropology of the kind which thickly bolster the myth of early times. Gawain's increased power of combat as the sun ascends to its zenith is retained; and twice ambassadors on difficult missions have to be virgins, one of them compulsorily attended by a dwarf. But the ladies who bring Arthur's body to be buried – Morgan not being mentioned by name – are conventionally presented, and pay in the usual way for prayers to be said for the dead king.

There may be some loss in this new and no doubt popular approach to romance material and conventions. In *The Rise of Romance* Vinaver notes, concerning both the poems in this volume, that their detachment from the Vulgate Cycle as a whole takes some meaning from their tragic endings. In the Cycle, the conclusion of the Grail Quest, which is mentioned but not discussed in the second stanza of this poem, removed divine protection from the Round Table, and that set in train the events which led to the final disaster. The first of these events, which is not mentioned here, was that Lancelot's adulterous affair with Guinevere, which had been suspended owing to religious scruple during the Quest, was resumed when the Grail no longer manifested itself. So the love between the King's favourite knight and his queen is here simply a popular *datum* which every listener knew about, and its consequences are worked out in terms of the conflict of human character without any divine planning or allegorical significance. One may agree with Vinaver about the profundity and grand harmony of the Cycle without denigrating the different quality and effect of this poem. It is a popular and graphically poetic reworking of a traditional story in its realistic essence. I do not use the word 'popular' in a pejorative sense; that would be to stigmatize the immortal elements in a great story which appeals to people of all kinds.

So we are left, in my view, with the best of the traditional lures of the medieval ballad, which are exercised on the unprecedented scale of almost four thousand lines. Archetypal characters of the kind traditionally moulded by the literary form engage in conflict among irreconcilable values: the perfect knight cannot be the perfect lover if his love-object is the queen of his royal master; kinship and blood-brotherhood among knights must give way to the law of the feud when brotherly blood is spilled within a fellowship such as the Round Table. What Vinaver describes as 'the most exalted mode of feeling and living ever devised' (*op. cit.*, p. 102) moves in pursuit of its objectives into subterfuge, covert ambush, the killing of kin, general slaughter and the destruction of the entire community. But of course all the main actors in the tragedy, with the exception of Mordred, make eventual peace with God and go to heaven. And the relentless verse, rhythmical, rhyming, alliterative and commonplace in diction, with its conventional adornments and violent though predictable expressions of emotion in speech and action, carries everything forward on its surge.

Archetypal characters in such a formal literary structure as this nevertheless have sharp individuality. They are archetypal because in what they do and say, they express the kinds of emotion, and press the kinds of action and solutions which, given the circumstances in which they are presented, the common mind understands and approves as in some sense inevitable.

Foremost among these individualities is that of the hero of the poem, Lancelot, from whose dual role as perfect knight and perfect lover the conflict arises. His capacity to exercise his limitless belief in the two ideals is narrowly bound by circumstance, like the foot of a classical Chinese beauty, which is shortened to deformity in the cause of making her desirable as a lover. A singular example of this fundamental paradox occurs at line 2190: when Sir Bors, one of Lancelot's best knights, has unhorsed the King in the battle outside the walls of Lancelot's castle, Joyous Gard, Lancelot and Arthur share an experience which expresses both the quintessence and the paradox of their chivalric relationship:

> 'Alas,' said Lancelot, 'What woe
> That ever I should see
> Unhorsed before my very eyes
> The King who knighted me!'
> And then, dismounting from his steed
> – So generous was he! –
> He horsed the King on it, telling him
> Out of harm's way to flee.
>
> The King, when mounted in the saddle,
> On Lancelot fixed his gaze,
> And knew there was never another knight
> Who had such courteous ways.

He thought how things had used to be,
    And tears from his eyes ran;
Sighing and groaning, he cried, 'Alas
    That ever this war began!'

                 (ll. 2190–205)

The treasonous adulterer, in spite of all, honours the cuckold for the very existence of his own chivalric persona and ideals; the royal cuckold, in spite of all, rises above his rôle of avenging king in battle to salute the chivalrous magnanimity of his sexual betrayer.

Lancelot's rôle of covert lover of the Queen necessarily involves him in subterfuge. He uses the forest as a place of concealment when his courtesy requires him to be absent from the scene, and as a refuge when he becomes, like that folk character, the wild man of the woods or *wodwose*, an outcast from society. This links him with Tristan, that other sylvan adulterer and redoubtable warrior. Twice he fights in disguise, on one of those occasions speaking with a foreign accent (l. 1564), and his concealment and rapid adjustment of his own position in the cause of preserving his courtesy are remarkable. Right at the beginning of the poem, when the court has left for the tournament at Winchester and he stays behind in order to make secret love to Guinevere, he adjusts his professed intention the moment that Guinevere warns him that Agravain is spying on them. He has come, he says, simply to take his leave of her before going to Winchester. Not dissimilarly, though unable to return the love of the Maid of Ascolot, he consoles her by leaving his armour with her; an act of courteous consideration which Guinevere and Gawain misinterpret as one of committed love. Guinevere's response, as she grievingly dismisses him, perfectly expresses the chivalric code:

'Alas, Sir Lancelot du Lake,
    Who have my heart in hold,
That you have taken the Earl's daughter
    Of Ascolot, as I'm told!
Now for her sake you cease to be
    A warrior daring-bold,
And I must wake and weep in woe
    Till clay shall clasp me cold.

'But Lancelot, I beg you now,
    Since it must needs be so,
Never to tell a single soul
    Of the love we used to know,
And never to let your love for her
    Enfeeble your knightly fame,
For though my fate is woe, I wish
    To hear you win acclaim.'

                                        (ll. 744–59)

Oddly enough, when one reflects on the whole course of events
in the poem, it appears probable that, after the return of Guinevere to court at the Pope's command, peace between Arthur and
Lancelot would have been restored with honour to all three, but
for Gawain's determination to avenge his brothers. If that is right,
this secondary cause of the tragic end of the Round Table is more
important than the primary one, the famous adultery. It suggests
that in this culture, as all over Europe in all ages, honour between
man and man takes precedence over honour between man and
woman. The latter can be patched up so that men's business can be
got on with.

The steadily increasing horror of the enmity between Gawain
and Lancelot, which dominates the middle of the poem, estab-
lishes the final tragic blackness, the sense of doom which pervades
the last thousand lines. It is lightened only by late shafts of light
from heaven, which figure first in Arthur's dream of the dead
Gawain who, surrounded by 'angelic folk' (l. 3199), advises him
on the conduct of the final battle against Mordred. Yet Gawain,
though he is inflexible in his feud, has been dragged forcibly into
the conflict against his better judgement and prophetic sense,
which are flexibly realistic at the initial point of crisis. It is the plan
of his brother Agravain to expose the adultery which sets Gawain
and the whole of the Round Table on an ineluctably fatal course,
and Gawain advises against it and refuses to join it:

'. . . You well know, brother Agravain,
    That harm is what we'd win;
So better to hide the thing than make
    Chaos and war begin.

'Lancelot's brave, the best of us,
   You well know, Agravain,
And but for him the King and court
   Would often have been slain.
And so I could never tell the love
   That lies between those two.
I shall never betray Sir Lancelot
   Behind his back, with you.'

(ll. 1692–703)

Gawain's insistence on his feud, which takes Arthur away from his seat of power and opens the way for Mordred's treason, falls exactly within his obligations as a knight. The rightness of his position cannot be faulted, but his attitude to the exposure of the adultery, quoted above, could be. It smacks more of political realism than chivalric ideal, though the latter is included in Gawain's reference to Lancelot's service to the King. Elsewhere, Gawain expresses a rigid personal idealism. His traditional courtesy to women makes him refuse to obey the command of Arthur that he attend the burning of Guinevere, but at the end he reaches from beyond the grave in loyalty to his king. In the highly sympathetic Gawain of this poem, the paradoxes inherent in the system often show.

The same is true of Arthur who, until the battles against Mordred, presents the shadowy persona of some French romances rather than the fierce sunlit warrior-figure of earlier literature. In his faith with the highest kind of chivalry, in which his sense of what might and ought to be tends to dominate his knowledge of what is, he seems to suffer a diminution of grandeur in which irresolution and complaisance play a part; but in government and justice he fulfils his function as king, and his defence of the Round Table in the face of fortune and circumstance turns him at the last into the kind of reckless chivalric hero who will ignore good tactical advice and actually court defeat and death – which is to put the matter in realistic terms.

The last of the four chief male characters, Mordred, is portrayed briefly as in the source, the *Mort Artu*; as a 'stirrer of trouble and pain' (l. 1675), and as a coward whose cowardice enables him to be the sole survivor of Lancelot's slaughterous irruption from the Queen's bedroom (l. 1863). The poet also follows the French in making Mordred the incestuous offspring of Arthur, so that the destruction of the Round Table may be seen as Arthur's punishment for incest, while Mordred's killing of the King may then be condemned as parricide. But in the final two battles Mordred is as brave as anyone, and there is a memorable image of him as politician when, between the two battles, there is a truce talk in which he considers Arthur's offer:

> Mordred stood still, his eyes searching;
>   Angrily up they went.
> He said, 'I would it were his will
>   To give me Cornwall and Kent!'
>
> (ll. 3264–7)

His villainy is always stressed. He gains power by spreading the lie that Arthur is dead; he wants to commit incest in his turn by marrying his father's wife, in which intention Guinevere frustrates him; and he dispossesses the Archbishop of Canterbury and threatens him with death for condemning his immorality.

To turn from the four men to the one woman among the principals is to confront the full complexity of 'fine amour' and the mysterious power of the story. Guinevere's attachment to her royal spouse is one of exemplary loyalty on every public occasion. From the opening lines of the poem, she guards and promotes the chivalric spirit of the Round Table, and rewards the achievements of its knights. She defines chivalrous conduct and insists on it in all knights, in Lancelot above all. Unlike the Maid of Ascolot, who lies to Gawain that Lancelot loves her, she is true to the chivalric system in everything she says and does, except in the crucial matter of the adultery.

In that, the formal requirement of the genre provides the justification, which is primarily artistic; the moral aspect, though not exactly in abeyance, has to take second place. The justification is this: the perfect lover must achieve his perfect love-object, and the hierarchical system requires that the woman must be of the highest possible rank, that of queen. In that rôle, as the mistress achieved by the lover, when Lancelot's success becomes known,

Guinevere achieves a dynamic subversion of the men's world despite her traditional passivity in it as a woman. A similar argument, though Lancelot is an operator of the system rather than an object within it, applies to the other basic factor, which is the knight-lover's ideal service to the chivalric master; Lancelot too is bound to subvert the system.

The irrationality of all this is exposed on the death of Arthur, when Guinevere becomes technically free to marry her lover but instead, as dictator of truly chivalric behaviour turned Christian penitent, she sends him away for ever after taking the veil. As once before, she urges him to marry someone else and continue his career of ideal chivalry. But the obligatory obedience of the lover to the lady is bound to be suspended if she commands him to end his fidelity to her, and so he, everlastingly faithful, emulates her tragic renunciation though not, at least in this poem I think, her heart's true penitence. If that is right, the act of renouncing love and accepting responsibility for the death of Arthur and the destruction of the Round Table is hers alone. Both she and Lancelot thus recognize consequence, but for different reasons, and each gains tragic status in accepting the loveless short future which will end in death.

In the Introduction to this volume, I suggest that the conclusion of the poem, like that of the alliterative *Morte Arthure*, is superior to Malory's, great though the latter is. This judgement is made not on the basis of meaning, which in Malory is more extensive as well as being copiously annotated and historically rounded off, but because successful expression and compression of material in poetry have a stronger effect than prose can achieve. The image of the poem is more intensely defined than that of the prose work, for all the latter's long rhythms, comprehensiveness of meaning and exalted sensibility.

The poem's sustained intensity, close succession of incident and dramatic mode of story-telling render it peculiarly suitable for oral performance, a characteristic which I have tried to preserve in the translation; diverse audiences have re-sponded enthusiastically to performance reading of both poems in this volume. That consideration is part of the reason for including the stanzaic *Le Morte Arthur*, the original of which, unlike that of *Morte Arthure*, scarcely needs translation. The further reason is to bring the poem out of the comparative obscurity of specialist reading, and to promote it independently of Malory studies, as a fine poem in its own right.

LE MORTE ARTHUR

Lords and ladies dearly loved,
   Listen while I tell
About our ancestors of old
   And what to them befell!
Many great events took place
   When Arthur was lord of all;
Much joy and woe his subjects knew,
   And I shall tell their fall.   8

When knights of the Round Table went
   In quest for the Holy Grail,[1]
Every adventure offered them
   They finished without fail.
Their enemies they beat and bound;
   No sparing life for gold![2]
Four years they lived and prospered then;
   Done were their exploits bold.   16

1. 10 The Holy Grail was the dish in which Joseph of Arimathea, who brought it to England, caught Christ's blood after the Deposition. It had powers to feed the starving and heal the wounded and sick, and stimulated virtue in the Arthurian fellowship when it was manifest. It was only manifest in the presence of pure people like Lancelot's son Galahad, who achieved it. The story is in Chrétien de Troyes's romance *Conte del Graal*, which Malory adapted in his *Le Morte Darthur* as *The Tale of the Sankgreal*. Galahad, who dies soon after his achievement, nevertheless survives in this poem.

2. 14 i.e. no giving of quarter.

It happened once about that time
   In bed lay King and Queen
Recalling many great events
   Their court and land had seen.
'Sire, give me leave,' said Guinevere,
   'To speak, and something strange
I'll tell you of your bravest knights:
   They leave in search of change.   24

'Your honour, Sire, which once was famed
   And through the wide world spread
By deeds of Lancelot and his like,
   Fails because not fed.'
'Then counsel me a cure for that,'
   Said Arthur, 'What's to do?'
'A tournament,' said Guinevere,
   'Will win renown for you.   32

'Announcing that event will set
   Men talking everywhere,
And knights by deeds of arms will seek
   Glory in jousting there.
Sire, your court must never cease
   To live for honour and fame.'
Arthur answered, 'Agreed! At once
   Advance the warlike game!'   40

The King announced the tournament
   At Winchester to be.
Young Galahad was great in deed:
   Head of the throng was he
Of all the nobly mounted knights
   For women and girls to see
Contending to be first in fight
   And vaunt the victory.   48

Then knights at once took warlike arms
    To the tournament to ride
With bucklers broad and helmets bright
    To win renown in pride.
But Lancelot stayed with Guinevere;
    Sick at the time he seemed.
The love between them was so great
    That that excuse he schemed.   56

The King went forth upon his mount
    To the tournament away.
Sir Agravain[1] with fixed intent
    Stayed home, most true to say,
Because all said that Lancelot
    With Arthur's high queen lay.
To catch them naked in the act
    He waited night and day.   64

To the Queen's chamber Lancelot
    Went in love and duty,
And knelt in noble style to greet
    That lady bright in beauty.
'The King's away, the court as well;
    Why meddle with me here?
The love that lies between us two
    Will be found out, I fear.   72

---

1. 59 Agravain is brother to Gawain.

'Sir Agravain has stayed to spy
    Upon us night and day.'
'If so, my honoured one,' said he,
    'He shall not have his way,
Because I come to take my leave
    Before I go from court.'
'Your dallying here offends me much;
    Go arm you as you ought!'   80

Lancelot went to his chamber where
    His splendid gear was laid,
And dressed himself in noble clothes
    And armour finely made.
He took his sword and shield, both tried
    And proved in many a war,
And leapt upon his grey, the gift
    Of Arthur long before.   88

That strong and noble knight rode off
    Following no known way,
And hurried on to the high city
    Not resting night or day;
To Winchester, for there it was
    The tournament should be,
With Arthur and his court in hall
    In high festivity.   96

Since all men looked for Lancelot
    And he wished not to be known,
He hunched his shoulders awkwardly
    And hung his head low down
As if he could not use his arms.
    No herald his call to blow
Had he, and very old he seemed;
    That knight, no man could know.   104

The King on tower-top called aloud
   To Ewain[1] at that sight:
'Sir Ewain, who's that riding there?
   Does any know that knight?'
Sir Ewain answered strict and straight
   (What's courtly, do not hide!):
'Some ancient knight, sir, come to see
   The young men joust and ride.'   112

They both stared on at him a while
   For the fine steed's sake,
Which stumbling then upon a stone
   Made Lancelot's body shake;
And by the way his brawn and bones
   Moved masterly to take
The bridle up, they both could see
   It was Lancelot du Lake.   120

King Arthur then to Ewain spoke
   These seemly words aright:
'Sir Lancelot is justly called
   The world's worthiest knight
For beauty and generosity;
   And since none has such might
In any deed, and since today
   He wants to hide his light,   128

1. 106 Ewain: hero of the Welsh *Owein* and Chrétien de Troyes's *Yvain*
(*Le Chevalier au Lion*). A minor figure in this poem. Unhorsed by
Lancelot at l. 270.

'Sir Ewain, we shall make him wait;
  He thinks we know him not.'
'Sir, better it is to let him ride
  And do what's in his thought.
Since he has come his course so far
  He'll stay close by the sport.
We'll know him by his noble deeds
  And by the horse he brought.'   136

The Lord of Ascolot[1] lived near,
  An earl of grace and might;
Lancelot to his castle rode
  And begged to stay the night.
With pomp and pride they hosted him
  And made a sumptuous meal:
He said he was a foreign knight
  Whose name he must conceal.   144

That earl possessed two noble sons
  Just knighted in the field.
The custom was, for the first year
  Of a knight's showing his shield,
It should be worn with no device,
  And be of one sole hue:
Yellow or blue or red or white –
  Thus men his status knew.   152

1. 137 Ascolot: in Malory and Tennyson, Astolat.

Said Lancelot to the Earl then
   As to their meat they went,
'Is there a young knight here, sir,
   Would try the tournament?'
'Two sons I have most dear to me,
   But one is sick, I declare;
If someone were to companion the other,
   I would that he were there.'   160

'Sir, if your son goes keenly forth,
   I'll partner him with a will,
And help him on with all my power;
   So none shall do him ill.'
Said the Earl, 'You seem a courteous knight
   With grace and noble pride,
So feast tomorrow and then prepare:
   Together you shall ride.'   168

Said Lancelot, 'One thing I crave
   If I am to succeed;
Arms and armour I require
   To borrow for this deed.'
'Sir, take the horse and battle gear
   Of my son who's sick in bed,
And so that my men shall know you both,
   You shall be clothed in red.'   176

A darling daughter had the Earl,
   Who gazed at Lancelot;
Like a wild rose or meadow flower
   She seemed, as like as not.
And it was bliss to her to be
   Beside that noble knight;
So fast her heart was fixed on him
   Her tears betrayed her quite.   184

At that the tender maiden rose
    And to her room she went,
Where falling down upon her bed,
    She felt her heart was rent.
Lancelot discerned her desire
    By every sign he saw:
He called her brother, and the two
    Entered her chamber door.   192

Upon the bed where the maiden lay
    He sat in courteous duty,
And for her sake he kindly spoke
    To comfort that sad beauty.
She twined her arms about him then
    And said to the knightly man,
'My lord, unless you save my life,
    There's no physician can.'   200

'Lady', he said, 'No more of this!
    Do not for me fall ill.
My heart is in another place
    And beats to another's will.
But nothing on earth stops me being
    Your knight through storm and still;
If we chance to meet again, it may
    Be fitter to speak your fill.'   208

'Since I cannot win more of you,
    Knight most noble and free,
I beg you, bear in the tournament
    An open favour from me.'
'Cut off your sleeve, which for your love
    I'll wear in chivalry.
I never did this before for any
    Bar one that most loved me.'   216

So Lancelot and the son next day
  Broke fast at morning-tide,
Prepared for jousting and set off
  Like brothers, side by side.
And soon they met a squire who spurred
  From the tournament away
And asked him which contending force
  Showed stronger in the fray.   224

'Sir Galahad has most knights, my lords,
  In his command to hold,
But Arthur's troop's more powerful,
  His knights are fierce and bold.
Like strong and savage boars are they,
  Lionel, Ewain and Bors.'
The Earl's son said to Lancelot,
  'With them we should join cause.'   232

But Lancelot thought otherwise:
  'Since they're such men of might,
How shall we then outshine a host
  So fierce and fell in fight?
We'll take the side that needs our help
  And fight against the best,
And if we do great deeds – well then,
  More honour to our quest!'   240

Thus Lancelot, brave and noble, spoke.
  'Tonight we'll lodge,' said he,
'Outside the city of Winchester
  Where crowds of knights must be.'
The Earl's son said, 'My aunt lives near,
  A lady of noble beauty;
If you will ride there she'll delight
  To pay us a hostess' duty.'   248

They quickly came to the castle high
   Of the lady fair and bright.
She gladly greeted them, in joy
   To have them stay that night.
At speed the supper was served in style;
   That night they dined in delight,
And again next day, then rode away,
   Lancelot and the knight.   256

At the tournament when they arrived,
   Great was the knightly play.
They watched a while how Arthur's troop
   Performed that festive day.
Galahad's troop was in retreat,
   His knights on foot away,
So sturdy Lancelot thought how he
   Could help without delay.   264

First at him like a savage boar
   Sir Ewain fiercely rode,
But Lancelot fought grimly back
   With weapons red as blood.
He struck Sir Ewain a blow which knocked
   That knight from saddle to ground,
And all men thought that he was dead,
   So grievous was his wound.   272

Seeing Sir Ewain unhorsed like that,
   Surcharged with grief, Sir Bors
At Lancelot leapt – I tell no lie –
   With a madman's mighty force.
But Lancelot hit him on the helm
   And swiftly laid him low;
And none being fit to fight with him,
   He thus thinned out the foe.   280

Sir Lionel[1] grieved and quickly got
  For battle grim arrayed:
With visor down at Lancelot
  He spurred with shining blade.
But Lancelot cut right through his helmet
  Deep into his crown;
And straight away all there could see
  Both man and horse were down.   288

The knights all gathered together then
  Some wise advice to take,
For there was never a knight like that
  But Lancelot du Lake;
And him they did not recognize,
  The sleeve being on his crest,
For favour like that he never bore
  Except at the Queen's behest.   296

'In Ascolot,' Sir Ector[2] said,
  'There never was a knight
Who did as this man's done today:
  I'll find him out in the fight.'
He picked himself a splendid steed
  And, glad to join the fray,
Met Lancelot amid the throng –
  For them, no children's play!   304

---

1. 281 Lionel: one of the three knights Lancelot loved best (see l. 449), the other two being Ector and Bors.

2. 297 Ector: Lancelot's brother.

Sir Ector struck at Lancelot
   In a furious forward ride;
Through helm he cut and gored his brow
   And almost quelled his pride.
Lancelot hit him on the hood
   And horse and man down reeled.
Then Lancelot, blind with streams of blood,
   Galloped fast from the field.   312

To a nearby forest high and hoar
   Galloped the two bold men,
And Lancelot, once they were alone,
   Took off his helmet then.
'I grieve to see you,' the Earl's son said,
   'By such great hurt oppressed.'
'Not so,' said Lancelot, 'but I wish
   We were where I could rest.'   320

'Sir, my aunt lives close at hand
   Where we two lay last night.
If you incline to take horse there
   She'll help with all her might;
She'll send for doctors straight away
   To heal your wounds aright,
And I myself shall stay with you,
   Your servant and your knight.'   328

They gently rode to the castle of
   The courteous countess fair,
Who sent for doctors far and near
   To heal his wounds, I swear.
But yet by dawn he was so ill
   He could not move in bed,
But lay in agony as one
   Soon to be counted dead.   336

King Arthur then with mighty pomp
   Had all his knights to him brought,
And said he'd stay in Winchester
   A month more with his court.
He sent out heralds to proclaim
   Another tournament.
'That knight,' he said, 'must be nearby:
   His wounds are of grave extent.'   344

The scrolls being written as was right,
   Forth with them heralds went
Throughout all England to announce
   Another tournament.
The message urged quick readiness
   On all who were strong on steeds,
And out it went to every knight
   Renowned for noble deeds.   352

And thus it chanced a herald came,
   As he traversed the way,
To lodge the night at the castle where
   The wounded Lancelot lay,
And said there'd be a tournament
   The following Sabbath day.
'Alas!' said Lancelot, and sighed
   In miserable dismay.   360

'Where knights are honoured and admired
   Ill chance keeps me away
And skulking like a craven thing.
   This tournament, I say,
Has been announced this very time
   For me to take part, I swear;
And though I die this very day,
   I'll ride and tourney there.'   367

At once the doctor said to him,
   'Sir, what do you intend?
All the healing art I've used
   Will serve to no good end!
By God who made all heaven and earth,
   There's not a living man
Could save your life if you took horse
   And a tournament began!'   375

'Although it bring my death today,
   In bed I shall not lie!
I swear I'd rather fight my best
   Than like a coward die!'
The leech at once got up and left;
   And Lancelot's every wound
Broke open as he lay in bed:
   Three times that noble swooned.   383

Half crazed with grief, the lady groaned,
   Certain he'd soon be dead;
The earl's son, sick with sorrow too,
   Called back the leech and said,
'I'll make you rich if you will stay
   With me and use your skill!'
He staunched the blood of Lancelot
   And bade him fear no ill.   391

The herald then went on his way
   As soon as it was light,
And swiftly spurred to Winchester,
   Arriving that same night.
King Arthur, and Sir Ewain beside,
   He there saluted both,
And what he'd heard and seen on quest
   He told them by his troth: 399

'Of all that ever struck my sight,
    Nothing amazed me more
Than the spectacle of a stupid knight
    Bedfast with gashes sore,
So weak he could not raise his head
    To win the world if he would –
Yet woe because he could not joust
    Made all his wounds spurt blood!'   407

Sir Ewain nobly spoke to the King
    These words: 'No coward knight
Is he! Alas that he is sick
    And lacks his lordly might!
He must be the man whose prowess unhorsed
    Us all at Winchester.
So best abandon the tournament:
    Then need he not be there!'   415

The tournament being abandoned thus,
    The throng all pressed away;
The knights their farewells made and went
    Each one his chosen way.
The King rode back to Camelot
    To Guinevere the Queen,
And thought Sir Lancelot would be there,
    But he was nowhere seen.   423

For Lancelot was laid up with wounds:
    Knights sought him far and wide,
While the Earl's son both night and day
    Watched ever at his side.
When he could sit a horse, the Earl
    Squired him with pomp and pride,
And made him mighty pleasure till he
    Could well both walk and ride.   431

Sir Bors and Lionel took their leave
   Of the King at Camelot,
And swore they'd not return to court
   Till they found Lancelot.
Sir Ector also went with them
   To seek his brother dear,
And many a land they travelled through,
   Searching far and near.   439

Until at last it happened that
   They went a certain way
And stayed to dine at the castle where
   The wounded Lancelot lay.
They suddenly saw him walking out
   Upon the castle wall,
Which filled them with such joy that on
   Their knees fell one and all.   447

When Lancelot saw the three men he
   In all the world loved best,
It was the merriest meeting ever! –
   He led them in to rest.
The Earl of Ascolot rejoiced
   At having such a guest,
The pretty maiden too whose love
   For him was manifest.   455

The boards were set on trestles then
   For supper and spread with white,
And the Earl placed his daughter beside
   Sir Lancelot, noble knight;
And both his stalwart sons were there
   To serve them with delight:
To give them joy, the Earl himself
   Served them with all his might.   463

But Bors turned over and over in mind
    The wound of Lancelot:
'Sir, if you'd hide it not, say where
    Such a savage stroke you got.'
'By the Creator of all this world,'
    Sir Lancelot then swore,
'That blow shall bitterly be avenged
    If ever I meet him more!' 471

Sir Ector sorrowed at those words;
    To hear them made him quail:
His knightly forces fell from him,
    His face went deathly pale.
Sir Bors then said in forthright style,
    'Why, Ector, such sad cheer?
For truly he's no coward knight
    Who menaces you here.' 479

Said Lancelot, 'So it was you
    Who hacked me with your sword?'
Ector frankly then replied,
    'I did not know you, Lord!
But I was grimly gashed by you;
    Never was I so sore!'
And Lionel too declared his scars
    Would be seen for evermore. 487

Sir Bors then swiftly intervened
    With knightly words profound:
'Not one of us got off scot free;
    I too was struck to the ground.
Sir, grudge your brother not that blow;
    Each knows the other's deed.
Now you can measure Ector's might
    To help you in your need.' 495

Lancelot laughed at Ector's dread
    With all his generous soul.
'Brother, grieve not, for I shall soon
    Again be hale and whole.
Though savagely you struck at me,
    I'll never grudge it you,
But ever love you more because
    You can strike a blow so true.'   503

Upon the third day after that
    The knights were on their way;
They took their leave to ride to court,
    But Lancelot had to stay.
'Greet Arthur well from me and tell
    The Queen I'm as you see;
Tell her I'll come as soon as I can;
    She's not to pine for me.'   511

They said farewell and galloped off
    With noble manly cheer,
Picking a private way to court
    To seek out Guinevere.
The King was hunting with his knights
    In the forest far away,
And so their errand to the Queen
    Unhindered they could say.   519

Before the Queen the knights kneeled down,
    Wise in their clever ways,
And said they'd seen Sir Lancelot
    And stayed with him three days.
They said that he was lying sick
    Of wounds from a contest grim;
'His message is, you'll see him soon:
    You must not pine for him.'   527

Guinevere laughed aloud to hear
 He lived and cried, 'Behold
How gracious God restores my joy!
 My husband must be told.'
The three bold knights to the forest rode
 And King Arthur, when he heard,
Thanked Jesus Christ, for never had he
 Such joy from just one word.   535

He called Sir Gawain to his side
 And said, 'So that was he
Equipped and clothed in red that day!
 He lives: what bliss for me!'
Sir Gawain, great in spirit and grace,
 Then said, 'I never got
Such joyful news! But how I long
 To see Sir Lancelot!'   543

Sir Gawain bade the King and Queen
 Adieu that very day,
And all the folk at court as well,
 Then proudly spurred away.
He rode as fast as he could ride
 Towards far Ascolot,
Sworn not to rest by day or night
 Till he saw Lancelot.   551

By then Sir Lancelot, fully healed,
 Made ready to depart.
The maiden wept at his farewell,
 With sorrow sick at heart.
'Since I may have no more of you,
 I beg you leave behind
Some token I may look upon
 When longing fills my mind.'   559

He comforted with noble words
 That sorrowing maiden fair:
'I'll leave my armour here with you;
 Your brother's I shall wear.
Grieve not for me when I am gone,
 For I may not remain;
Yet one day I shall either come
 Or send you word again.'   567

So Lancelot, ready, rode away
 And soon Sir Gawain came
And asked if they had seen a knight,
 Sir Lancelot by name.
They welcomed him and feasted him
 With pomp and mighty show
And said, 'True hearts may nothing hide:
 He left two weeks ago.'   575

Sir Gawain sat by the lady sweet
 Some pleasant talk to make,
And mentioned Earth's most perfect knight,
 Sir Lancelot du Lake.
She spoke of him, that pretty one,
 'I love him, I declare!
He's taken me for his own lover:
 I have his armour in there.'   583

'I'm glad to hear it's so, lady,'
 Sir Gawain then replied.
'For such a lover as yours there's none
 In all the world beside.
There's not a woman of flesh and bone,
 Perfect in wind and limb,
Who, though her heart were steel or stone,
 Could help adoring him.   591

'But show me the shield of Lancelot,
  Lady, I beg of you,
For if it's his, then be assured
  I'll know it by its hue.'
With lofty courtesy she led
  Gawain to a chamber new
And showed him the shield of Lancelot,
  And all his armour too.   599

Gawain spoke courteously in turn,
  'Your word for truth I take:
This is the shield, let all be sure,
  Of Lancelot du Lake.
And I rejoice that Lancelot
  Has taken you for his love,
And I shall serve you as your knight
  Therefore, by God above!'   607

Thus Gawain vowed to the pretty one,
  His heart in what he said;
And they hosted him in highest pleasure
  Till it was time for bed.
The following day soon after dawn
  He bade farewell to all,
And lastly to the lovely girl,
  Then rode out from the hall.   615

He did not know which way to go
    To seek Sir Lancelot;
The world to search, and not one clue!
    He'd surely find him not.
And so he rode straight back to court;
    The swiftest way went he,
And King and knight there welcomed him,
    Their pattern of courtesy.[1]   623

Soon after it happened that the King
    Stood talking to the Queen
With Gawain beside, and both complained
    How wretched they had been
Waiting woefully for the return
    Of Lancelot du Lake.
None hid their grief in pride at court,
    So sad were they for his sake.   631

'Surely if Lancelot were alive
    He'd quickly come to court!'
But Gawain answered them at once,
    'No wonder, is my thought,[2]
For he has picked the prettiest girl
    On earth his love to be,
And none of us but would delight
    Such a beauty to see.'   639

1. 623 In English romances, Gawain often sets the standard of courtesy.

2. 635 Gawain's behaviour is mysteriously equivocal. Here he insults Guinevere by describing Lancelot's lover as 'the prettiest girl on earth', but later he owns up to his error in thinking Lancelot loved the girl (l. 1128), and tries to prevent the love between Lancelot and Guinevere being exposed (l. 1688).

Great was King Arthur's gladness then
  At hearing Gawain's news.
'But who,' he quickly asked the knight,
  'Is the girl he came to choose?'
Gawain replied, 'The daughter of
  The Earl of Ascolot.
They dined me there, and she showed me
  The shield of Lancelot.'   647

The Queen said not a single word,
  But to her chamber fled,
And there, demented at the news,
  Fell down upon her bed.
'Alas that ever I was born!'
  She cried, 'The loveliest knight
That ever sat a steed in battle
  Is lost to me this night!'   655

Her ladies, knowing her secret well,
  Tried hard to give relief
Lest men should see her sorrowing face
  And guess her cause of grief.
They made her bed afresh and laid
  Her down with tender care,
But still she sobbed, quite lost to sense:
  They pitied her despair.   663

Guinevere lay a long time sick,
  With sorrow overwrought,
Until one day Sir Lionel
  And Ector rode from court.
The forest was sweet with flower and leaf,
  And there they went for sport;
And there, while spurring on their way,
  They met Sir Lancelot.   671

No wonder, when they saw their lord,
  They hailed him with delight,
And kneeling gladly, there and then
  Thanked God with all their might.
What joy it was to see and hear
  Them meet the noble knight!
The first words Lancelot framed were these:
  'How fares my Lady bright?'   679

The knights replied that Guinevere
  Was ill beyond belief:
To see and hear her sorrowing
  It was the greatest grief.
'Because you come to court no more
  The King is sick with dread,
And he, and all men high and low,
  Suppose you must be dead.   687

'Return with us and greet the Queen,
  If it be your will;
One sight of you will gladden her
  And cure her spirit's ill.
The King and all the court besides
  Are sick and sad with care,
Believing you no longer live
  Because you come not there.'   695

At once he granted their request
  That homeward he would ride.
They turned their horses' heads at that
  And spurred in joy and pride,
Fast pressing on to Camelot,
  Not pausing day or night.
The King and court received that news
  With limitless delight.   703

The King on tower-top with Gawain
   Saw Lancelot far away,
And never in the whole wide world
   Were men as glad as they.
Out at the gates all ran to him
   As fast as they could go,
And King and courtiers kissed him, glad
   Such happiness to know.   711

They led him to a lofty room
   Locked in their soft embrace,
And seated him on cloth of gold
   On a bed with utmost grace.
Not one man grudged to serve him there
   Or give what made him glad,
And afterwards he told them all
   The adventures he had had.   719

Three days he stayed, but could not speak
   To Guinevere the Queen;
King Arthur hosted him, and the court
   Were all the time between.
And she, most lovely, longed to see him,
   Lonely in her plight;
She wept and wept, but dared not send
   A message to her knight.   727

And then one day the King set forth
   To hunt with all his knights;
They rode to the forest for the chase,
   The sport and its delights.
But Lancelot planned to see the Queen
   And so lay long in bed,
Then went to meet her in her room,
   And gracious greeting said.   735

First he kissed her courteously,
    That lady full of grace,
And then her maids, whose joy ran down
    In tears on every face.
'Ah, Lancelot,' said the Queen, 'that ever
    I set my eyes on you!
Alas that it is gone for ever,
    The love that once we knew!   743

'Alas, Sir Lancelot du Lake,
    Who have my heart in hold,
That you have taken the Earl's daughter
    Of Ascolot, as I'm told!
Now for her sake you cease to be
    A warrior daring-bold,
And I must wake and weep in woe
    Till clay shall clasp me cold.   751

'But Lancelot, I beg you now,
    Since it must needs be so,
Never to tell a single soul
    Of the love we used to know,
And never to let your love for her
    Enfeeble your knightly fame,
For though my fate is woe, I wish
    To hear you win acclaim.'   759

Lancelot stood transfixed at that,
    His heart a heavy stone;
It seemed to him that all was lost,
    And grieving made him groan,
'My lady, by the body of Christ,
    What means your mighty moan?
For by the blood He shed for me,
    Your news I quite disown.   767

'But from your words it seems to be
    You wish I were away:
And so farewell, my noble love,
    For ever and a day.'
He left the lofty chamber at once –
    How great his cause to grieve!
Three times the lady swooned and strove
    Almost this life to leave.   775

To his quarters then went Lancelot
    His noble gear to find;
He dressed and armed himself, though not
    To knightly sport inclined.
Yet like a live coal leapt he forth,
    Face set and ashen grey,
At once bestrode his saddled horse,
    And rode to the woods away.   783

That Lancelot was on his horse
    Word came into the hall,
And out as if they'd lost their wits
    The knights ran one and all.
Bors de Gawnes and Lionel
    And Ector trusty–true
Mounted swift steeds and blew their horns
    As after him they flew.   791

But none could overtake him there
    As he spurred to a forest green,
And greatly grieved those knights for him,
    Though they were brave and keen.
'Alas!' they cried, 'Lancelot du Lake!
    That ever you saw the Queen!'
They cursed her on account of the love
    That lay that pair between.   799

But none of them knew where they should search,
   Or where he wished to go,
And so that noble troop returned
   To court with sighs of woe.
They found the Queen there, swooning still,
   All lank and loose her hair,
And they were so sad they could not speak
   To ease her pain and despair.   807

The King came quickly back to court
   And arrived that very day
To ask after Lancelot du Lake
   And be told, 'He has gone away.'
In her chamber crying, the Queen in bed
   Naked and sorrowing lay;
The King so grieved that not one knight
   Would exercise or play.   815

King Arthur called Gawain to him
   And spoke his sadness and pain:
'Now Lancelot has left us thus,
   He'll never come back again.'
He cried, 'Alas!' and made himself
   Sick with his sorrowing thought.
'That lord whom we have always loved,
   Why stays he not at court?'   823

Sir Gawain answered Arthur then,
   'Sire, do not grieve or fear,
But stay in your castle here at home
   With comfort and good cheer,
While we on horseback and on foot
   Search all lands far and near
So secretly that somehow we
   Shall something of him hear.'   831

They looked for Lancelot far and wide,
   But nothing did they hear.
Lovely as wild rose blossoming,
   One day Queen Guinevere
Sat at supper with Sir Gawain
   Beside her with, I swear,
A Scottish knight she well esteemed
   On the other side of her.   839

A certain squire at court had planned,
   If he could, that very day,
With a poison that he'd had prepared,
   The good Sir Gawain to slay.
Before the fairest Guinevere
   He had it placed in the fruit:
Yes, topmost on the brim-full bowl
   The poisoned apple he'd put.   847

The squire believed the lovely Queen
   Would give Sir Gawain the best,
But she offered the fruit to the Scottish knight,
   As he was a foreign guest.
No diner dreamed of treason there
   As the Scot that apple bit,
Then lost all vital strength, collapsed
   And quickly died of it.   855

The meaning of it none there knew,
   But Gawain leapt upright,
The others too, and on the board
   They stretched the Scottish knight.
'Alas, alas!' then cried the Queen,
   'Jesu, what can I say?
All will believe that I'm the cause
   This knight has died today.'   863

Guinevere strove to save his life,
   And medicines were brought out,
But nothing they did could help the knight:
   He was dead without a doubt.
Great pity it was to see and hear
   The sorrowing Queen lament:
'O Lord, misfortune follows me!
   Shall I never know content?'   871

The knights could do nothing but bury him
   With grief and anguish keen
Beside a richly-candled chapel
   In a forested ravine.
They had prepared a splendid tomb,
   And a clerk inscribed it clear,
How there was laid the Scottish knight
   Poisoned by Guinevere.   879

Not many days had gone before
   A knight to the high court came,
The brother of the Scottish knight,
   And Mador was his name.
He was a hardy and active man
   In tournament and fight,
And greatly loved to live at court,
   Being a valiant knight.   887

One day the dauntless Mador rode
   To the forest near the court,
Where flowers flourished and branches spread,
   To seek some knightly sport.
He chanced on the chapel in the ravine
   Where his own brother lay dead,
And thereupon made up his mind
   To stay till Mass was said.   895

And soon he found that splendid tomb
   Inscribed with clerkly art.
He stood and slowly read the words,
   And sorrow struck his heart.
He read that the Queen by poison's means
   Had dealt his brother his doom;
His senses left him, and he fell
   Swooning upon the tomb.   903

When he awoke from that dread swoon,
   Lead-heavy his heart grew;
He grieved and sighed for his brother's sake,
   But knew not what to do.
Then quickly he galloped back to court
   And cried aloud to the Queen,
Challenging her for his brother's death,
   No meekness in his mien.   911

Most fearful was the King because
   He could not oppose the law;
The Queen went almost mad although
   No stain of guilt she bore:
She must find a knight to fight for her
   Or else admit the deed.
She knew, if judged by Arthur's knights,
   Her death would be decreed.   919

King Arthur had to uphold the law:
   For the trial he set a date
When either a knight with spear and shield
   Must duel for her fate;
Or she to death her body must yield;
   Or by court of knights be tried.
The Queen and Mador held up their hands
   And swore by this to abide.   927

The day of judgement thus being set,
    The terms of trial made clear,
News swiftly spread through every land
    Of the grief of Guinevere,
And word soon reached the wounded knight,[1]
    Sir Lancelot du Lake:
Men told him the trouble where he lay;
    Of the whole sad case they spake;   935

How Guinevere the gracious Queen
    Had killed a Scottish knight
With poison at the festive board –
    He took but a single bite;
And how a day was set when she
    A brave defender must find
To fight her case, or else be burnt,
    No ransom being assigned.   943

He listened to every word they said,
    Did Lancelot du Lake,
And a mighty sadness surged in him
    For the sorrowing Queen's sake.
If he could live to see that day,
    He would avenge her, he swore.
He fought his grief off then, and grew
    As fierce as a wild boar.   951

---

1. 933 Lancelot's wound came from a hunting accident detailed in the *Mort Artu*, but not mentioned by this poet, unless on the missing page of the manuscript (see note to l. 1198).

Now leave we Lancelot where he was,
   With the hermit in the wood,
And tell of matters touching Arthur,
   The King so brave and good.
He summoned Sir Gawain, and both
   For the Queen made much lament.
To a tower they went, and there discussed
   Best policy in the event. 959

And as they stood in solemn talk,
   With the sparkling river below,
Thinking how best to handle things,
   They saw on the current's flow
A little boat of graceful line
   Towards them floating free:
No finer boat of timber built
   They thought could ever be. 967

When King Arthur saw that sight
   He marvelled much because
The boat was rich with ornament;
   Most wonderful it was.
Its vaulted shape in cloth shone gold
   And glittered on the tide.
'This boat is dressed in splendid style!'
   The gracious Gawain cried. 975

'It's truly so,' the King replied,
   'I never saw such a sight;
Let you and I go down there now,
   For adventure seems to invite.
For if the ornament inside
   Is as rich, or still more fine,
I safely swear some high adventure
   Shall then be yours and mine.' 983

Down from the tower the two then came,
   King Arthur and Sir Gawain,
And swiftly strode towards the boat –
  No others, just the twain.
And when they came to where it stopped,
   They scanned it steady-eyed,
Till Gawain raised the covering cloth,
   And both men stepped inside.   991

Once in, they found it finely decked
   With riches glittering,
And in the midst a bed was set
   Fit for a Christian king.
They quickly lifted the coverlet –
   No pause had they in mind! –
And a dead woman was lying there,
   The fairest man could find.   999

Then said the King to Sir Gawain,
   'Ungallant, graceless Death,
To waft such beauty from the world
   And stop her youthful breath!
So noble she looks, I'd like to know
   Her kinsfolk and her name,
And how she lived, and from what court
   The darling creature came.'   1007

Sir Gawain gazed upon the girl
   Intently, blinking not,
Until he surely saw that she
   Was the Maid of Ascolot,
Whom once he'd wooed to be his love,[1]
   But no good answer got
Because she said she'd never incline
   To any but Lancelot.   1015

And so he said to Arthur, 'Sire,
   Do you recall the day
When you and I were with the Queen
   Passing the time away,
And I spoke of one to whom Lancelot
   His love eternal swore?'
To which the King replied at once,
   'I remember that for sure.'   1023

'This is the sweet one I spoke of then,'
   Said Gawain, 'and no mistake;
Above all men in the world she loved
   Sir Lancelot du Lake.'
'I mourn her death for Lancelot's sake,
   And long,' King Arthur said,
'To learn the cause. I think that grief
   Is the reason she lies dead.'   1031

1. 1012 See ll. 606–7.

Then the good Sir Gawain at once
   Searched all about the girl,
And found a fine embroidered purse
   Banded with gold and pearl.
It seemed, when Gawain held it up,
   That something was inside:
A letter it was, and both men wondered
   What it signified.   1039

Its contents they were keen to know,
   So Gawain gave it the King
And asked him to open it at once,
   And he did, no dallying.
Unfolding the paper, there he found
   The entire tale conveyed
In writing, so I have been told,
   Of the death of the lovely maid.   1047

'King Arthur and all his warrior knights
   Who belong to the Round Table,
Noble and courteous princes of power,
   In battle bold and able;
Most honourable in helping those
   Who to misfortune fall,
The Maid of Ascolot with justice
   Greets you one and all.   1055

'To each of you I make my plaint
   Of the great wrong done to me –
Though not to claim that you avenge
   Me and my misery,
But simply to say for this thing's sake
   That, search the world entire
For noble grace, to rival yours
   No others could aspire.   1063

'So hereby have it! – That because
   For many and many a day
I loved in truth and loyalty,
   Death has fetched me away.
And if you wish to know for whom
   Thus languishing I lay,
Since nothing's had by hiding it,
   The truth I'll not delay.   1071

'To tell you truly of the man
   For whom I suffered so,
I say I died a fearful death
   For the noblest knight I know.
None was so regal or richly graced
   Or dealt a braver blow,
Yet baser in field and hall I never
   Met as friend or foe.   1079

'Yes, such discourtesy friend or foe
   Has never shown, I say.
His manners were of churlish mode,
   All courtliness cast away.
I knelt and wept with woeful moans,
   But to every plea I made,
He replied he would not be my lover:
   He'd none of that, he said.   1087

'So for his sake my sad heart, lords,
   Was stricken with grieving sore,
And at the last death took me off,
   For I could live no more.
For truly loving I suffered so,
   My life bereft of bliss,
And all for Sir Lancelot du Lake,
   For he it was did this.'   1095

When royal and noble Arthur had read
   The letter and learned the name,
These words to Sir Gawain he said:
   'Lancelot is to blame!
For since she died for such great love,
   That he shunned it brings him shame;
Implacable reproof is his
   For ever, and evil fame.'   1103

Then Gawain, grieving, told the King,
   'I lied to you, my lord,
That Lancelot belonged to a lady
   Or other whom he adored.
And then, remember, you declared
   His love he would not waste
On one so low, but would lavish it
   On a beauty nobly graced.'   1111

Then Arthur said to Sir Gawain,
   'Give me your good advice!
What must be done with the maiden now?'
   Said Gawain, 'Let it suffice,
If you assent, that reverently
   We bear her to the court,
She being the daughter of a duke,
   And bury her as we ought.'   1119

The King agreed, and Gawain then
   A band of warriors brought,
Who in utmost honour took her up
   And carried her to court,
Where Arthur announced to all his knights –
   No detail did he hide –
That Lancelot would not be her love,
   And so for sorrow she'd died.   1127

Gawain then went to the Queen to tell
   The truth of the case all through:
'Great is my guilt for the offence
   I now confess to you.
I told an utter lie to you here
   When I said that Lancelot
Had a ready love in the daughter of
   The Earl of Ascolot.   1135

'I told you the Maid of Ascolot
   Was Lancelot's paramour.
I smart for that lying sin, but now
   Here is the truth, for sure:
It's clear he would not have her, and hence
   That swan-white girl has died.
This letter proves it, for to all
   Of his cruelty she cried.'   1143

As wild as wind the Queen then raged
   At Gawain: 'Truly, sir,
Most base you were to mark a man
   With such a slanderous slur,
Unless you knew that it was true,
   For only truth should be said.
Yes, when you started saying such things,
   Your courtesy was dead.   1151

'You ruined your honour, sir, with wrong
   In blaming that good knight.
He never did you so much evil
   That you, against all right,
And churlishly behind his back,
   Should lie to everyone.
So, sir, conceive the harm you caused,
   And the more that may be done.   1159

'I thought you steadfast, firm and true
   And full of courtesy,
But now I find your manners fit
   For a man of low degree.
Yes, now you play your tricks on knights
   By lying jealously.
Who honours you will rue it: hence,
   And forsake my company!'   1167

Seeing the Queen aggrieved so sore,
   Gawain went wisely away,
Expecting her anger for evermore:
   There was nothing he could say.
As for the Queen, she wrung her hands
   And cried, 'Alas the day!
That I was born to wretchedness
   Nobody could gainsay!   1175

'Oh why, my heart, so mad to think
   That Lancelot du Lake
In fickle falseness would go off
   And another lover take?
No, not for all this world's rewards
   Would he do such a thing
As slyly swear his love elsewhere
   And leave me suffering.'   (1183)

Meanwhile the King most nobly caused
   A sumptuous tomb to be made
In the cathedral at Camelot,
   And there the girl was laid.
HERE LIES THE MAID OF ASCOLOT
   Was graven in blue and gold,
WHO DIED FOR LOVE OF LANCELOT.
   Thus is the story told.   (1191)

Now leave we King and leave we court,
   And leave we girl and Queen,
And let us speak of Lancelot,
   That knight so noble and keen.
He'd had to dwell in a stony cell
   Far in the forest hoar
With a hermit who could heal the wound[1]
   That he from hunting bore.   (1199)

At last Sir Lancelot could ride,
   And came to a fountain fair
With two trees towering over it:
   A knight was sleeping there.
He tethered his horse to one tall tree
   Beside the sleeper's steed,
And waited till the knight should wake,
   Thus courteous in his deed.   (1207)

Not long they kept that quietness;
   Their horses fell to fight.
The din and drumming of their hooves
   Awoke the sleeping knight,
Who, seeing Lancelot sitting there,
   Wondered what would ensue.
'Who are you? Whence do you come?' he asked:
   'Tell me, if you be true.'   (1215)

---

1. 1199 This reference to Lancelot's wound is versified from the *Mort Artu*.

223

Said Lancelot, thus unrecognized,
  'I come from Western Gaul.'
'And I from Logres,'[1] the other replied,
  'The loveliest land of all;
But now I come from Camelot.
  In Arthur's court I've been,
Where noble hearts are grieved, not glad:
  The cause concerns the Queen.'   (1223)

'Tell me how so,' said Lancelot,
  'I greatly long to know.'
And the other told of the poisoning
  And Guinevere's great woe
That none would defend her against the charge
  Of Mador de la Port,
And said if none came by the fortieth day,
  The knights must doom her in court.   (1231)

Sir Lancelot inquired of him,
  'Will none defend the Queen?'
The other said, 'By no means, since
  Her crime by all was seen.'
Then Lancelot: 'Yet one there is
  Will shield the Queen from shame,
Rebut the charge in deadly duel,
  And honour Arthur's name.'   (1239)

1. 1219 Logres: the old name for England.

'No honour will accrue from that,'
  Said the other, 'for this reason:
If won, such a fight gainsays the right,
  Gives victory to treason.'
'Yet tell me,' said Sir Lancelot,
  'When is the fortieth day?'
The knight then told him, saluted him,
  Mounted and went his way.   (1247)

The tale is now of Guinevere
  In terror twisting and turning
To find a man to fight for her
  Or yield to bale-fire burning.
She knew that judgement by the knights
  Would bring her death and shame;
Though utterly innocent, she'd end
  Her life in evil fame.   1323

The King, sighing and sick with anguish,
  Went to Sir Gawain,
To Bors de Gawnes and Lionel
  And Ector of warrior strain,
To ask if any in his need
  Would help and do him ease.
Almost out of her wits, the Queen
  Before them fell on her knees.   1331

The knights replied with little pride,
  Hearts full of sorrow and pain,
'We sat beside the knight and saw
  Him die from the apple-bane;
And then Sir Gawain laid him out
  Upon the festive board.
We will not ride against the right:
  We saw the truth, my lord.'   1339

Weeping and sighing, then the Queen
    To Bors de Gawnes went first,
Fell on her knees to plead with him
    As if her heart would burst.
'Mercy, Lord Bors, of your grace!' she cried,
    'Today to death I go
Unless it's your will in honour bold
    To give me life from this woe!'   1347

But Bors de Gawnes replied in rage,
    His fierce eyes downward turned,
'By the body of God on the Holy Cross,
    You well deserve to be burned!
The noblest body of flesh and blood
    That ever breathed here below
Was forced by your vile capricious mind
    Away from us to go.'   1355

Fevered with weeping, secondly
    To Gawain the Queen made cry,
Fell on her knees to plead with him,
    Out of her wits wellnigh.
'Mercy!' she cried out loud and shrill,
    'As I'm guiltless of the deed,
I beg you, make it your honour's task
    To help me in my need.'   1363

Gawain replied with little pride:
    Heart sorrowing, he said,
'Was I not seated beside the knight
    When your poison struck him dead?
Did I not lay his body out
    Upon our festive board?
I will not ride against the right:
    Truly, truth's the word.'   1371

Thirdly she went to Lionel,
   Ever her loyal friend,
And fell before him on her knees,
   Her strength near its end.
'Mercy!' she cried out loud and shrill,
   'Lord, as I am guiltless quite,
To save my life, for honour's sake
   Will you not take this fight?'   1379

'Madam, how can you demand of me,'
   He answered, 'when you know
That you with ill-will forced Lancelot
   Away from us to go?
When noble knights in troops we see,
   Great sadness comes to us.
By Christ who created me a man,
   We are glad you suffer thus!'   1387

Then she was seized by dread of death;
   She knew that she must die.
She knelt a fourth time to a knight,
   To Ector, with this cry:
'By Christ who wore the crown of thorns,
   And died for us on high,
Unless you help me in my need,
   Then surely I shall die!'   1395

Said Ector, 'How can you come to us?
   Or I take on this fight?
Consider Lancelot du Lake,
   Who was ever your own knight.
Because of you my own dear brother
   Is ever out of my sight.
Cursed be he who takes up arms
   For you against the right!'   1403

So no man there would fight her cause.
   To her room she went apart,
Making such miserable lament
   She almost burst her heart.
'Alas!' she sobbed, and started then
   To shiver and to shake,
'No court could kill me had I here
   Sir Lancelot du Lake.   1411

'Evil and useless was my wont
   To honour so many a knight,
Since in my need, for love of me,
   No man will dare to fight.
Lord King of Nations, whose high rule
   Directs the world aright,
Preserve Sir Lancelot, of whom
   I shall nevermore have sight!'   1419

Ill with terror when she saw
   The bale-fire burning high,
And grieving greatly, Guinevere
   To Bors again made cry.
She begged him, if he would, to help
   Her in her great despair,
Then fell before him in a swoon,
   Stark and speechless there.   1427

Bors gazed at Guinevere so fair
   And, pitying her grief,
Held her upright in his arms
   And offered this relief:
'Madam, unless one better comes
   To bear the battle for you,
As long as life and limb shall last,
   I'll fight your cause right through.'   1434

Then was the Queen so struck with joy
   That Bors would take the fight
That she'd have fallen in a faint
   But that he held her tight.
To her ladies-in-waiting she was led,
   Full of relief and delight.
Yet he told her, 'Tell no man at all
   Until I am armed to fight!'   1442

Then Bors, that bold and hardly noble,
   Called his brother knights
To take their counsel in this affair
   With all its wrongs and rights.
He told them he had truly sworn
   For Guinevere to fight
Against Sir Mador's furious challenge,
   And save her if he might.   1450

The knights responded with much pain,
   'For a certainty we know
That Guinevere forced Lancelot
   Away from us to go.
We'd all have fought for her before
   She did that dreadful thing,
But we'll not wish her joy until
   She's had due suffering.'   1458

Then Bors and Ector and Lionel,
   Brave any battle to dare,
Rode to the chapel in the forest
   In order to offer prayer
To God the Lord, mighty in power,
   That through His grace Sir Bors
Might gain the victory in the fight:
   They feared Sir Mador's force.   1466

And as they rode by the forest side
   To offer up their prayer,
The noblest knight ever created
   They saw riding there.
His armour, horse and all were white,
   His reins in the sheen did shake.
In no way can I hide his name:
   It was Lancelot du Lake!   1474

No wonder was it they were glad
   To see their master thus;
They knelt to give their greatest thanks
   To God all-glorious.
Delight it was to see and hear
   The knights encounter him there;
Yet quickly did Sir Lancelot ask,
   'How does my lady fair?'   1482

Sir Bors then told him all the truth;
   No detail did he hide
Of how the Scottish knight had died
   Sitting at the Queen's side:
'No longer may there be delay;
   For her life she must be tried.
Today's the day that I must fight
   This matter to decide.   1488

'Sir Mador in the duel will prove
   His fierceness and his might.'
Sir Lancelot at once replied,
   'To me belongs this fight.
You three, go quickly back to court
   And cheer my lady bright,
But see you say no word of me;
   I shall come as a foreign knight.'   1495

And so Sir Lancelot, brave and strong,
 Stayed in the forest green,
While those three others went to court
 To comfort the sad Queen.
They jollied and joked among themselves
 And bade her be of good cheer;
They tried to make her happy and said
 There was nothing she should fear.   1503

The cloths were spread, the board was laid,
 The King in place was set;
The Queen was to the table led,
 Her cheeks all wan and wet.
So sick with sorrow were they both,
 They neither drank nor ate;
Her **dread** of death so shook the Queen
 She shed more grim tears yet.   1511

And as the King and court were ready
 The third course to begin,
With helmet, shield and hauberk bright,
 Mador came striding in
Among them all before the dais,
 And called on Guinevere
Without deceit to grant his right
 Defined in covenant clear.   1519

Greater still was the King's grief:
 He looked at every knight,
But saw not one ready in arms
 Against Sir Mador to fight,
While Mador swore by his fierce heart
 And by God's holy might
To kill the Queen in presence there
 Unless he had his right.   1527

Then Arthur, strong and courteous King,
   Politely spoke his mind:
'Sir, let us eat, and later, treat;
   The day's not yet declined.
God willing, a champion may appear;
   Your challenge may be met,
And you shall have your fill of fight
   Before the sun is set.'   1535

Sir Bors then laughed at Lionel:
   None knew of their secret word.
Seeking his chamber, quickly then
   He silently left the board,
Put on his hauberk in much haste,
   Took helmet, spear and sword,
Then quietly came back again
   And sat down at the board.   1543

The King, when he saw Sir Bors prepared,
   Let fall glad tears to his knee,
Then, generous-hearted, leapt to his feet
   And embraced him courteously.
'May God reward you, Bors,' he said,
   'For taking on this fight!
You well repay me for the honour
   I make for many a knight.'   1551

As Mador accused the Queen of treason
   With loud and furious call,
Sir Lancelot du Lake came riding
   Right into the hall.
His horse and armour were all of white,
   His visor hid his eyes;
Many a knight quaked at the sight:
   All made a dread surmise.[1]   1559

On all occasions high King Arthur
   Was brave and courteous.
'Good sir,' he said, 'alight in peace,
   And eat and drink with us!'
Sir Lancelot spoke like a foreign knight:
   'I heard there was some strife.
No feasting here for me! I come
   To save a lady's life.   1567

'The Queen has used her time not well
   In honouring many a knight,
Since none of them, when she's in need,
   For her life will dare to fight.
You who accuse her of treason: quick!
   Be ready to stand and smite!
Your wits are wanting, but today
   This trial shall test your might.'   1575

1. 1559 'A dread surmise' that he was a ghost-knight, presumably.

233

That made Sir Mador as rapturous
  As dawn-bird at end of night;
He swiftly strode to his great war-horse,
  That man of mettle and might.
Not pausing, they rode to the duelling-place:
  The King and every knight
Followed to see and hear the battle,
  For never did stronger men fight.   1583

The first charge felled both furious knights,
  They met with such mighty force,
And then they fought with their keen-edged swords
  On foot, neither on horse.
In all the battles in which he'd been
  In fell and violent strife,
Sir Lancelot had never come
  So close to losing his life.   1591

Thus foot to foot, not giving an inch
  In that most fierce fight,
They dealt each other dreadful wounds
  From morn till late at night.
Sir Lancelot then struck Mador down
  Most savagely with his sword.
So hurt that he could not fight on,
  Mador cried, 'Mercy, lord!'   1599

Though raging like a foaming boar,
  Lancelot stood upright
And flung his sword away from him:
  With no more strokes would he smite.
Sir Mador swore, 'By God, I've fought
  In lands both far and near
With knights of every rank and sort,
  But never yet met my peer.   1607

'So sir, for the sake of the thing you love
    The most in every way,
And for Our Sweetest Lady's sake,
    Tell me your name, I pray.'
Lancelot raised his visor so
    That Mador his face might see:
When Mador knew it was Lancelot,
    Then most content was he.   1615

'Most happy am I, lord,' said he,
    'This great boast may I make:
I bore a blow from you, and fought
    Sir Lancelot du Lake.
For your sake, free of my brother's death
    May the Queen be found!'
Sir Lancelot warmly kissed him then
    And raised him from the ground.   1623

From amongst his knights the King cried out
    To the Queen, 'No mistake!
If ever I set eyes on him,
    That is Lancelot du Lake!'
They all then rode or ran to him
    With but a single thought.
Arthur kissed him in his arms,
    And so did all the court.   1631

Seeing Sir Lancelot du Lake,
    The Queen was glad beyond words,
And would have fallen in a faint
    But for support from her lords.
The knights all wept and laughed for joy
    As they talked in company,
And with Sir Mador they made their peace
    Quickly and happily.   1639

No point in delaying matters then:
    They rode to the castle at speed.
The trumpeting and the pomp they made
    Were pleasure to hear indeed.
Since Mador could not walk or ride,
    Most carefully was he brought
By knights who held him on each side
    And carried him to the court.   1647

Then the squires who had served in hall
    When the knight by poison was slain
Were taken and tortured to tell the truth,
    Put to the utmost pain,
And one confessed before them all
    That he'd put the venomous bane
In an apple placed upon the dish
    To poison Sir Gawain.   1655

When Mador heard the whole truth
    And the innocence of the Queen,
He fell before her on his knees
    In grief and anguish keen;
But Lancelot for love of him
    Lifted him upright,
And Mador exchanged the kiss of peace
    With Arthur and every knight.   1663

The squire was put to death at once
  By right and by the law,
Disembowelled, hanged and burnt
  In front of Sir Mador.
Then in the castle Joyous Gard[1]
  That company all stayed.
To Lancelot for his chivalry
  The highest honour they paid.   1671

One day the knights were talking together,
  Gaheriet and Gawain,
And others with them, Mordred too,
  Stirrer of trouble and pain.
'Alas, why do we deal in falsehood?'
  Cried Sir Agravain,
'Why this treason of Lancelot
  Do we hide and thus sustain?   1679

'We know King Arthur is our uncle;
  True nephews we should be.
Since Lancelot lies with Arthur's Queen,
  Traitor to the King is he.
His treachery, people of the court
  Daily hear and see,
So we should tell it to the King.
  Take this advice from me.'   1687

1. 1668 An inexplicable sudden shift to Lancelot's castle.

'Right well we know,' said Sir Gawain,
    'That we are the King's kin;
But Lancelot's strong, and such words are
    Worse out and better in.
You well know, brother Agravain,
    That harm is what we'd win;
So better to hide the thing than make
    Chaos and war begin.   1695

'Lancelot's brave, the best of us,
    You well know, Agravain,
And but for him the King and court
    Would often have been slain.
And so I could never tell the love
    That lies between those two.
I shall never betray Sir Lancelot
    Behind his back, with you.   1703

'Lancelot is the son of a king,[1]
    A knight of breeding high,
And if he needed, many a land
    He'd have as his ally.
There'd be for sure much shedding of blood
    When the story spread about.
Sir Agravain, he'd be enraged
    If such a thing came out.'   1711

---

1. 1704 Lancelot's father was King Ban of Benwick.

As Gawain and the other knights
    Contended without cease,
In came the King in gentle mood.
    Cried Gawain, 'Fellows, peace!'
But Arthur raged at once to know
    Their cause of disaccord.
Agravain answered, 'By Christ's cross
    I'll tell you all, my lord.'   1719

Gawain went swiftly to his room;
    He would not hear one word.
Gaheriet and Gaheris
    With their brother both concurred.
They well knew all was lost in ruin:
    Gawain was moved to swear,
'What's now begun will not be done,
    By God, for many a year.'   1727

Sir Agravain told Arthur all
    With innocent-seeming cheer:
'Sir Lancelot lies with the Queen,
    And has done many a year;
And all the court are well aware,
    And daily find it true;
And Sire, we have been treacherous
    In never telling you.'   1735

'Alas!' then sighed the sorrowing King,
    'That were a mighty shame
For a man so fine and generous
    And of such splendid fame.
There never was another man
    Of such nobility.
Alas! what grief if he were proved
    So treasonous to be!   1743

'But since it's so, Sir Agravain,
   And taken as a fact,
Advise me how we may proceed
   To catch him in the act.
I dread his great accomplishments
   And mighty fighting force;
Not all the court could best him if
   He were armed and on his horse.'   1751

'Sire,' said Agravain, 'tomorrow
   Make it a hunting day
For all your court, and tell the Queen
   You'll spend the night away.
And I'll remain with twelve brave knights
   In secret, armed to fight;
And rest assured that we shall take him
   Before the next day's light.'   1759

So King and court were early out
   To hunt the following day,
And Arthur to the Queen sent word
   He'd spend the night away.
But Agravain remained behind
   With twelve knights brave and keen,
And hid so close that all the day
   Not one of them was seen.   1767

The Queen rejoiced because the King
   Was far away in the wood,
And sent to Lancelot to come
   As quickly as he could.
Sir Bors de Gawnes heard the message
   And thought it boded ill.
'Sir,' he said, 'a word with you
   If it be your will.   1775

'Stay in tonight, I counsel you:
    Some plot's afoot, I fear,
From Agravain of evil mind
    Who day and night lurks near.
Of all the nights you've gone to her,
    Not one disturbed my calm
Or made my heart as sick as this,
    Which fills me with alarm.'   1783

Said Lancelot, 'Be patient, Bors;
    You must not say me nay.
I only go to Guinevere
    To hear what she will say,
And find out what she wants of me;
    There is no cause for pain.
I shall not stay there long, but soon
    Return to you again.'   1791

So thinking that he'd soon be back,
    Not purposing to stay,
He wore no armour, only a robe
    Made in a marvellous way.
He feared no treason, so he took
    His sword as his only arm;
No man beneath the moon, he thought,
    Would dare to do him harm.   1799

He kissed and embraced that brilliant queen
   Upon arriving there.
For treason or betrayal both
   Took neither thought nor care.
They could not think of parting then,
   Their love was such delight.
To bed went Lancelot with the Queen,[1]
   Intent on staying all night.   1807

Barely was Lancelot in bed
   In the boudoir of the Queen
When Agravain and Mordred came
   With twelve knights brave and keen.
They called him traitor to the King,
   A false and shameless one;
Strong was the imminent attack,
   But armour had he none.   1815

'Ah Lancelot!' exclaimed the Queen,
   'What shall become of us?
Alas, alas that such a love
   As ours should finish thus!
Through Agravain so fierce and harsh,
   And night and day our foe,
I know it now beyond all doubt:
   Our joy is turned to woe.'   1823

1. 1806 It is rare, in romances which mention the two lovers, for there to be a bedroom scene between Lancelot and Guinevere.

'Peace, lady!' answered Lancelot,
  'Their words will soon be rife;
But have you any armour here,
  That I may save my life?'
'I know I've none,' she cried, 'Ill luck
  Have we in this grim strife,
For I've no helm or hauberk here,
  Nor any sword or knife.'   1831

And Agravain and Mordred still
  Called him a traitor knight,
And goaded him: 'Get out of bed
  And face us in the fight!'
Then Lancelot put on his robe,
  Not the armour he would,
And furiously drawing his sword,
  Close to the doorway stood.   1839

In came the first armed knight, intent
  On killing Lancelot,
But Lancelot gave him such a blow
  He felled him on the spot.
The others paused, not daring to
  Advance upon the floor,
So Lancelot leapt forward then
  And double-barred the door.   1847

He found the armour of the knight
  Whom he had slain was good;
He stripped him of it, put it on
  And fully armed upstood.
'Now then, Sir Agravain,' he cried,
  'No prison for me tonight!'
Then strong and raging out he sprang
  Against them all to fight.   1855

Exultingly Sir Lancelot fought –
   Mark well, I tell you true!
Sir Agravain went down in death,
   And all the others too.[1]
Too weak they were to fight with him
   In any sort of strife;
But Mordred fled like one run mad,
   Eager to save his life.   1863

Back to his room went Lancelot,
   Where Bors stood fully armed.
He had not been to bed at all,
   Being so much alarmed;
While Lancelot's company of knights
   Dreamed violent dreams that night.
But all their doubts and fears vanished
   When their master came in sight.   1871

Said Bors, that hardy warrior, 'Sir,
   For you we had much dread,
And fearing you might come to harm,
   I dared not go to bed.
Some knights leapt naked out of sleep
   From dreams of direst fright,
Because we all had promptings deep
   Of treason traps this night.'   1879

---

1. 1859 In the *Mort Artu* (Chapter 90) Lancelot kills only two before the rest stand back in fear and let him pass.

'Fear nothing, Bors,' said Lancelot,
   'But be of resolute heart!
Go now and wake up every knight
   You know will take our part,
And see that all are fitly armed.
   Indeed the truth you told:
Tonight is done a deed will leave
   Many men dead and cold.'   1887

Then, greatly grieving, Bors replied,
   'Sir, since that is so,
We shall, the days of joy being done,
   Fearless face the woe.'
The knights put all their armour on
   As quickly as they could;
At dawn a hundred with their squires
   Before Sir Lancelot stood.   1895

All being prepared, at gentle pace
   Those brave men rode from court,
And in the forest not far away
   For the present made resort.
Sir Lancelot drew up his knights
   And lodged them one and all
Till he should hear of Guinevere
   And what might her befall.   1903

Fast to the forest Mordred fled
   To Arthur and his court,
And what had happened that grim night
   He started to report.
'But Mordred, is that traitor dead?
   Is all now done to rights?'
'No, sir, for Agravain is dead,
   And all our other knights.'   1911

When that dread word Sir Gawain heard,
   The knight both strong and bold,
'Alas!' he said, 'Is my brother dead?'[1]
   And his heart with grief went cold.
'I warned Sir Agravain of this
   Before the tale was told,
For Lancelot is far too strong
   And much too hard to hold.'   1919

It was no time to take their ease:
   Arthur in anguish drew
His knights to him in conference
   To deem what they must do.
They all were keen to doom the Queen
   The fate that she had earned;
That very day, without delay,
   They said she must be burned.   1925

Then in the field they built the fire
   And brought the lady fair,
And all arms–bearing knights were bidden
   To be in presence there.
But Gawain, Gaheriet and Gaheris
   Firmly refused that part,
And went to their chambers cherishing
   Pity for her at heart.   1933

---

1. 1914 Significantly, Gawain does not take up the family feud on behalf of Agravain, presumably because he disapproved of the action in which Agravain died. But it is quite another matter when his other two brothers are killed during Lancelot's rescue of Guinevere from the burning (l. 2008).

For Gawain and Sir Gaheris
  King Arthur sternly sent,
But their reply was clear and plain:
  They said they'd not consent.
Gawain would never in all his life
  Be by when a woman was burned;
But, ashamed and unarmed, the other two
  To the burning-place returned.   1941

A squire whom Lancelot sent to court
  To find out these things then
Galloped back fast to the forest base
  Of Lancelot and his men.
'The Queen's led out to be burnt!' he cried,
  'Hurry to rescue her!'
To arms and horse each warrior leapt,
  Not sparing steed or spur.   1949

The Queen was standing by the fire,
  All ready in her smock;
Powerful lords and barons were there,
  All knights of noble stock.
Then Lancelot, berserk, launched his charge
  And thrust apart the throng,
And after his fierce first assault
  None stood up stout and strong.   1957

Not long they fought, and all their steel
  Stood them in little stead;
Many mighty barons bold
  Fell on the field dead.
Gaheriet and Gaheris both were slain.
  Then away to the forest green,
Leaving the dead and wounded lying,
  Lancelot took the Queen.   1965

King Arthur sorrowed that Lancelot
   Had taken the Queen away,
And greatly grieved that his noblest knights
   Had died in the affray.
He swooned and sank upon the ground
   In mighty grief and pain,
And, pitying him, the people thought
   He'd never live again.   1973

Was never man so sad as he,
   And when he could speak, he said,
'In all the world there'll come no more
   Such knights as now lie dead.
Of Gaheriet his brother's death
   Let not Sir Gawain know.
Ah, wretched the kingdom that I rule
   Now Lancelot is its foe!'   1981

Sir Gawain stayed in his chamber still;
   From there he would not go,
And when a squire brought the news,
   No wonder he felt much woe.
'Alas!' he cried, 'Gaheriet gone?
   My brother brave and bold?'
At that he almost slew himself;
   His heart went dead and cold.   1989

The squire in desolation spoke
   To comfort Sir Gawain,
'Gaheriet is well, my lord;
   Soon he will come again.'
Sir Gawain went at once with him
   To where the dead men lay
In pools of gore on the chamber floor
   And cloth of gold array.   1997

He lifted up the cloth and looked
  At the dead knights lying there;
No wonder that the sight of them
  Filled him with despair;
And when he saw his brother's body,
  No word could he say,
But lost all strength and fell on it
  And fainting swooned away.   2005

When from that swoon Sir Gawain rose
  And stood up wide awake,
The good man swore, 'By God, between
  Sir Lancelot du Lake
And me, there is no man on earth
  Could peace or fair truce make
Till one of us has killed the other.'
  Thus brave Sir Gawain spake.   2013

A squire whom Lancelot sent to court
  The latest news to learn
Told Lancelot in his forest base
  These things on his return:
That lords most rich in land and rent
  And many more were dead;
Gaheriet and Gaheris too.
  Then Lancelot felt dread.   2021

He cried, 'Lord Jesus, can this be?
  Stands the matter so?
Could that long love of ours end thus?
  Gaheriet my foe?
By that I know for certain now,
  A sad man is Gawain.
Never again will there be peace
  Till one of us is slain.'   2029

So Lancelot led his party forth
    In sad and gloomy mood,
And sent to queens and countesses
    And ladies of noble blood,
Saying he'd often saved their lands
    When they had asked for aid.
Each granted him some help, and thus
    His force was stronger made.   2037

Many a queen and countess sent
    An earl with a warrior band,
And ladies of less power than they
    Put knights at his command.
His force was frightening to see,
    So greatly did it swell.
He took them all to Joyous Gard,[1]
    And held that citadel.   2045

Most sad at heart was Lancelot
    For Guinevere so fair.
He bade a virgin richly robe
    And for a journey prepare;
An urgent message she must take
    To the King most high in might:
He'd prove the accusation false
    By trial in a fight.   2053

1. 2044 Joyous Gard seems to have been near the Humber, and
Arthur's first campaign against Lancelot there was based on Carlisle.

The maiden was ready to ride away
   In fine habiliment
Of samite, choicest silk, in green,
   Wrought in the Orient.
She had to have a dwarf as squire
   By Lancelot's decree:
Such was the custom when a virgin
   Went on embassy.   2061

The girl arrived at Camelot,
   Dismounted by the court
And quickly gave the King and Gawain
   The message she had brought:
'True to the King is Guinevere,
   And Lancelot, loyal knight,
To prove all else an empty lie,
   Offers trial by fight.'   2069

Sharply King Arthur made reply,
   'Prove it or prove it not,
He'd do to death some of my men:
   What gain would then be got?'
Then King and Gawain pledged their word.
   'By Christ,' they swore with zeal,
'His deeds shall cost him dear unless
   He can't be killed by steel!'   2077

The girl returned to Joyous Gard
   With the answer she had got,
And told the King's exact words
   At once to Lancelot,
Who sighed with sorrow and sadly wept;
   The tears fell to his feet.
But Bors de Gawnes then swore, 'By God,
   On the battlefield we'll meet.'   2085

King Arthur in no time at all
   Acted with all his might.
He made his messengers ride forth,
   Not pausing day or night,
All over England, everywhere,
   To baron, earl and knight,
Requiring them to come at once
   On horse, with armour bright.   2093

So, grieving for their gallant dead,
   Yet sternly ready for war,
At Camelot King and company stood,
   Three hundred knights and more.
From England, Ireland, Scotland, Wales,
   The best were gathered then
In boar–like fury of heart to kill
   Sir Lancelot and his men.   2101

When that host was wholly armed
   And all their needs supplied,
They raised their spears and banners high
   As men of mighty pride.
With shining hauberk, helm and shield
   Sir Gawain was first to ride;
He led them to the Joyous Gard
   And besieged it on every side.   2109

They stayed for seventeen weeks and more
   Till one day Lancelot
Told them to raise the siege and go
   Back home to Camelot.
'Great pity it were to kill you all,
   So take your force away!
That ever this grievous quarrel began,
   Alas and woe the day!'   2117

But still the King and Sir Gawain
   Called him a traitor knight
Who had killed his comrades and brothers-in-arms,
   And was false by day and night.
They taunted him to prove his power
   On the battlefield in fight,
But Lancelot sat still and sighed:
   That was a sorry sight.   2125

They called on Lancelot with shouts
   And hideous braying of horns.
Lancelot pulled a sour face,
   And then said Bors de Gawnes,
'Why should we listen to them while
   These fleering words are said?
You come on, sir, just like a coward,
   As if we were afraid.   2133

'So let us put our armour on
   And taking sword and shield,
Ride out as quickly as we can
   To face them in the field.
I'll not surrender my arms today
   Nor live to know defeat;
We two, I wager my life on it,
   Shall make them all retreat.'   2141

'Alas!' said Lancelot, 'woe is me
   That ever I should see
The noble king who made me knight
   And be his enemy!
Sir Gawain, noble and great in mind,
   I beg you let it not be
That Arthur my lord is in the field,
   Or you battle with me.'   2149

So there was nothing for it then
    But to get in fighting gear,
And when they were all ready to ride
    They brandished sword and spear.
When those forces met head-on
    With shout and trumpet sound,
Both sides greatly grieved to see
    Good men struck to the ground.   2157

On Lancelot's side Sir Lionel
    With spear was to the fore;
Sir Gawain charged him, and to the ground
    Both horse and man he bore.
Sir Lionel then was thought to be dead;
    They carried him from the field,
Thinking his wounds so wide and deep
    They never could be healed.   2165

In all that battle there was none
    Dared face Sir Lancelot,
Who spurred about the field at speed;
    The foe he slaughtered not.
Close to Lancelot kept the King,
    Hewing with fervour grim,
But Lancelot was so courteous
    He struck not back at him.   2173

Observing this, Sir Bors attacked
    The King with all his might,
And hit him on the helm so hard
    He lost his power to fight.
His horse's back broke under him;
    Recover he could not.
Then loudly with these words Sir Bors
    Reproached Sir Lancelot: 2181

'Why do you freely let the King
   Assault you thus all day,
When you can see his heart's so hard
   Your courtesy cannot pay?
If you will do what I advise,
   All wars are over and done:
Allow us, lord, to slaughter them all,
   For sure, this battle is won.'   2189

'Alas,' said Lancelot, 'What woe
   That ever I should see
Unhorsed before my very eyes
   The King who knighted me!'
And then, dismounting from his steed
   – So generous was he! –
He horsed the King on it, telling him
   Out of harm's way to flee.   2197

The King, when mounted in the saddle,
   On Lancelot fixed his gaze,
And knew there was never another knight
   Who had such courteous ways.
He thought how things had used to be,
   And tears from his eyes ran;
Sighing and groaning, he cried, 'Alas
   That ever this war began!'   2205

The two sides slowly separated,
   So many knights were slain,
And on the following day the fight
   Was set to start again.
Yes, the armies drew apart
   In noble style, I swear:
Was he not a sinner who started
   This miserable affair?   2213

Yet Bors, as furious as a boar,
  Charged at Sir Gawain,
Wishing to avenge his brother's wounds,
  For great was Lionel's pain.
Sir Gawain charged him in return
  With all his might and main;
Each ran the other's body through
  And both were nearly slain.   2221

Tangled together, they fell to the ground,
  Which many saw with dismay,
And Arthur's men came hurrying up
  To take them both away,
But Lancelot intervened himself
  And bravely rescued Bors.
Both wounded men were carried off;
  Such was that duel's course.   2229

Even to men who know of war
  It would be hard to tell
How knights were mangled with grim blows
  And from their saddles fell,
And horses speedy and high-mettled
  Ambled about in the blood.
By vesper-bell Lancelot's side
  With some advantage stood.   2237

The battle stopped for the time being:
  Folk led friends away
If they were wounded, and they carried
  The dead from where they lay.
Lancelot entered Joyous Gard,
  The fight won, so to say,
But great was the grief, many the tears:
  That was no child's play.   2245

North and south the word went out
  About this grisly war,
And in Rome too the people knew
  The anguish England bore.
The Pope in pity wrote a letter
  And sealed it with his hand:
'Unless you truly swear a peace,
  I'll interdict your land.'[1]   2253

The Bishop of Rochester was in Rome,
  And came as emissary
To Carlisle where the King was lying,
  Bearing the Pope's decree.
Before high table in the palace
  Arthur thus he addressed:
'Obey the arbitrament of the Pope;
  Give England peace and rest!'   2261

He read the letter of the Pope
  For everyone to hear:
'The King must agree with Lancelot
  And take back Guinevere;
Their peace must be a lasting one
  Or else, through their despite,
All England shall be interdicted
  And fall in wretched plight.'   2269

---

1. 2253 Throughout medieval wars, it was common for a Papal messenger to be on hand to enjoin peace on the contestants. An interdict would have denied the whole country all ecclesiastical functions and privileges.

King Arthur said, 'I shall be pleased
   To obey the Pope's command
And have back Guinevere, my queen:
   I do not wish the land
To be denied the sacraments.'
   But Gawain would not agree:
His heart was hard, and while he lived
   He'd Lancelot's foeman be.   2277

At length with the consent of all
   The Bishop went to take
A letter from the noble King
   To Lancelot du Lake,
Inquiring if he would entrust
   The Queen to him again;
Or England under interdict
   Must suffer grief and pain.   2285

Most humbly Lancelot made reply,
   'Your Grace knows I have been
In many a battle bearing the brunt
   For both the King and Queen.
His strongest castles would have fallen
   If I had not been there.
Scant honour for that constant service
   He pays me, I declare.'   2293

Boldly spoke the Bishop then:
   'Those battles that you won
Came to you by grace of God.
   In what shall now be done
Take my advice and think of Him
   Who saved your soul, my son.
Women are frail and weak: let not
   Fair England be undone!'   2301

'Know well, Sir Bishop, I've no need,'
   Sir Lancelot replied,
'Of castles, since I could be king
   Of Benwick's province wide,[1]
And take possession with my knights.
   But if we end our strife
And I give up the Queen to them,
   I'd fear for her life.'   2309

'By Mary, Sir, that maiden-flower,
   And God who makes all right,'
The Bishop said, 'She shall have honour:
   Thereto my troth I plight.
Back to her bower she shall be led
   By ladies in delight,
And honoured more than ever before
   Both by day and night.'   2317

'If I agree to such a thing
   And send back Guinevere,
Sir Bishop, Gawain and the King
   Must give assurance clear,'
Said Lancelot, 'to obey a truce
   And to its terms adhere.'   2323

---

1. 2305 Benwick is thought to have been in Brittany, but one school of thought places it in the far south-west of France, near Bayonne, which was under English rule for at least two centuries before and during the Hundred Years War.

That answer made the Bishop glad,
    And in a little while,
His palfrey being brought, he mounted
    And cantered to Carlisle.
The news of Lancelot's word announced,
    The King and all his court
Rejoiced and swore to set a truce
    And keep it as they ought.   2331

Yes, all agreed a goodly truce,
    And even Sir Gawain
Was not against a truce which brought
    The Queen back home again.
But, that apart, his hardened heart
    Refused to promise peace
To Lancelot till the sword of one
    Made the other's heart-beat cease.   2339

They wrote the truce in binding terms
    And sealed it all by hand,
And gave it to three bishops then,
    The wisest in the land.
To Lancelot at Joyous Gard
    The three delivered it,
And Lancelot to all its terms
    Swore he would submit.   2347

The bishops went upon their way
    To Carlisle and the King,
And said that he would come next day,
    And the regal lady bring.
Then Lancelot rightly robed himself
    In nobly rich array,
And took a hundred of his knights;
    The choicest men were they.   2355

The Queen and Lancelot were clad
   In silvered samite bright;
Their saddles were of ivory,
   Their horses both were white.
Their saddle-cloths were samite too,
   Made in a heathen land.
The French book says that Lancelot led,
   Her bridle in his hand.   2363

The attendant knights were nobly dressed
   In robes of samite green
And rode unarmoured, on each head
   A garland also green;
Their saddles were set with precious stones.
   That host lit up the land
As they advanced with sweetest song,
   Olive branches in hand.   2371

And when they came to Carlisle castle,
   At the court did they alight;
Lancelot lifted the Queen down
   From her palfrey, gracious sight,
And made obeisance to the King
   In all his courteous might.
Fair words were said, but weeping there
   Stood many and many a knight.   2379

Lancelot spoke to the powerful King,
   'Sire, as I am a knight,
Here is your queen, whose life I saved,
   As was truly right.
For she is beautiful and pure
   And faithful day and night.
If any doubts her virtue, Sire,
   I challenge him to fight.'   2387

King Arthur answered, fierce and hard:
   'I never thought that you
Would cause me damage, Lancelot,
   As you have come to do,
Or that beneath our comradeship
   You were my secret foe.
Yet all the same, that we two warred
   Gives me the greatest woe.'   2395

Sir Lancelot replied to him
   When he had listened long,
'Sire, you blame me for the bad,
   Though knowing that is wrong.
I never was far away, Sire, when
   Your griefs or foes were strong;
But false men make their fables, and you
   Believe their lying song.'   2403

Sir Gawain was the next to speak,
   A knight of spirit high:
'That you killed all my brothers three
   You never can deny.
Therefore in battle we must meet
   The consequence to try;
Till one of us has killed the other,
   In peace I shall not lie.'   2411

Heart faint with sadness, not with fear,
   Thus answered Lancelot,
'Though I was there, your brothers fair
   Myself, sir, I slew not.
Many a knight was there to whom
   This war has brought much woe.'
Lancelot sighed, and from his eyes
   The tears began to flow.   2419

Then yet once more Sir Lancelot spoke
   To the King and Sir Gawain:
'Shall I never know reconcilement
   And we be friends again?'
And Gawain, fierce and hard of heart,
   Repeated his promise plain:
'No, you never shall have peace
   Till one of us is slain.'   2427

'If peace can never be between us,
   May I yet safely ride
With all my knights to my own lands?'
   Thus asking, Lancelot sighed,
'Why then, at once I'll leave you all;
   Wherever I may go
In this wide world, this English land
   I never again shall know.'   2435

In tears King Arthur then declared
   Before the knights in hall,
'By Jesus Christ who made this world
   And won it for us all,
No living man shall hinder you
   When to your lands you go.
Alas that ever this war began!'
   He sighed in grievous woe.   2443

But Lancelot still asked Gawain,
   'May I safely remain
In my own lands, and will you not
   Make war on me again?'
Sir Gawain answered, 'No, by Him
   Who made the sun and moon!
Prepare yourself as best you can,
   For we shall assault you soon.'   2451

Sir Lancelot took his leave at once:
   No point in any delay.
His horse was ready; he quickly mounted
   And led his knights away
To the castle gate, and grimly they
   Their galling tears let glide.
Both sides wept in open grief:
   In that parting was no pride.   2459

To Joyous Gard, that famous fort,
   Rode Lancelot, noble knight,
Then with his force prepared to leave,
   Men of spirit and might.
With spears in hand and banners raised,
   They spurred by night and day
To Caerleon where, all ready to sail,
   Their splendid galleys lay.   2467

And now they floated on the flood,
   Lancelot and his force,
With fairest winds and fine weather
   To help them on their course,
For Christ it was who guided them
   To Benwick all the way,
And happy were they to reach that haven,
   And eager there to stay.   2475

And all the waiting crowds rejoiced
   As they stepped upon the strand.
To Lancelot then quickly came
   The great lords of the land,
Acknowledged him to be their lord
   And kissed his foot and hand,
And promised to obey his laws
   And to his judgements stand.   2483

He crowned Sir Bors King of Gawnes
 By lawful high decree,
And Lionel he made King of France
 (Or Gaul as it used to be).
He advanced his henchmen, gave out lands
 To every loyal knight,
And stocked his castles with arms and stores,
 Knowing he'd have to fight.   2491

Sir Ector, the book truly tells,
 He crowned with his own hand;
Made him prince over powerful lords
 And king of his father's land,
Forbade all men to stand against him,
 Made all men call him king.
Himself, till he was sure of peace,
 He sought no further thing.   2499

King Arthur's heart ached night and day;
 No longer could he wait.
Through England's length and breadth he sent
 His urgent couriers straight
To earls and barons, telling them
 To prepare in utmost haste
To ride to the lands of Lancelot
 To burn, kill and lay waste.[1]   2507

1. 2507, 2537 Arthur and Gawain make a *chevauchée* (see note to l. 1251 of *Morte Arthure*) through Lancelot's lands.

The King took counsel with his knights
    Concerning who would make
Best steward while they were away,
    And be for Britain's sake
Best guard and ruler of the land,
    For they were much afraid
That when their forces were in France
    Foreigners might invade.   2515

The knights at length advised the King,
    They being of one mind,
Sir Mordred was the trustiest man
    That any of them could find
To rule the realm and keep the peace:
    On the Book before him laid
They swore him as steward; and for that, later,
    Hosts of bold men paid.   2523

The order that all should be well armed
    Was not to be denied:
With pennants streaming and spears raised
    They all were ready to ride.
To Caerleon haven straight they spurred,
    Riding in pomp and pride,
Where great galleys of many kinds
    Were rigged by the river side.   2531

Now are they shipped upon the sea,
   Sailing the waters wide.
On Benwick beach that mighty band
   Landed and started to ride.
Not stone nor tree withstood their sallies;
   They burned and slaughtered at will,
While Lancelot bided his time for battle
   In his fortress, strong and still.   2539

Lancelot called his knights together,
   His earls and barons too,
And said they must decide the matter:
   What did they wish to do?
Attack, or as a besieged force
   Behind their strong walls stay?
For Arthur's army, as well they knew,
   Could not be dreamed away.   2547

Sir Bors de Gawnes, noble knight,
   Sternly spoke his mind:
'Brave henchmen, have yourselves prepared
   With hearts to battle inclined,
With spear and shield and armour bright
   To fight against the foe.
For king and duke and earl and knight
   We'll conquer and lay low.'   2555

Then in his turn Sir Lionel spoke,
   In war most wise and bold:
'My lords, I counsel that we stay
   And this fine fortress hold.
Let them spur about in pride
   Till they are starved and cold.
Then we'll ride out and cut them down
   Like sheep penned in a fold.'   2563

Sir Bangdemagew, mighty king,
   To Lancelot spoke thus:
'Sir, your courtesy and suffering
   Have brought great woe to us.
Take careful counsel about this case:
   If they lay waste our land,
They'll gain while we are holed up here,
   A shamed, inactive band.'   2571

Next Galahad the Good spoke out
   To Lancelot, 'Sir, here
Are knights of royal blood and fame
   Who will not cringe in fear.
For Christ's sake, let me lead a sally,
   For though they have the gall
Of desperate outlaws, yet my men
   Shall kill and strip them all.'   2579

There were seven brothers from North Wales,
   Marvels of strength and pride;
Few better in battle could be named,
   It cannot be denied.
With single voice they cried aloud,
   'Lords, enough of debate!
Lancelot, let us with Galahad
   Spur to the conflict straight!'   2587

Then spoke Sir Lancelot du Lake,
   Most courteous of them all.
'Lords, let us stay here yet a while
   Guarding the castle wall,
While I request of them a truce,
   That battle now may cease.
King Arthur is so gentle and kind,
   I still have hope of peace.   2595

'Though we might well with honour win,
   Of one thing I despair.
My land is full of starving folk;
   Battles have burnt it bare.
To let more Christian men be killed
   You know would be a sin,
But God will guide us to good ends
   If gently we begin.'   2603

All gave assent to this and set
   A watch upon the wall –
Knights as dangerous as dread dragons,
   And grim as boars with gall.
They wrote a letter and picked the girl
   By whom it'd be conveyed,
For she who took an offer of truce
   Must be a virgin maid.   2611

Lovely to look at was the girl
   When seated on her steed;
Gowned in velvet green she was,
   And prettiest to plead.
That none should stop her in her quest
   She bore the branch of green
By which men knew a messenger
   Whenever one was seen.   2619

The King was camped in a fair meadow
   Beside a river wide:
She paused on seeing the bright pavilions
   Pitched on every side.
The pole pommels shone like gold
   On every elegant tent:
On one there hung King Arthur's shield,
   And thither the maiden went.   2627

The royal standard was flying there,
   And to that tent she came,
And met at once a noble knight,
   Sir Lucan the Butler by name.
She gently greeted him, and he
   With welcome word replied;
He knew she was a messenger
   Who must not be denied.   2635

Sir Lucan helped the girl dismount
   And on his arm led her forth,
Saying politely, as a knight
   Of sterling manners and worth,
'You come from Lancelot du Lake,
   Best ever to straddle a steed;
May Jesus for his Mother's sake
   Give you grace and God-speed!'   2643

On the chief pavilion pitched there
   The maiden made her call.
The King himself and Sir Gawain
   Were seated as in hall.
She knelt to the King, bending down
   As low as she could fall.
Her letters she did not conceal;
   They were read out to all.   2651

Then graciously the girl spoke out,
   Most eager to succeed:
'Sire, Lord save you from suffering,
   And give you all God-speed!
Greetings from Lancelot du Lake,
   Who ever helped you at need!
A twelvemonth truce to live in peace
   He asks you to concede.   2659

'And afterwards, your word being given,
   Faithfully he'll swear
An everlasting peace with you,
   And then in haste prepare
To travel to the Holy Land,
   Not seeking any strife,
And live there till his days are done
   And ended is his life.'   2667

King Arthur called for counsel then
   From all his valiant knights
And said, 'We must consider this
   And settle it to rights.
Only a fool would spurn her speech
   And this fair offer ignore,
For it would be great pity if
   All were to end in war.'   2675

Sir Gawain denied it. 'Never!' he said;
   'Many a grievous thing
He's done, and falsely killed my brothers
   For love of you, Sir King!
I'll not return to England till
   He's hanged upon a tree,
For while I live and my powers last,
   There are folk who'll fight for me.'   2683

The King spoke next, then every lord
  Gave his opinion plain,
And each one advocated peace,
  Yes, all except Gawain.
He'd bound himself by oath to battle
  Or never return again;
So all prepared to launch an attack.
  For that men sorrowed in vain.   2691

The King strode back into the hall
  And sat upon his throne.
He bade Sir Lucan fetch the girl;
  He'd make his message known.
'Tell Sir Lancelot and his knights
  I repeat to him my oath
That we shall never be deterred
  Till battle grips us both.'   2699

Having her answer, the girl prepared
  To leave with heavy heart;
Sir Lucan led her to her horse,
  And it was time to part.
She galloped through forests to Benwick Castle
  As fast as she could go;
When Lancelot and his knights saw her,
  Their trumpets began to blow.   2707

The gracious girl in gown of green
  Entered the castle wall,
Then, helped off horseback by a knight,
  She paced into the hall.
She read King Arthur's message out
  To the princes proudly dressed,
And since no counsel could avail,
  To arms each warrior pressed.   2715

As men with minds made up to fight,
   From the field they'd never flee.
At dawn next day they found themselves
   Besieged by the enemy,
And both sides, bent on fatal battle,
   Formed up their chivalry.   2721

At dawn the trumpeters took their stand:
   To the castle walls they went,
And saw from there pavilions proud
   And many a noble tent,
For Arthur with his battle host
   Was there with fixed intent
To make assault on Lancelot
   With crossbows charged, bows bent.   2729

Sir Lancelot was amazed to see
   That host by his redoubt.
He'd rather have known of their attack
   Than let his knights rush out.
He said, 'Hold still, my princes all!
   No rash ill–planned foray!
I mean, if they won't raise their siege,
   To make them rue the day!'   2737

Then Gawain, up to every wile,
   Put armour on, took arms
And mounted on a battle horse
   Well used to war's alarms.
He leapt forth like a living coal
   Before the barbican,
And challenged any knight within
   To prove himself a man.   2745

Sir Bors de Gawnes took up the challenge,
    Donned helmet, hauberk, shield,
And on his steed with spear in hand
    Went forth into the field.
Sir Gawain knew the arts of war:
    Blow after mighty blow
He struck at Bors both man and horse,
    And quickly laid them low.   2753

Sir Lionel, grieving for his brother,
    With all his might and main
Sallied out upon his steed,
    Meaning to kill Gawain.
Sir Gawain, countering, strong and calm,
    Struck man and horse to earth,
Then day after day did the same
    To many a knight of worth.   2761

And so for more than half a year,
    While they did there remain,
Men beaten in battle could be seen,
    Some wounded and some slain.
However in the world it was,
    Such grace had Sir Gawain,
He never suffered a single wound,
    And they fought him all in vain.   2769

One day, according to the book,
    Sir Gawain, courteous man,
Riding forth ready for battle,
    Called out at the barbican,
Accusing Lancelot of treason
    In killing his brothers three;
And Lancelot knew he must reply,
    Or else a coward be.   2777

And so this honourable knight,
   Sir Lancelot du Lake,
Above the tower-gate to the King
   This forced excuse did make:
'My royal lord, God save your honour!
   I grieve now for your sake
That I must fight against your kin:
   This battle I needs must take.'   2785

Sir Lancelot then equipped himself,
   As truly he had need,
With helmet, hauberk and all of steel,
   Then leapt upon his steed.
Of arms and armour he'd no lack
   To do a daring deed,
So, like a spark from living coal,
   He spurred to battle at speed.   2793

Both high commands then ordered that
   Wherever Fortune led,
None must go near those two till one
   Had yielded or was dead;
So both the armies then withdrew.
   On the field broad and bare,
Where all could see the blows they struck,
   They met, that famous pair.   2801

Now Gawain had this special gift
　　By a holy hermit's boon:
In morning sun his strength would grow[1]
　　From nine o'clock till noon
Whenever he was in a fight;
　　And so Sir Lancelot hence
For twenty blows returned not one,
　　But stuck to firm defence.　　　　　　　2809

Sir Lancelot knew that that was Fate;
　　He had to await his chance,
And many a fearful knock he felt
　　As the sun made high advance.
But noon being past, he straightened up
　　And gave Gawain a blow
Which made the blood run down his face
　　And laid him sideways low.　　　　　　2817

So savagely was Gawain struck
　　Through helmet to the head
That he could hardly move at all,
　　So nearly was he dead.
And yet he waved his sword about,
　　As ever brave and bold;
But Lancelot left him lying there,
　　Unwilling to kill him cold.　　　　　　2825

1. 2804 Gawain was given this quality by the hermit who christened
him. In the *Mort Artu* (Chapter 152) it operates at midday, but not for
three hours. It is a rare instance of magic in this poem.

Sir Lancelot drew back from him,
   His sword as yet unsheathed.
'Traitor and coward, come again!'
   The fallen Gawain breathed,
'When I am hale and whole once more,
   I'll fight you yet again;
And if you now come nearer me,
   You'll know I am not slain.'   2833

'Gawain,' said Lancelot, 'many a stroke
   When you were strong I stood,
And always I held back through love
   And regard for the King's blood.
When you are whole in heart and hand,
   I beg you change your mood.
May God preserve my living soul
   From deeds that are not good!   2841

'So have good day, my lord the King,
   And valiant warriors all.
Go home, give up your feud! Your hope
   Of victory is small.
If I brought out my knights to battle,
   You'd suffer grief and gall;
So ponder that, my lord, and think
   How many in death would fall.'   2849

So Lancelot to his castle went
   Boldly, at steady pace,
And all his good knights welcomed him
   With courteous embrace.
King Arthur's men took up Gawain
   And washed his wound with care.
Before his blood and spirit came back,
   He almost died, I swear.   2857

A fortnight sick and fretting then
   Wounded lay Gawain,
Treated by doctors and attended
   Till he was strong again.
And then one day he rose from bed,
   Put feet upon the floor,
Mounted his horse, rode to the gate
   And challenged yet once more: 2865

'Come forth and prove your manly strength,
   You traitor, Lancelot!
My three brothers you have killed
   In false and treacherous plot.
I shall pursue this feud till death
   With all my strength and art:
No peace shall be between us till
   You are pierced to the heart.'   2873

These words brought woe to Lancelot,
   Who thought it an evil thing.
He stood above the tower-gate
   And spoke thus to the King:
'Sire, I grieve that Gawain's heart
   Is fixed in such despite:
By the crucified Body, could I be blamed
   If I killed him in the fight?'   2881

So Lancelot prepared for combat
   With helmet, hauberk and shield.
None better or bolder in the world
   Fought on the battlefield.
With spear in hand and pennant flying
   And noble sword at his side,
He spurred out at a rapid pace
   When he was ready to ride.   2889

Gawain gripped his goodly spear
   And grimly spurred his horse,
But Lancelot proved his warlike skill
   And met him with equal force.
Truly it was a marvellous thing,
   The fury of their fight:
They dealt out gashes deep and wide
   With every savage smite.   2897

Towards midday Sir Gawain's strength
   Greater and greater grew;
His terrible blows Sir Lancelot
   Kept out with much ado.
But seeing that Gawain would not cease,
   He gripped his sword anew
And hit him so hard, the watching knights
   Their breath in pity drew.   2905

Yes, seeing Gawain would never cease,
   Forward Sir Lancelot drove.
And through Sir Gawain's gilded helm
   His mighty sword-cut clove.
On his old wound he hit Gawain,
   Who fell from his saddle down,
Groaning horribly on the ground.
   Thus Gawain lost renown.   2913

Yet Gawain, swooning where he lay,
   Held fast to sword and shield
And said, 'By Him who has the power
   Through all the world to wield,
As long as life shall last in me
   To you I'll never yield:
But do the worst that ever you wish,
   I'll defend myself on the field.'   2921

At that Sir Lancelot stood still,
   The man of marvellous might.
'Gawain, it saddens me to hear
   Such words from a noble knight.
Do you think me mad enough to offer
   A fallen warrior fight?
By Christ on cross, I shall not now,
   Nor ever did, day or night.   2929

'So have good day, my lord the King,
   And all your stalwarts dear!
Go home and give up thought of strife;
   You'll win no honour here.
For if I brought my knights to battle
   You'd none of you be glad.
So bear in mind, good lord, the love
   That we two always had.'   2937

And then it was a full two months,
   So nobles understand,
Before Gawain could walk or ride
   Or had the strength to stand;
And then a third time he was ready
   To battle with heart and hand.
But then from England they were called
   Back to their own land.   2945

Not one man thought the message good
   That to the King was brought;
Most full of sorrow was his mind
   And wretched was his thought
That they must home across the sea
   To counter treason at court.
Enraged, they broke the siege and then
   Their homeward way they sought.   2953

Sir Mordred, traitor false and vile,[1]
   King Arthur's sister's son
(And Arthur's too, as all believe,
   And that is why he won
The stewardship), was to the land
   A wily, treacherous lord:
He wished to wed his father's wife,
   Which many men abhorred.   2961

Great were the gifts and feasts he gave
   With lavish pomp and show,
And people said his rule brought joy,
   Arthur's but grief and woe.
So good allegiance turned to bad:
   The hearts of Englishmen
Deserted Arthur and their vows
   Were made to Mordred then.   2969

Sir Mordred had false letters written,
   Which he made heralds bring,
Saying that Arthur had been killed:
   They must choose another king.
The people spoke their minds and said
   Arthur loved only war,
And since he'd lost his life in battle,
   He had deserved no more.   2977

1. 2954 In the *Mort Artu*, Gawain is further wounded in a battle against the Romans, just before the treason of Mordred is revealed. The messenger is sent by Guinevere. Gawain dies full of guilt. This poet's selections and emphases are especially unerring hereabouts.

Then Mordred summoned parliament:
  Great was the gathering,
And there they all with full consent
  Crowned Sir Mordred king.
At Canterbury for two whole weeks
  The revels never ceased,
And then he went to Winchester
  To hold the wedding feast. 2985

In summer when the sun shone bright
  His father's wife he'd wed,
And her he'd hold in warm embrace
  And bring as bride to bed.
Dismayed, she begged a fortnight's leave
  To buy of London's best
In clothes, that she and her cortège
  Might be the better dressed. 2993

The Queen was white as lily-flower:
  With knights of her own kin
She hurried to London to the Tower
  And shut herself within.
Mordred rode after, pale with rage:
  His archers shot off showers
Of arrows, but to win those walls
  Was much beyond his powers. 3001

The Archbishop of Canterbury
  Rode there with cross on high:
'By Christ crucified, think again!'
  Was the holy man's loud cry.
'You cannot wed your father's wife!
  You must be mad in mind!
And come the King across the sea,
  You'll pay for it, you'll find!' 3009

'A foolish priest!' then Mordred said,
   'Do you think to thwart my will?
By Him who suffered pain for us,
   You words will work you ill.
I'll have you dragged by wild horses
   And hanged upon a hill!'
The Archbishop fled, leaving him
   His mad plan to fulfil. 3017

He cursed him then with book and bell
   At Canterbury in Kent.
As soon as Mordred heard of that,
   For the Archbishop he sent.
But he had fled, leaving his treasure –
   No time for argument!
While Mordred seized his gold and silver,
   To the wilderness he went. 3025

Thus the Archbishop fled the world
   And its joys for evermore.
He had a chapel built between
   Two copses high and hoar,
And as a hermit in the woods
   Black cowl and habit wore.
He often lay awake and wept
   For England's sorrows sore. 3033

Sir Mordred still maintained his siege,
   But attacking with his power,
Or starving it, or using guile,
   He could not take the Tower.
He feared his father might arrive,
   Yet still he sinned the more,
Intending wrongly to deny him
   The land whose crown he wore. 3041

To Dover and the coasts he knew
   Mordred set out to ride,
Sending letters and giving gifts
   To earls on every side.
He placed blockades by land and sea
   With archers bold supplied,
Meaning to keep his father out
   Of England's acres wide.   3049

King Arthur with his host of knights
   Sailed on the Channel flood;
A hundred galleys had in hold
   His barons of noble blood.
He aimed to disembark at Dover,
   As seemed both right and good,
But there he met a mighty force,
   Which strong against him stood.   3057

Upon the land he loved to live in
   Arthur put foot to ground,
But many a former faithful friend
   As foeman there he found.
So, mad with anger, Arthur then
   Came fighting up the shore:
So hard they battled on that beach
   That many lived no more.   3065

Alas! Sir Gawain armed himself
   To fight on the battlefield,
But his head, so long unhelmeted,
   Was not yet wholly healed,
And he was hit on the old wound
   By the handle of an oar.
So Gawain the Good fell to the ground
   And was silent evermore.   3073

Sir Mordred's bowmen bravely shot,
   His knights to the galleys rode
And through the hauberks hacked and hewed
   Until the red blood flowed;
Yes, sharpened spears cut through the mail.
   It was a day of dread,
And when they finished that grim fight,
   The waves all ran with red. 3081

King Arthur fought so fiercely then
   That none against him stood;
He hacked their hauberks and their helms
   Until their breasts ran blood.
So some were killed, some ran away,
   And some of the treacherous horde
Fled to Canterbury to warn
   Mordred, their traitor lord. 3089

Sir Mordred then prepared to fight
   With heart and spirit stout;
With helmet, shield and hauberk brown
   He led his army out.
They met next day at Barlam Down
   As soon as it was light;
With banners flying and spears couched
   They clashed with furious might. 3097

Richly arrayed was Arthur's host:
   The horns blew high and loud.
Mordred attacked in furious joy,
   That traitor false and proud.
The whole day long they stood and fought
   Till evening turned to night,
And those who saw it said they'd never
   Again see such a sight. 3105

Boldly and fiercely Arthur fought;
   There never was knight so good.
Through helmets into heads he struck
   And stirred both bone and blood.
Mordred rallied his hard-pressed men:
   'Fight back, or by Holy Rood
Alas, we shall have lost the day!'
   So raged he, mad in mood.   3113

Such deeds were done that many a lord
   That day bade life adieu;
The ghastly dead on the bare ground lay,
   By shining swords stuck through.
To Canterbury Sir Mordred went
   In woe the following day,
But Arthur kept the field where all
   His noble dead still lay.   3121

King Arthur early on the morrow
   Ordered horns to blow,
And called in many stalwart men
   To bury the dead in a row.
They dug them pits both deep and wide
   And made each grave a mound
Well marked to ensure that afterwards
   By friends it might be found.   3129

King Arthur went to dinner then,
   His nobles following fast,
But when he found Sir Gawain dead
   Beside a galley's mast,
His heart nigh broke a hundred times
   Before his fit was past.   3135

They bore Sir Gawain on a bier
   To a nearby castle fair,
And buried that noble in a grave
   In the choir of the chapel there.
King Arthur's face went grey with grief:
   No wonder his heart was sore!
His noble nephew whom he loved
   He never would see more.   3143

King Arthur would not there remain:
   Foul dreams destroyed his rest.
He marched along the southern coast
   Towards Wales in the west,
But at Whitsuntide he made a stay,
   As then appeared right,
In Salisbury, and there called to him
   Bold barons keen to fight.   3151

And many a valiant knight arrived,
   For word had spread about
That Arthur was right and Mordred wrong:
   Men knew it without doubt.
The armies gathered ominously;
   Arthur's was strung out long,
But Mordred by munificent gifts
   Had made his forces strong.   3159

Trinity Sunday being past,
   There came the dread event,
The mighty battle which was due
   And no man could prevent.
King Arthur's heart was well content
   To fight this deadly war,
And Mordred massed his army there
   With allies fetched from far.   3167

As Arthur lay in bed that night[1]
  Before the battle morrow,
He was beset by dreadful dreams
  Of the ensuing sorrow.
It seemed he sat all clad in gold,
  And as a true king crowned,
Upon a huge revolving wheel,
  With all his knights around.   3175

The wheel was wondrous fine and round,
  The biggest there could be;
He sat with rings and bezants crowned
  And precious jewellery.
When he looked down upon the ground
  He saw a black lake there,
With dragons raging there unbound:
  Approach them, none would dare.   3183

He feared to fall among those fiends
  Fighting under him,
But the wheel turned and each dragon
  Seized him by a limb.
Like one half mad, with mind unhinged,
  The King cried out in dread.
His chamberlains woke him and he leapt
  Distracted out of bed.   3191

---

1. 3168 In the *Mort Artu*, the dreams are in reverse order. This poet's order is more dramatically effective.

All night he lay awake and wept,
    Groaning with regret,
But near first light he fell asleep,
    Seven tapers round him set.
Waiting for him by a river
    Was Gawain, so he dreamed,
Accompanied by countless people:
    Angelic folk they seemed.   3199

Most joyful was King Arthur then
    His sister's son to see.
'Welcome!' he cried, 'But were you alive
    How happy I should be!
But friend, inform me: who are these
    Who keep you company?'
'In heaven here,' Gawain replied,
    'Dwelling in bliss are we.   3207

'Lords and ladies were they all
    Who lost their earthly life;
While I still lived, I took their part
    Against their foes in strife.
And now my greatest friends, they bless
    The day that I was born.
They begged my leave to come with me
    To meet you on this morn.   3215

'A month of truce you must obtain
    And then to battle go,
For Lancelot du Lake is coming
    To help you fight the foe.
If you take the field tomorrow,
    Death will lay you low.'
Then Arthur, weeping, awoke and said,
    'Alas for England's woe!'   3223

He hurriedly put on his clothes
   And to his knights he said,
'From dreamings dire I know that joy
   Has gone, and all is dread.
We must make Mordred seal his word
   To fight another day,
Or I shall die. This truth I dreamed
   Whilst I sleeping lay.   3231

'Sir Lucan, go to Mordred now
   With guile of wit and word;
Take with you bishops and barons bold,
   The better to be heard.'
And so they rode forth all together,
   Numberless knights and lords,
To Mordred and his battle force,
   As the book with truth records.   3239

And soon the bishop and warriors brave
   Before Sir Mordred stood.
They greeted him with great respect,
   Being barons of noble blood:
'King Arthur greets you graciously
   And asks in gentle mood
If you will grant a one-month truce,
   For the sake of Holy Rood.'   3247

Sir Mordred, raging-keen for battle,
   Foamed like a boar at bay,
And swore by Judas who sold Jesus,
   'Such words he should not say:
Let him keep the promise he made!
   He or I must die today.
So tell him truly what I said:
   I'll batter him, come what may.'   3255

'Sir,' they replied, 'if you and he
  To deadly battle go,
There's many a powerful knight will grieve
  Before its final blow.
Much better it were to abandon war
  And let him wear the crown;
And after him, then you shall rule
  All England, tower and town.'   3263

Mordred stood still, his eyes searching;
  Angrily up they went.
He said, 'I would it were his will
  To give me Cornwall and Kent!
Let me meet him on yonder hill
  And talk with true intent;
To good agreements of such a kind
  I'll quickly give consent.   3271

'And if our speeches prosper well,
  Being in good faith meant,
And the pact proposed promises
  To give me Cornwall and Kent,
True love shall bless it, and remain;
  But if we fail to agree,
Let Arthur leap upon his horse
  Sternly to battle with me.'   3279

'Sir,' they said, 'How will you come?
  With twelve or fourteen men?
Or with all your mailed and helmeted knights
  To parley with us then?'
'Neither,' replied the other, 'but truly
  Expect no treachery;
Between our armies, but alone,
  Arthur and I shall be.'   3287

They took their leave without delay
    And on their way they went,
Returning to seek out the King
    Where he sat within his tent.
'Sir,' they said, 'we have offered peace,
    If you will thereto assent:
Let Mordred succeed you as King, and have
    In your lifetime Cornwall and Kent. 3295

'If you will grant that grave request,
    And pledge to it your word,
Then have each valiant knight prepared
    With hauberk, helmet and sword,
For you must meet upon that hill
    In both the armies' sight;
And if you fail to agree, then nothing
    Can follow but deadly fight.' 3303

When Arthur heard those fateful words,
    His oath he truly swore,
And drew up seven ranks of battle
    With banners to the fore.
They gleamed as bright as lightning flash
    On the morrow when they met:
None ever saw a finer sight
    Than that, in order set. 3311

But far more men had Mordred then,
    Master of many fights;
He had twelve to Arthur's two,
    All battle-hardened knights.
So Arthur and Mordred were prepared
    To meet in open ground,
With wise men passing to and fro,
    To seek agreement sound. 3319

King Arthur pondered in his heart,
    Then to his lords spoke thus:
'In yonder traitor I have no trust,
    For he'll play false with us
If we can come to no accord.
    So as men of might and main
Attack if you see a weapon drawn
    So that all of them are slain.'   3327

Sir Mordred, fierce and keen to fight,
    Said to his nobles all,
'Since Arthur has lost his throne and lands,
    His heart is full of gall.
With fourteen knights and not one more
    We meet at yonder thorn:
To guard against tricks, have broad banners
    Ready for battle borne.'   3335

So Arthur and his fourteen knights
    Footed it to the thorn,
Wearing helmets and hauberks bright,
    With shields before them borne.
And as they came, an adder glided
    Forth upon the ground
And stung a knight on Mordred's side,
    Who fell with poisoned wound.   3343

Out he whipped his weapon bright;
    The adder he meant to kill.
When Arthur's party saw that sight
    They responded with a will,
Attacking at once, for what they saw
    Was treason, so they thought.
That day died many a noble knight
    And barons to death were brought.   3351

King Arthur, seeing no other course,
   Quickly mounted his steed,
And Mordred, almost out of his mind,
   Leapt to his saddle at speed.
No talk of peace, but levelled spears
   Clashed with a splintering sound,
And many a daring knight in death
   Was dashed to the bitter ground.   3359

Sir Mordred wounded many a man
   As he fought that battle's course;
He cut through many a company,
   So hard he galloped his horse.
In ceaseless strife King Arthur dealt
   Wounds that were deep and wide.
Starting at dawn, the battle raged
   Till almost eventide.   3367

Many a spear was thrust and splintered,
   Many a stern word spoken;
Many a sword was hacked and bent,
   Many a helmet broken;
Noble companies clashed together,
   Battering helmets bright.
A hundred thousand fell to the ground;
   The boldest were quelled ere night.   3375

Since Brutus voyaged out of Troy
   And Britain for kingdom won,
No war so wonderfully fierce
   Was fought beneath the sun.
By evening not a knight was left
   Could stir his blood and bone
But Arthur and two fellow-knights,
   And Mordred, left alone.   3383

King Arthur's knights were Lucan the Butler
    And Bedivere, his brother.
Sir Lucan bled from grievous wounds:
    No better was the other.
'Shall we not fell this thief to earth?'
    King Arthur fiercely raged,
And gripping his spear with grim intent
    His foeman he engaged.   3391

His spear hit Mordred in the chest
    And through his backbone bore;
So Mordred lost his life at last
    And never word spoke more.
But as he died, he raised his arm
    And clove King Arthur's head
Through crest and helmet. Thrice he swooned
    Like one that's almost dead.   3399

Between them Lucan and Bedivere
    Held the King upright,
And the three went forth among the dead
    Killed in the long day's fight.
The valiant king they loved so much
    Could hardly move for pain.
They took him to a nearby chapel:
    All other cure was vain.   3407

All night long they lay in the chapel
    Which stood by the sea-side.
To Mary for her matchless mercy
    With sorrowing hearts they cried,
And to her Son they offered prayer:
    'By thy Names, the Seven,
Jesu, guide his soul, that it
    Lose not the bliss of heaven!'   3415

Then Lucan watched the body-robbers
   Hurrying to the plain
And wrenching coins and rings and brooches
   From nobles lying slain,
And went at once to warn King Arthur
   Where he lay in pain.   3421

He spoke in sorrow, soft and still,
   To Arthur where he lay,
'Sire, there are people on the hill
   On which we fought today.
Whether they mean us good or ill
   We ought to ride away
And find a town, if it be your will,
   For safety's sake, I say.'   3427

Said Arthur to Lucan, 'Let us so:
   Lift me up while I last.'
Sir Lucan put his arms round Arthur,
   Lifted, and held him fast.
Arthur, bleeding to death, looked up,
   Wounded and swooning with pain.
Lucan held him a while, and then
   His heart burst with the strain.   3437

When Arthur woke there from his swoon,
   Beside an altar he stood,
But Lucan, whom he dearly loved,
   Lay dead and foaming with blood.
The bold Sir Bedivere, his brother,
   Mourning and deathly sad,
For grief could not go near to him:
   He wept as if he were mad.   3445

The King then turned to Bedivere
    And said with sorrowful mien,
'Take Excalibur, my good sword!
    A better was never seen.
Go, cast it in the salty sea
    And then return to me.
Hurry, by Holy Rood, and tell me
    What wonder there you see.'   3453

The knight rejoiced because he thought
    He'd save that splendid sword:
'Should I be better if nobody
    Possessed it afterward?
To waste that weapon in the sea! –
    No man could be so mad.'
He hid it under a tree and said,
    'Sire, I did as you bade.'   3461

'What saw you there?' inquired the King.
    'Truly,' the knight replied,
'I saw nothing but the blear waves
    And the waters deep and wide.'
'You have broken my bidding!' said the King;
    'Why did you, perjured man?
Bring me a better message than that!'
    Bedivere busily ran,   3469

Still thinking that he'd save the sword
    And throw the scabbard instead.
'If any adventure comes from this,
    I'll see a sign,' he said.
He slid the scabbard into the sea
    While on the shore he stood,
And then went back to the King and swore,
    ''Tis done, Sire, by the Rood!'   3477

'What wonder saw you?' asked the King.
  'Nothing,' the knight replied.
'You treacherous traitor!' cried the King,
  'My will you've twice defied.
Greatly shall you regret that act,
  And pay for it, be sure!'
Bedivere begged for mercy then,
  And took the sword once more. 3485

He thought it best to obey the King,
  And so with the sword he went
And flung it far, and closely watched
  To see what sign would be sent.
Out of the water there came a hand
  Which seized the sword from the spray
And brandished it as if to break it;
  Then gleam-like glided away. 3493

Then Bedivere went back and said,
  'Sir, I saw a hand
Come out of the water, and three times
  It shook your shining brand.'
'Help me thither,' said Arthur then.
  He led his lord to the strand,
And there was an oared and masted ship
  Full of ladies close to land. 3501

Those beautiful and noble ladies
  Gently took the King;
The loveliest of them wrung her hands
  And wept in her sorrowing.
'Alas, dear brother!' she said, 'Too long
  You have lacked good doctors' care:
I know, and great is the grief to me,
  Your pain is hard to bear.' 3509

Sadly Bedivere, standing there
  Wounded and full of woe,
Said to the King, 'Are you leaving me?
  Alas, where will you go?'
And Arthur, sorrowing, answered him,
  'This day I must be gone
To heal my grievous wounds awhile
  In the vale of Avalon.'[1]   3517

The ship sailed slowly from the land
  Till it was lost to sight.
Then searching forests and gloomy hills
  Galloped that grieving knight,
Caring nothing for his life
  And ever weeping sore,
Until one dawn he came to a chapel
  Between two copses hoar.   3525

And there he saw a marvellous sight
  As to it he made his way:
Before a fine tomb freshly built
  Praying, a hermit lay.
The tomb was cased in marble grey
  And inscribed in lettering bright.
A noble coffin was on it, lit
  By a hundred candles' light.   3533

1. 3517 '. . . the Isle of Avalon (*Mort Artu*, Chapter 50), which is the dwelling-place of the ladies who know all the magic of the world' (trans. James Cable).

He went to the hermit and inquired,
  'Who is the coffined man?'
The hermit rose to his feet and said,
  'I'll tell you all I can.
At midnight came a troop of ladies;
  I knew not who they were.
They brought this badly wounded body
  And laid the coffin here.'   3541

'They gave me a hundred pounds and more
  In bezants[1] golden-bright,
And bade me offer holiest prayer
  To Our Lady day and night
For him who lies mouldering there,
  That she his soul guard well.'
Then Bedivere read the words inscribed:
  In grief to the ground he fell.   3549

'Hermit,' he said, 'Here lies my lord,
  Arthur, now lost to me,
The best king ever born in Britain,
  The best there'll ever be.
By him who wore the crown of thorns,
  While I have life and limb,
Let me live here in hermit's garb
  And ever pray for him.'   3557

1. 3543 Bezant: a gold coin from Byzantium. Bezants were widely
current in Europe from the ninth century. In England they were
superseded by the noble, a coin of Edward III.

This holy hermit was the Archbishop
  Whom Mordred hunted away,
And who then chose to live in the woods:
  He agreed without delay,
And thanked the Lord that Bedivere
  In quiet peace had come.
He welcomed him with heart and hand
  Into his forest home.   3565

Guinevere, learning of the battle
  And the deadly ruin done,
Took five ladies and went away
  To Amesbury as a nun,
And there she remained in holy prayer,
  Weeping evermore.
She never would be happy again:
  Yes, white and black she wore.   3573

When Lancelot heard of Mordred's claims,
  No wonder it grieved his heart;
Wise men and friends all rallied to him,
  People from every part.
They put their galleys in perfect trim;
  No detail did they miss.
To help King Arthur was all their thought,
  And to mar Sir Mordred's bliss.   3581

Sir Lancelot had crowned seven kings,
  All earls and barons bold;
Innumerable were his knights and squires,
  Too many to be told;
All glittered like the lightning-flash.
  The friendly breezes blew
Them fast to Dover, where they landed
  And formed their ranks anew.   3589

There Lancelot heard the hateful news
– To hide it was in vain –
About the Battle of Barlam Down
    And the death of Sir Gawain;
How Mordred coveted Arthur's crown,
    And how they both were slain;
How all who'd fought at Salisbury
    Lay dead upon the plain.   3597

Sir Lancelot – this grieved his heart –
    There also heard it said
That Guinevere the Queen had lived
    In sorrow, pain and dread.
With five ladies she'd gone away,
    And none knew where they'd fled.
Worse still for him, nobody knew
    If she was alive or dead.   3605

Sir Lancelot called his kings together,
    And Bors was at his side.
He said, 'My lords, I leave you now,
    But you must here abide
For fifteen days should I return,
    Whatever may betide.
Do not ride rashly forth to find
    Which knights in battle died.'   3613

He galloped forth in grief of mind
    Knowing neither peace nor rest;
His senses numb to good or ill,
    For three days he rode west,
Then came to a tower beside a stream,
    And there he thought it best
To pause and ask the people within
    For food and drink, and rest.   3621

As he came through a cloister pure,
   With weeping almost mad,
He saw a beautiful lady there
   In nuns' clothing clad.
Three times she swooned on seeing him,
   So great her pain and dread.
Nuns helped her up, and to her room
   The lady was gently led.   3629

'By Jesus, King of Bliss!' they cried,
   'Who has angered you?
Some maiden from the bower or hall?'
   'No,' was her answer true.
They called Sir Lancelot to her,
   The abbess and every nun,
In council, and Queen Guinevere
   Said before everyone: 3637

'Abbess, I acknowledge to you here
   That through this man and me
Being lovers came this woeful war
   And all calamity.
My lord is dead, the best of men,
   And many brave knights slain:
That's why I almost died of grief
   At seeing him again.   3645

'For when I saw him, truth to tell,
   My heart went faint and cold.
That I should live to see this day,
   Knowing those barons bold
Were killed and buried on our account!
   For our lust a hundredfold
Revenge has come; but God has set me
   Where my resolve shall hold.   3653

'To await the healing of my soul
   I am set in such a place
That through the mercy of His wounds
   God may grant me grace
To atone my sins, and of their tarnish
   Take off every trace,
That I may be at His right hand
   At the Doom, and see His face.   3661

'Therefore, Sir Lancelot du Lake,
   For love of me, I pray,
Forsake my company for ever.
   To Benwick take your way
And rule your realm in peace and quiet!
   Marry, and love your wife;
Delight in her, and may God give
   You both a joyful life!   3669

'I pray to God, almighty King,
   To bind you both in bliss.
I charge you, beyond everything,
   That never, after this,
You come to me for comforting
   Or send me secret word:
And may my prayers to amend my life
   By God on high be heard!'   3677

'Sweet Madam, never shall I be false
   To you,' said Lancelot,
'Though all the world were my reward!
   Christ grant I do it not!   3681

'May God forbid that ever I should
   Do such a wrong to you,
Since day and night upon this earth
   We have been lovers true.
I pledge to God my promise now:
   The destiny you embrace
Shall in a monastery be mine,
   So please Him in His Grace!   3689

'To gladden God as best I can
   Hereafter is my intent,
And specially to pray for you
   While life to me is lent.'
'Ah, will you hold to that high oath?'
   Queen Guinevere returned.
'If I said not,' said Lancelot,
   'I'd well deserve to be burned.   3697

'Worthy to burn I well should be
   If I refused a life
Of penance such as you give to God,
   Suffering woe and strife.
Since we have lived and loved, by Mary,
   Mother, maiden and wife,
Until God severs us by death,
   To penance I yield my life.   3705

'Gladly shall I take this penance,
   And find an anchorite
Who'll give me shelter for God's sake
   And robes of black and white.'
So sorrowing and sighing they spoke;
   Between them was great woe.
'Madam,' said Lancelot du Lake,
   'Kiss me, and I will go.'   3713

'No,' said Guinevere, 'that I will not;
   Think about that no more.
We must resolve to deny ourselves
   What brought us bliss before.
Consider this world, its war and ruin,
   Its strife and battles grim,
And let us think of Christ who saved us,
   Please God, and pray to Him.'   3721

Why lengthen out my history longer?
   The two prepared to part;
No living man could measure then
   Their agony of heart.
They wrung their hands and cried aloud
   And swooned as if for ever.
If any saw, they'd tell the tale,
   And stint it would they never.   3729

The ladies sadly carried the Queen
   Still swooning to her cell,
And strove to ease her of her grief
   And make her spirit well.
But many stayed with Lancelot
   Until that brave man stirred;
And when he awoke, he stood at once,
   And went without a word.   3737

He knew he'd rather have lost his life;
   His heart was heavy as lead.
'O righteous God, what can I do?
   Why was I born?' he said.
To a deep forest in front of him
   He went as one that fled.
He longed to tear his rich clothes off,
   And wished that he was dead.   3745

All night like a demented man
  He wandered in the wood
Weeping, and then at dawn of day
  He saw where a chapel stood.
He heard its bell and thither went
  As quickly as he could:
The priest sang mass, and Lancelot
  Heard it in dreary mood.   3753

This hermit was the very Archbishop
  Sir Bedivere had found.
He sighed in grief as he sang the mass;
  Their sadness was profound
At Mordred's treason, Arthur's death
  And all the ensuing woes.
The darkness lifted; they knew each other
  As soon as the sun rose.   3761

Mass being sung, the Archbishop came
  And welcomed Lancelot;
He knelt as courtesy required
  And kindliness spared not:
'To us and to our lonely house
  Be welcome as a friend!
Stay one or many nights, and we
  Shall to your wants attend.'   3769

They both embraced Sir Lancelot
  On knowing it was he:
He asked them how King Arthur was
  And all his company.
His heart near burst a hundred times
  At what he then was told:
He struggled to King Arthur's tomb,
  His spirit dead and cold.   3777

He flung his arms against the wall,
  Those weapons nobly bright,
And falling before the bishop there,
  Knelt as a sinning knight,
Confessing all his sins and praying
  That he his brother might be,
And serve the Lord in bower and hall:
  Thus he addressed his plea.   3785

The holy man did not refuse,
  Being glad to grant his boon,
But giving thanks to Christ enthroned,
  Confessed Sir Lancelot soon.
He shrove the knight so clean of sin
  That every stain was gone,
And then he kissed him on cheek and chin
  And put his habit on.   3793

Meanwhile his men at Dover stayed,
  Waiting for him in vain,
And then it happened that Lionel,
  That man of might and main,
Set out with fifty fierce knights
  To find his lord again,
And took the road direct to London,
  And there, alas! was slain.   3801

Sir Bors de Gawnes could wait no more:
  He called the host together
And sent them home by ship and horse:
  God grant them wind and weather!
Different ways went he and Ector
  Looking for Lancelot.
Bors rode westwards: good or ill,
  Being dazed, he pondered not.   3809

At first light on the morrow morn
   In a forest he found a well,
And riding by the river side,
   Upon a chapel he fell.
He thought that he would stay for Mass:
   Sadly he heard the bell,
Then in delight saw Lancelot,
   And with him prayed to dwell.   3817

Before another half year's end,
   Of Lancelot's men came seven.
Each one had searched to find his friend,
   And by God's will in heaven,
Though sad their hearts and loud their cries,
   Yet finding Lancelot,
They stayed together as banded brothers
   And thence departed not.   3825

For seven years Lancelot was priest;
   At Mass he led the song.
In prayer and penance time went by
   And life did not seem long.
Sir Bors and his fellows read books, rang bells
   And worship solemnized.
So thin they grew of body and face
   They'd scarce be recognized.   3833

Sir Lancelot sickened suddenly
   Early one eventide;
He called the bishop and his fellows
   Swiftly to his side.
'Brothers,' he said, 'My end is near,
   My baleful life-blood fails.
My foul flesh yearns for the grave's earth:
   To hide it, nothing avails.   3841

'I beg you, brothers, that tomorrow,
   When you find me dead,
I may be placed upon a bier
   And to Joyous Gard be sped.
I promised, alas! to be buried there,
   Swore to it long ago:
For God's sake bear my body there
   And bury it, even so.'   3849

'For love of Him that died on the cross!'
   The other three replied,
'It is but heaviness of the blood
   That makes you mortified.
When did your strength not conquer harm?
   Soon you shall better be!'
Thus cheerfully they spoke to him,
   But straight to bed went he.   3857

To shrive him of his sins he called
   The bishop to his room,
And spoke or whispered all his shames
   In readiness for his doom.
Then shrived of sin, he willingly
   Received the Sacrament,
Sir Bors de Gawnes weeping the while:
   And then to bed all went.   3865

A little while before the day,
   The bishop being in bed,
A laughter took him where he lay
   And all were filled with dread.
They woke him and asked him how he was,
   And sighing aloud, he said,
'Alas and woe! Deep in my dreams,
   Where have I been led?   3873

'Why did you come and wake me now
  When I in sleep was lost?
Lancelot bright of face I saw
  With a mighty angelic host.
They opened heaven's gates for him
  And bore him through on high!
This great unearthly sight I saw,
  And still it dazzles my eye.'   3881

'Sir,' they said, 'By the Holy Cross,
  Put words like that away!
Sir Lancelot shall be well again
  Before the break of day.'
They caught up candles and went to him
  And found him dead, I say,
With face and flesh still flushed with blood,
  As if he sleeping lay.   3889

'Alas!' said Bors, 'That I was born!
  That ever I should see
The best of knights that ever battled
  Dead in front of me!
Lord Jesus, save his soul in heaven
  As you were crowned with thorn!'
They did not cease their prayer and song
  Until the fifth day's morn.   3897

Soon afterwards they built a bier,
  The bishop and warriors bold;
Then forth they went to Joyous Gard,
  That mighty fortress-hold.
And there in the chapel, in the choir,
  They dug a grave for him.
They kept the lykewake three whole days:
  Their mood was sadly grim.   3905

And as, about to bury him,
   They stood around the hearse,
In came Sir Ector, his brother dear
   Who'd sought him seven years.
He looked for grace towards the choir;
   To hear a mass, he thought:
But being entranced, both he and they
   Knew each other not.   3913

Embracing Ector, noble Bors
   Wept aloud and sang;
The bishop and the bold men too
   Wept with many a pang.
Sir Ector thought, then wished to know
   Whose corpse lay still and cold.
His heart near burst a hundred times
   Before the tale was told.   3921

Sir Bors said courteously to him,
   'Welcome, Ector, to us.
Here lies Sir Lancelot du Lake,
   Whom we are mourning thus.'
Sir Ector gathered the body up,
   Embraced it with many a kiss,
And begged that he might watch all night
   Through Jesu, King of bliss.   3929

Sir Ector trembled like a madman,
   Wrung his hands and sighed;
His mind was fixed in sad lament
   And sorrowfully he cried.
When Ector took the body up,
   His tears stinted not.
At length their weeping had to cease:
   They buried Lancelot.   3937

Then all went down upon their knees,
  Most sorrowful the sight:
'Of Jesus Christ we ask a boon,
  And also of Mary bright:
Lord, as thou madest sun and moon,
  And hast in heaven the might,
Bring this soul in bliss to your throne,
  If ever you pitied knight.'   3945

Sir Ector cared not whether his horse
  Stood still or ran away:
He only wished to stay for ever
  And for his brother pray.
He put on hermit's weeds at once:
  On foot they made their way
Back to the forest chapel, taking
  A fortnight, truth to say.   3953

And when they came to Amesbury
  They found Queen Guinevere dead,
And bore her forth among them all,
  Her cheeks still rosy red.
They buried her at Arthur's side;
  Glastonbury is the name
Of the noble abbey where they lie,
  A place of purest fame.   3961

No more of Lancelot du Lake,
  But hermits know it's true
That Arthur's body still lies there,
  And Queen Guinevere's too,
With gentle monks in holy wisdom
  Reading and singing this:
'May Jesus who suffered grievous wounds
  Grant us heavenly bliss!'   3969

    Here ends the Death of Arthur   AMEN

BIBLIOGRAPHY

Texts of the Poems

Benson, L. D., ed.: *King Arthur's Death*, New York 1974 (containing *Morte Arthure* (Alliterative) and *Le Morte Arthur* (Stanzaic))

Brock, E., ed.: *Morte Arthure*, Oxford 1871

Bruce, J. D., ed.: *Le Morte Arthur*, Oxford 1903

Hamel, M., ed.: *Morte Arthure* (Alliterative), New York 1984

Hissiger, P. F., ed.: *Le Morte Arthur*, Paris 1975

Krishna, V., ed.: *The Alliterative Morte Arthure*, New York 1976

Barron, W. R. J.: *English Medieval Romance*, London 1987

Brewer, D. S. and Owen, A. E. B., eds: *The Thornton Manuscript*, London 1975

Chambers, E. K.: *Arthur of Britain*, London 1927

Chrétien de Troyes: *Arthurian Romances*, trans. and ed. Owen, London 1987

Everett, D.: *Essays on Middle English Literature*, Oxford 1955

Frappier, J., ed.: *La Mort le Roi Artu*, Paris 1964

Geoffrey of Monmouth: *The History of the Kings of Britain*, trans. and ed. Thorpe, London 1966

Goller, K. H., ed.: *The Alliterative Morte Arthure: A Reassessment of the Poem*, Cambridge 1981

Keen, M.: *Chivalry*, Yale 1984

Knight, S.: *Arthurian Literature and Society*, London 1983

Krishna, V.: *The Alliterative Morte Arthure, a New Verse Translation*, Washington 1983

Lacy, N. J., ed.: *The Arthurian Encyclopaedia*, New York 1986

Loomis, R. S.: *The Development of Arthurian Romance*, New York 1964

McKisack, M.: *The Fourteenth Century, 1307–1399* (*The Oxford History of England*, Vol. V), Oxford 1959

Malory, Sir T.: *Works*, ed. Vinaver, Oxford 1977

Preminger, A., ed.: *Princeton Encyclopaedia of Poetry and Poetics*, London 1974

Stephens, J.: *Medieval Romance*, London 1973

Turnbull, S.: *The Book of the Medieval Knight*, London 1985

Vinaver, E.: *The Rise of Romance*, Oxford 1971

Wilson, R. M.: *Early Middle English Literature*, London 1939

FOR THE BEST IN PAPERBACKS, LOOK FOR THE 🐧

In every corner of the world, on every subject under the sun, Penguin represents quality and variety – the very best in publishing today.

For complete information about books available from Penguin – including Puffins, Penguin Classics and Arkana – and how to order them, write to us at the appropriate address below. Please note that for copyright reasons the selection of books varies from country to country.

In the United Kingdom: Please write to *Dept E.P., Penguin Books Ltd, Harmondsworth, Middlesex, UB7 0DA.*

If you have any difficulty in obtaining a title, please send your order with the correct money, plus ten per cent for postage and packaging, to *PO Box No 11, West Drayton, Middlesex*

In the United States: Please write to *Dept BA, Penguin, 299 Murray Hill Parkway, East Rutherford, New Jersey 07073*

In Canada: Please write to *Penguin Books Canada Ltd, 2801 John Street, Markham, Ontario L3R 1B4*

In Australia: Please write to the *Marketing Department, Penguin Books Australia Ltd, P.O. Box 257, Ringwood, Victoria 3134*

In New Zealand: Please write to the *Marketing Department, Penguin Books (NZ) Ltd, Private Bag, Takapuna, Auckland 9*

In India: Please write to *Penguin Overseas Ltd, 706 Eros Apartments, 56 Nehru Place, New Delhi, 110019*

In the Netherlands: Please write to *Penguin Books Netherlands B.V., Postbus 195, NL–1380AD Weesp*

In West Germany: Please write to *Penguin Books Ltd, Friedrichstrasse 10–12, D–6000 Frankfurt/Main 1*

In Spain: Please write to *Alhambra Longman S.A., Fernandez de la Hoz 9, E–28010 Madrid*

In Italy: Please write to *Penguin Italia s.r.l., Via Como 4, I-20096 Pioltello (Milano)*

In France: Please write to *Penguin Books Ltd, 39 Rue de Montmorency, F-75003 Paris*

In Japan: Please write to *Longman Penguin Japan Co Ltd, Yamaguchi Building, 2–12–9 Kanda Jimbocho, Chiyoda-Ku, Tokyo 101*

FOR THE BEST IN PAPERBACKS, LOOK FOR THE 🐧

PENGUIN CLASSICS

Saint Anselm	**The Prayers and Meditations**
Saint Augustine	**The Confessions**
Bede	**Ecclesiastical History of the English People**
Chaucer	**The Canterbury Tales**
	Love Visions
	Troilus and Criseyde
Marie de France	**The Lais of Marie de France**
Jean Froissart	**The Chronicles**
Geoffrey of Monmouth	**The History of the Kings of Britain**
Gerald of Wales	**History and Topography of Ireland**
	The Journey through Wales and **The Description of Wales**
Gregory of Tours	**The History of the Franks**
Henryson	**The Testament of Cresseid and Other Poems**
Walter Hilton	**The Ladder of Perfection**
Julian of Norwich	**Revelations of Divine Love**
Thomas à Kempis	**The Imitation of Christ**
William Langland	**Piers the Ploughman**
Sir John Mandeville	**The Travels of Sir John Mandeville**
Marguerite de Navarre	**The Heptameron**
Christine de Pisan	**The Treasure of the City of Ladies**
Marco Polo	**The Travels**
Richard Rolle	**The Fire of Love**
François Villon	**Selected Poems**

FOR THE BEST IN PAPERBACKS, LOOK FOR THE 🐧

PENGUIN CLASSICS

ANTHOLOGIES AND ANONYMOUS WORKS

The Age of Bede
Alfred the Great
Beowulf
A Celtic Miscellany
The Cloud of Unknowing and Other Works
The Death of King Arthur
The Earliest English Poems
Early Irish Myths and Sagas
Egil's Saga
The Letters of Abelard and Heloise
Medieval English Verse
Njal's Saga
Seven Viking Romances
Sir Gawain and the Green Knight
The Song of Roland